THE ANTIQUARY BOOK MURDERS

The Hunt for Little Dorrit

A Novel

By

Arno B. Zimmer

Author of Reservoir Man and The Severed Finger

Copyright © 2023 Arno B. Zimmer
All Rights Reserved

No part of this publication may be reproduced, stored in or introduced into a retrieval system, or transmitted, in any form or by any means (electronic, mechanical, photocopying, recording or otherwise), without the prior written permission of the copyright owner, except by a reviewer who may quote brief passages in a review.

This book is sold subject to the condition that it shall not, by way of trade or otherwise, be lent, re-sold, hired out or otherwise circulated without the author's prior consent in any form of binding or cover other than that in which it is published and without a similar condition including this condition being imposed on the subsequent purchaser.

The caricature on the cover is from an 1857 edition of *Little Dorrit* and is now in the public domain, having been identified in the United States as being free of known restrictions under copyright law, including those rights of all related and neighboring countries, where one hundred years has passed since the death of the author.

ISBN: 9798393318819 (paperback)

OTHER NOVELS BY
ARNO B. ZIMMER

*THE PARLOR CITY BOYS
*RETURN TO PARLOR CITY
*A MURDER IN PARLOR HARBOR
*DEATH COMES TO THE TORPEDO FACTORY
*THE SEVERED FINGER: A THIMBLE ISLANDS MYSTERY
*RESERVOIR MAN: THE DISAPPEARANCE OF TOMMY DWYER

Dedication

For Bridget, Caitlin, Flannery, Quinn and Maeve
"Thanks for the memories ...."

Acknowledgements

I want to thank the advance readers and reviewers of my previous work, including family, friends and former colleagues – but also strangers – who have urged me to keep writing after my debut novel, *The Parlor City Boys*, was released in 2015.

Once again, special thanks to Tim Dailey, Cheryl Hardy, Beverly Morrill and Rita Zimmer. They made helpful suggestions on clarifying the plot and timeline but also caught numerous typographical and grammatical errors that have, hopefully, all been exorcised, any remaining ones the sole responsibility of the author.

Table of Contents

Prologue 1
Chapter One: The Assignment 10
Chapter Two: A Murder In Graniteville 17
Chapter Three: Buried Treasure 22
Chapter Four: Finders Keepers 28
Chapter Five: Near Fine 36
Chapter Six: An Education In Antwerp 45
Chapter Seven: The Making Of A Biblioklept 52
Chapter Eight: Sleight of Hand 56
Chapter Nine: Old Friends United 66
Chapter Ten: The Temptation 72
Chapter Eleven: Hitlerian Obsession 77
Chapter Twelve: The Seduction 85
Chapter Thirteen: Down Memory Lane 93
Chapter Fourteen: The Dresden Connection 98
Chapter Fifteen: A Dead End 104
Chapter Sixteen: Dead Or Alive? 110
Chapter Seventeen: A Gothic Moment 118
Chapter Eighteen: The Escape 124
Chapter Nineteen: Goodnight, My Lovely 130
Chapter Twenty: Secret Codes 135
Chapter Twenty-One: A Gang Of One 142
Chapter Twenty-Two: From High to Low 149
Chapter Twenty-Three: A New Mistress 156
Chapter Twenty-Four: The List 163
Chapter Twenty-Five: "Run For Your Life!" 169

Chapter Twenty-Six: Targeted For Extinction 174
Chapter Twenty-Seven: Small Town Thief 181
Chapter Twenty-Eight: Where It All began................................... 186
Chapter Twenty-Nine: A Momentous Discovery 190
Chapter Thirty: The Actor... 197
Chapter Thirty-One: Buried In Books.. 203
Chapter Thirty-Two: No Way Out 209
Epilogue.. 217

Prologue

It was 1937 when an industrial accident at the Erla Machinenwerks in Leipzig shattered the left leg of 21-year-old Heinz Kammler, a technician in one of the aircraft factories gearing up for production of the Messerschmitt Bf 109 fighter plane. Kammler was sent home to Berchtesgaden to recuperate but it was tacitly understood that he would never return to the factory floor.

It was two more years before World War II officially started with Hitler's attack on Poland, but the Fuhrer had already signaled his aggressive intent in 1936 by occupying the strip of land known as The Rhineland, a buffer zone created by the Treaty of Versailles, which ran along Germany's border with France, Belgium and the Netherlands.

Then, in 1938 and under pressure from Hitler, Britain brokered an agreement to avoid war by sanctioning the return to Germany of the section of Czechoslovakia known as the Sudetenland.

Heinz was bitter and depressed as he limped around Berchtesgaden in constant pain. He gazed up at the Berghof, Hitler's heavily guarded retreat in the Bavarian Alps, and fantasized that he would somehow make his way up the mountain and get an audience with the Fuhrer to plead his case for a return to Leipzig.

As Heinz Kammler stewed and bemoaned his fate, he could hardly imagine the dramatic turn that his life would take in a few years. Due to the secret machinations of his younger sister, he would embark on an improbable journey that would take him thousands of miles from his beloved Germany.

BACK IN 1936, teenager Gerda Kammler reluctantly went to work as a chambermaid at what was once Hitler's modest chalet. It was he who named it Berghof, or mountain farm. She was ashamed but desperate, as jobs were scarce. Her parents were dead and she was all alone, her older brother Heinz still far away in Leipzig. On her first day, she was warned by one of the other housemaids to hold her tongue unless spoken to and to avoid the watchful eye of Angela Raubal, a large, intimidating woman. Raubal was Hitler's older half-sister who functioned as the Berghof housekeeper but also intervened with authority well beyond her domestic duties.

Gerda hadn't forgotten how a few years earlier her uncle, Karl Schuster, had been first harassed and threatened, then thrown in prison – at what would later be known as the infamous concentration camp at Dachau – because he refused to sell his beloved and popular Berchtesgaden hotel. With the encouragement of Raubal, the property was targeted by Hitler's chief lackey, Martin Bormann, as an ideal location to serve both as a communications center as well as the barracks for the Fuhrer's burgeoning *Schutzstaffel*, better known as his SS bodyguards, now numbering over two thousand strong in the area.

During his imprisonment at Dachau, Schuster was persuaded to sell the Hotel zum Türken and leave the area. He had been a loyal member of the National Socialist Party in its early years but had made the mistake of openly criticizing Hitler as he consolidated his dictatorial power. If Schuster stayed in Berchtesgaden, it was explained, he would be made to disappear.

OUTWARDLY SHY AND deferential, Gerda was clever and calculating beyond her years. She became increasingly resentful as she observed the opulence of the Berghof. Like her uncle, she despised Hitler and cringed at the incessant newspaper photographs of him posing with Blondi, his German shepherd dog, and groups of small children. It was just one of the devious campaigns of propaganda chief Josef Goebbels to make the Fuhrer appear as the benevolent father figure of the country.

Like her uncle's hotel, the private houses and cottages surrounding the Berghof were seized by Nazi party leaders in order that they might have vacation homes close by their leader. Eventually, an ever widening area surrounding the Berghof was fenced off with barbed wire and patrolled by Gestapo and SS troops. The expansion went miles beyond Hitler's chalet and eventually extended to dozens of buildings for Nazi officials, aides-to-camp, adjutants and hangers-on.

Walking through the Berghof, Gerda couldn't help but notice the hand-woven rugs and the sanded wainscoting, the red marble fireplace, the heavy Teutonic furniture. Then, there was the expensive tapestries and artwork that adorned the walls of the Berghof, much of it borrowed or simply taken from German museums. Intermixed with the priceless art treasures, one could see amateurish watercolors from Hitler's brush.

Hitler had been coming to the picturesque Obersalzberg, as the mountainous region was known, for over a decade, first renting a modest cottage before acquiring it when *Mein Kampf* became a best seller and made him wealthy.

It was common knowledge among the staff that the best French cheeses and wines, along with other delicacies, were brought in regularly from Dallmayr's specialty food store in Munich. It was even whispered that Hitler added a little Beluga caviar to his vegetarian diet. It all made Gerda burn with the desire to exact small measures of defiance and revenge. When her brother came home from Leipzig, crippled and depressed, she started to formulate a grander scheme.

———

The Berghof was a luxuriant haven not just for the Nazi elite but also for the foreign dignitaries who came to fawn over and curry favor with Hitler. Guests could indulge in the sumptuous food and choice wines as they took in the breath-taking views of the mountains overlooking Austria to the south. The Duke and Duchess of Windsor were guests along with the Italian dictator Benito Mussolini and even a delegation from China. The Aga Khan, the spiritual leader of a large Muslim sect, came to pay homage and allegedly offered Hitler 30,000 Arab troops to encourage his invasion and occupation of Egypt, Syria and Palestine. For much of the world, Hitler was an idol, but for Gerda Kammler he was evil incarnate.

One day in the Spring of 1938, Gerda was scrubbing the floor in the back of the Berghof library, shielded by a large chair, when she saw a military officer enter the room and pull a book from one of the shelves. Gerda froze in place. His back was to her and she peered from behind the chair to watch. His movements were partially obscured but he appeared to leaf through the book and turn it over several times before putting it back on the shelf and exiting the library.

Gerda waited a few minutes then went over to examine the book with the title of *Little Dorrit* on the spine. She frowned when she opened the book and saw the swastika and Adolf Hitler in bold lettering on the inside cover. Turning to the title page, even with her very limited command of English, she recognized the name of the author. It struck her as odd that there was an English language novel by Charles Dickens in the Fuhrer's library. Before she could place the book on the shelf, Hitler's valet walked in, snatched the novel and shooed her out of the library.

When Heinz heard about his sister's library encounter, he asked Gerda for details about the officer. As she described the grey-green uniform with its collar patches, yellow shoulder straps and yellow cuff insignias, Heinz grabbed his sister's arms and exclaimed, "My god, Gerda, you were in a room with a Gestapo officer, possibly a general. If the valet reports that you were snooping, the consequences could be dire."

Gerda wanted to placate her brother so she nodded her head and said she would be more careful. She had seen many military officers and dignitaries come and go from the Berghof and wasn't intimidated. She was a pretty, blue-eyed girl and reacted to admiring glances with a carefully rehearsed, coy smile.

Heinz would have been mortified if he knew that Gerda had been taking increasing amounts of cash, Reichsmarks as well as American dollars and other currencies, from the bedrooms of Berghof guests, normally on the day of their departure. By the end of 1938, she had accumulated a sufficient amount to further her secret plan.

Gerda kept other secrets from her brother. She knew that a crippled young man would never have an opportunity to succeed in the Third Reich of the future. Heinz Kammler no longer embodied the ideal Aryan man and would be reduced to a menial, caretaker existence. It would be difficult to convince him but Gerda believed that the only chance for her brother's happiness was outside of Germany.

Before Heinz had been sent home to Berchtesgaden, Gerda had noticed the young man walking into the Nazi communication center which was once her uncle's hotel. When he smiled at her, she scowled and looked away. He was handsome and young but he was the enemy, she said to herself.

These chance encounters would continue until one day the young man approached Gerda as she was heading up to the Berghof. His name was Anton Albrecht and he was from Munich. He knew no one in Berchtesgaden and hoped he might go for a walk with her one day. Gerda liked the way he talked, his gentle manner and it flustered her. She turned away quickly and headed up the mountain.

It was not long before Gerda acquiesced to Anton's blandishments. Soon thereafter, they became secret lovers. She eventually told him about her concern for Heinz and her plan to help him. The objective was simple: get her brother out of Germany. Anton was madly in love with Gerda and would do anything she asked.

By 1939, emigration from Germany was becoming more restrictive and the United States had significantly curtailed the number of people who could enter the country. The bureaucratic obstacles were daunting and Kafkaesque.

As fortune or happenstance can intervene, for good or bad, in anyone's life, Heinz Kammler was the beneficiary of Gerda's serendipitous relationship with Anton. As luck would have it, Anton's father was the proprietor of the Albrecht Cafe in Munich, a favorite of the city's mayor, Karl Fiehler. The mayor was also a Nazi party official who enjoyed doing favors for anyone who showed fealty to the Fuhrer – and him. Fiehler had enjoyed the cuisine at Albrecht's ever since he became mayor in 1933 but had never once been handed a bill. He had reciprocated by using his party influence to get young Anton assigned to the communication center at Berchtesgaden. Now, the elder Albrecht, at the pleading of his lovestruck son, would ask Fiehler for a second favor.

Normally, it would take months on a waiting list to get permission to exit Germany in the late 1930s. Once the war began, it would be nearly impossible for the average German citizen to emigrate to England, the United States or any other Western country. In 1939, obtaining a passport was just the beginning of the process.

After confirming that Kammler was not a malingerer, and that the injury at the Leipzig factory was genuine, Fiehler contacted the consulate office and made his wishes known. Afterwards, one of the mayor's deputies would handle the labyrinthine details while a frequently intoxicated Heinz Kammler stumbled around Berchtesgaden, oblivious to the future that was being engineered for him.

For the traveler with no political connections, there was a seemingly endless list of forms to be completed and supporting documents to be secured. An inventory list of possessions, tax and medical records, police certificate, recommendation letters, and a transit stamp with evidence of a boat ticket. Finally, there was the favorable interview at the American consulate in Munich, in Kammler's case a perfunctory session pre-arranged shortly before his departure, at which time the coveted visa would be stamped into his passport.

One evening, in the Spring of 1939, Gerda brought Anton home to dinner and introduced him as a friend who had picked up some troubling news that came through the communications center. A plan was afoot, engineered by Heinrich Himmler, head of the SS, to transport to slave labor camps all men physically unable to fight on the front lines or work in the factories. There, they would work long, arduous hours under life-threatening conditions.

With her brother now sufficiently mortified, Gerda laid out the plan which she had finalized with the assistance of Anton and his family. Heinz would take a train to Munich then proceed to the North Sea port of Bremerhaven, there to board an ocean liner bound for New York. From there, he would travel by train to his ultimate destination, Baltimore, Maryland, where there was a large population of German immigrants, some of them from the Berchtesgaden area.

It was urgent that Heinz leave Berchtesgaden as soon as possible. To assuage Heinz' concerns, Gerda promised her brother that she would be following him to America before the end of the year.

In early August, with Gerda's cash hoard and his travel documents, Heinz took the train to Munich. As he was boarding, his sister handed him a package wrapped in newspapers. "It is a book that you can sell once you get to America if you find yourself in need of money," she said, smiling before giving him a tearful embrace.

On August 22nd, Heinz Kammler was on board the *S.S. Bremen* when it departed from the Bremerhaven Columbus Quay. Little did he know that the *Bremen's* crew included a Nazi Party contingent along with a unit of the infamous SA, the notorious Brown Shirts who terrorized Hitler's opponents and detractors.

Once safely at sea, after stops in Southampton and Cherbourg to pick up additional passengers, he took Gerda's package from his satchel, unwrapped the newspapers and stared in disbelief at *Little Dorrit* and the Hitler bookplate. By the time the ship docked at the Hudson River pier in New York City on August 28th, he had decided that his defiant and intrepid sister had gone back into the Berghof library and taken the book, her way of assuring him that she could not be intimidated by the Fuhrer or his sycophants.

WHEN HE GOT to Baltimore, Heinz would read in the German-language newspapers about his dramatic voyage to America. Three days out of Bremerhaven, and with war imminent, the captain defied orders to return to port and sailed on to New York City. After passengers disembarked and the ship was refueled, the captain heeded a new set of orders and agreed to return to Germany.

The *S.S. Bremen* was in the waters of the North Atlantic when word was received on September 1st that Germany had invaded Poland. Two days later, when Britain declared war against Germany, the *Bremen* was near Iceland, now trying to evade enemy ships. It would not be until mid-December, after several close encounters and with the aid of the Russian navy, that the *Bremen* made it back to the Bremerhaven Quay.

So it was that Heinz Kammler, through the resourcefulness of his sister and a defiant boat captain, had made it out of Germany on the last passenger ship before the outbreak of World War II. While others might be elated by their good luck, Heinz was as morose and dispirited as he had been while limping around Berchtesgaden. Now, he worried about what would become of Gerda and wished he was back home to watch over her.

CHAPTER ONE
THE ASSIGNMENT

———◆———

It was the middle of May in 1995 when Theo DeBruycker got a call from the owner of the auction house in Hamburg. He was not simply good but the absolute best in the arcane world of rare book theft and, because he could afford to be selective, it was his habit to ask questions about a proposed assignment before accepting it. But when he listened to Otto Von Paulus' voice, it sounded more like an urgent summons and he decided to comply without pressing for details. DeBruycker had provided Von Paulus with a number of rare books over the years, "stole to order" was how he described his modus operandi, and it had paid off handsomely for both of them. It was understood that most of the purloined books would disappear into the private collections of wealthy individuals, trophies to be enjoyed by select people, and would never be seen in public again.

With his ability to don multiple disguises, Theo was a "gang of one," a shadowy figure who haunted libraries, museums, book shops and trade shows, targeting a specific book such as a first edition of Kafka's *The Metamorphosis* or Mann's *The Magic Mountain*. Or, he would snatch hard to find or out of print books for which he knew there would always be eager collectors. After scrubbing them clean of any ownership markings, he would ship them on consignment to Von Paulus or to the Reinhold auction house in Dresden, confident he would be compensated when the item was sold.

"Your passport has not expired, I presume?" Otto asked. When DeBruycker assured him it had not, Von Paulus added, "Be here first thing in the morning. My intuition tells me that you are about to go abroad to pursue the opportunity of a lifetime."

DeBruycker left his apartment in the Belgian city of Bruges, known as the "City of Canals," and, after a short train ride, caught the first flight out of Brussels the following morning. As the plane passed over the Elbe River, he gazed at the intricate network of canals that dominated Hamburg's port area. It made him think briefly of his hometown of Ghent, but he quickly pushed those painful memories aside. Thirty minutes after landing, he was in the Altstadt, the old town district of the city where Von Paulus maintained his offices and warehouse.

As the two men sat across from each other, there was an uneasy silence which was uncharacteristic of their cordial but business-like relationship. To Theo, Von Paulus seemed detached, almost distracted, as he fingered the nine-by-twelve yellow envelope he held in his hands, twisting it back and forth before pushing it to the middle of his desk. Von Paulus was a squat, dense man with a thick grey mustache that disguised his upper lip, making it difficult to determine his mood or demeanor. The dome of his head was freshly shaved and oiled and beamed from the reflection of the overhead light.

"Why me?" DeBruycker asked, with false modesty. Von Paulus smiled, causing his mustache to spread out across his cheeks. "Ve have a verd in German – *unerschutterlichkeit* – that fits you perfectly.

The Americans vood say you have ice in the veins or are cool under pressure. Also, I told the client's representative that you ver the master of disguises. My description of you vas sufficient. Then, this envelope arrived yesterday via courier. So, it is time to get down to business.

"You vill note, in case you are questioned, that the envelope vas sealed and taped ven you received it. I therefore have no knowledge of its contents. If you accept, I vill receive my instructions separately. So, you must ask me no questions since none can be answered. Of course, I can logically assume that your task involves the acquisition of a rare book or map. I can only repeat vat I told you yesterday on the telephone – that you vill be handsomely revorded. On such scant information, you have a decision to make."

DeBruycker paused for only a moment and then reached for the envelope when Von Paulus' hand came down firmly on top of it. "If you trust me and take possession of the envelope, there is no turning back. It vill hopefully ease your mind, if you are troubled, to know that this assignment came to me from a prominent individual in Munich by the name of Augustus Gottfried who is acting on behalf of someone who chooses to remain anonymous. Such secrets are to be expected in our business. If vill do us vell to please both of them."

After this admonitory speech, Von Paulus slid his hand away from the envelope and sat back in his chair. DeBruycker nodded his assent and picked up the brass antique letter opener, shaped like a dagger, laying on the desk, causing Von Paulus to spring forward and exclaim, "Vait! I am forbidden from knowing its contents. My advice is not to open it until you are back home, in the privacy of your apartment. Ve vill not speak of this matter anymore today nor ven ve meet again unless our instructions otherwise direct us."

At the door, DeBruycker said, "We have been partners for several years and have always treated each other fairly, Otto. When this assignment is completed, you will receive your portion of the compensation." Von Paulus touched DeBruycker's arm and smiled. "I have already been taken care of, also most handsomely, for my small contribution. Now, good luck to you, Theo DeBruycker, and take care out there, verever you go, okay? I vill be in need of your services upon your return."

AFTER ARRIVING BACK in Brussels, DeBruycker took the train to Bruges and went straight to his apartment. He poured a shot of genever with a beer chaser before sitting down on the couch. All the way back from Hamburg, he fiddled with the envelope but did not break the seal.

Theo stared at the envelope for a minute and then took a deep breath before slicing it open. "I'm committed now," he said aloud in a voice of resignation. He then pulled out a sheet of paper and three smaller, sealed envelopes. The first envelope contained three thousand dollars in U.S. currency. Theo's eyebrows went up and his heart beat a little faster. He had never been to America.

The next envelope was a shocker and caused DeBruycker to finish off the remaining genever. It contained a French passport with his picture but was in the name of Alexandre d'Arblay. In addition, there was a French driver's license plus a credit card, both in d'Arblay's name, along with a prepaid international calling card. Who was this Gottfried that Von Paulus was so certain could be trusted? Certainly, someone powerful, highly organized and well-connected, enough so to get his picture and produce false identification documents. Perhaps, a high official in the German or French government? If so, did that make Theo the *de facto* agent of a foreign government? Theo was intrigued and excited.

The final envelope contained a one-way ticket for d'Arblay from Paris to Montreal the following week. He ran his fingers over the pile of U.S. bills, twenties and fifties divided by rubber bands. Why not

Canadian currency, he wondered, if his destination was Montreal? In a minute, he would have his answer.

THEO PICKED UP the sheet of paper, reading and rereading it until he had committed the details to memory.

BURN AFTER READING

- Leave all personal identifications in your apartment
- Fly to Montreal
- Wait one day and purchase a train ticket to New Haven, Connecticut
- From New Haven, travel to the town of Graniteville (approx. ten miles distance)
- Go to the *Alt Germania* shop on the edge of town owned by Heinz Kammler
- Secure the 1857 first edition copy of *Little Dorrit* by Charles Dickens
- Immediately return to New Haven and take the next train to New York City
- Check into the Mohawk Hotel near the Pennsylvania Train Station
- Call Von Paulus when the Dickens novel is secured and leave the following message: Frederick the Great
- Using the d'Arblay credit card, purchase a ticket on the next flight to Hamburg and deliver the book to Von Paulus
- Upon your return, a cash payment of 50,000 euros will be made
- If there is a problem or a delay, leave Von Paulus the following message: Compiegne.

Theo walked to the window holding the sheet of paper. He scanned the street below. Von Paulus had been so uncharacteristically cautious, even mysterious, and it made him wonder if he would be watched until he boarded the flight in Paris. Turning away, he crumbled up the paper and squeezed it into the palm of his hand. Grabbing a box of matches from the fireplace mantel, he walked into the bathroom and watched as the flaming ball came apart in the toilet bowl.

IT HAD BEEN a few days since he had opened what he thought of as the "d'Arblay envelope." Those unaccustomed nerves that he felt then, and which had briefly embarrassed him, had vanished. He was now anxious to begin his journey, despite all its uncertainties, and was looking past the acquisition of the Dickens novel to the brief time he would spend in New York City. He thought ahead and envisioned the look on Otto's face when he showed up in Hamburg with the prize.

To understand the choice of messages he was allowed to leave, he went to the library and read about Frederick the Great and Compiegne. Frederick's success as a Prussian soldier and statesman was undisputed but Compiegne was the town where Germany's ignominious surrender at the end of World War 1 took place. It all made sense.

Before leaving for Paris, Theo went to the library to learn what he could about Augustus Gottfried. He was not shocked to learn that Gottfried was a minister in the Bavarian government in Munich, confirming his earlier suspicion that Otto's mystery client and his surrogate were power brokers at the highest levels.

Theo went to the post office and had his mail held until his return. Using a pay telephone out front, he called the auction house in Dresden where he frequently did business. As it turned out, Reinhold had a long-standing request for a prized map that was housed in a library at Yale University in New Haven, Connecticut, the procurement of which would be amply rewarded.

Theo DeBruycker saw no reason why he should not take full advantage of this fortuitous coincidence. He was unknown in America, would be operating under a French alias, and could plunder as much as discretion allowed before returning to the continent. What would an extra day or two matter to Gottfried or his client? The idea that he might be thwarted in his efforts to secure the Dickens novel or that he might face his own Compiegne never crossed his mind.

———•———

SIX MONTHS BEFORE Theo received his assignment, a German couple from Munich was visiting relatives in Hartford, Connecticut. They drove down to the coast one day to see the Thimble Islands when they spotted the Alt Germania shop on the outskirts of Graniteville. Upon returning home, they told friends and relatives about the peculiar, reclusive shop owner named Heinz Kammler. It wasn't long before the story of Alt Germania reached the ears of Augustus Gottfried.

CHAPTER TWO
A Murder In Graniteville

———◆———

Since arriving in Graniteville in 1977, 50-year-old high school teacher Jerry Kosinsky regularly drove past the *Alt Germania* shop on the edge of town.

Cyrus Trowbridge, the retired lawyer who befriended Jerry when he first showed up in town on the quixotic pursuit of a missing person, told him back then that the owner was an eccentric old German by the name of Heinz Kammler who was seen limping around in public on rare occasions. "I had to go to town hall to examine his business registration just to learn his name. I'll bet that only a handful of people in Graniteville know it – and now you're one of a select group," Trowbridge explained.

On the one occasion that Cyrus engaged Kammler in conversation outside the Post Office, the old man spoke haltingly and with such a thick accent as to be almost unintelligible. "Makes a buttoned-up curmudgeon like me seem voluble. He's a shop owner who keeps unpredictable hours and who doesn't believe in capitalism," Trowbridge had observed wryly.

THE CONVERSATION WITH Cyrus provoked Jerry's curiosity and he started visiting Kammler's shop every few months, always buying at least one book while attempting to engage in banter with the old man. One day, Jerry got the idea to introduce a German novelist in one of his classes and approached Kammler for advice. The old man suggested *The Tin Drum* by Günter Grass and when Jerry went to pay, Kammler smiled faintly and said, "My gift," in his gruff German accent.

After this unexpected display of generosity, Jerry made it a point to stop by Kammler's shop on a regular basis. He watched him limp around the shop and wondered if it was from an old war injury. There would be no endearing friendship, like the one he had developed with Cyrus Trowbridge, but Jerry saw signs that his visits added a touch of joy to the old man's lonely and isolated existence.

IT WAS NEAR the end of May of 1995, when an antiquarian book dealer and collector from Massachusetts saw Kammler's shop as he drove through Graniteville one morning, on his way to spend a weekend with friends on the nearby Thimble Islands, just off the Connecticut coast. When he found the door to the shop ajar, he pushed it open and called out for the proprietor. The lights were off and receiving no response, he started to back out when he noticed a leg protruding from an overturned bookshelf. Later that day, the coroner confirmed that old Kammler had been bludgeoned to death with a blood-stained porcelain figurine depicting a Bavarian farmer.

The police were baffled by the crime. The shop had been ransacked but since no listing of the shop's inventory was discovered, it was impossible to determine what might have been stolen, if rare book or antique thievery was the motive. Behind the counter, Kammler's cash box was undisturbed and contained less than $100, making robbery by opportunity implausible. As for the murder weapon, it had been either wiped clean of prints or the perpetrator had worn gloves, either possibility making the crime more sinister than a mere robbery gone bad.

———◆———

A FEW DAYS later, Graniteville police received a report from their counterparts in New Haven. A janitor at the train station had seen an elderly man with a shock of white hair and a drooping mustache washing blood from his shirt the night of the murder. Then, there was the report of a vehicle stolen near the campus of Yale University, later found abandoned at the train depot. Again, no fingerprints were found.

A senior investigator from the state police was called in to render his expertise to the Graniteville police but he was stumped as well when DNA testing of the blood found at *Alt Germania* produced no matches in the state's criminal database. There was no evidence that the Graniteville and New Haven cases were even linked. As a result, Kammler's murder investigation quickly stagnated.

———◆———

THEO DEBRUYCKER FROWNED as he looked at his reflection in the window as the train rumbled and rocked in route from New Haven to New York City. Uncharacteristically, he had lost his temper. When old Kammler sneered and refused to give up the book, Theo grabbed the figurine and raised it over his head, intending it to be nothing more than an intimidating gesture. But the old man had shown contempt, had actually spit at him – and Theo had lost it. For a man who prided himself in being circumspect, always exhibiting self-control, he knew that it was a dangerous slip. The rage came on him suddenly and he had acted impetuously.

DeBruycker was shaken by his confrontation with Kammler. He left New Haven without completing his second assignment for the Dresden dealer, realizing that since he had no choice but to return to Graniteville, he would visit the Yale library at that time.

It had puzzled Theo, beginning on the flight from Paris, why he had been sent all the way to Connecticut from Belgium to seize a novel, even if a rare edition, which could easily be procured at any number of antiquarian shops in London. How valuable could this particular edition or any Dickens novel be, he had asked himself more than once? Was it possible that the great Victorian writer had inscribed it to his good friend, the novelist Wilkie Collins, or some famous patron? All he knew was that an enigmatic German insisted on this particular copy of *Little Dorrit*, allegedly in the possession of Heinz Kammler. It was an unfortunate inconvenience, as DeBruycker viewed it. If the old man had already sold the novel to another secret buyer, why didn't he say so and give up the name? His intransigence along with his final, vulgar act of defiance had resulted in his vicious beating. Before leaving the shop, Theo took one last look at Kammler. His eyes were blinking and he was actually smiling scornfully up at him.

DeBruycker now felt certain that the novel was valuable for reasons other than its historical rarity, accounting for Kammler's extraordinary obstinance. A signed, first edition of the novel's very first printing – assuming it would be in mint condition- would certainly command a premium price. But could its intrinsic value equal or exceed the 50,000 euros that he was being paid to steal it? Outside of

London, what better place to ascertain the true worth of *Little Dorrit* than from a prestigious rare book dealer in New York City who specialized in Victorian literature?

On a practical basis, DeBruycker had to confront additional challenges if Kammler died. Would the shop reopen under a new owner or would it be shut down permanently, the inventory sold to another dealer? Of the two, the latter possibility was the most worrisome and would require quick action.

Except for the brief encounter with the janitor in the train station, De Bruycker did not recall any situation where he had come face to face with anyone else. Still, he would take no unnecessary chances. He looked around at the few passengers in his train car and walked to the bathroom. There, he peeled off the bushy white mustache and eyebrows and detached the matching wig before wiping off the dark lines under his eyes and the translucent powder that he had applied to his cheeks. When he returned to his seat, he was transformed, no longer an old man. No one seemed to notice. He would metamorphize again once in that city known everywhere in the world as the Big Apple.

CHAPTER THREE
BURIED TREASURE

TWO DAYS AFTER the murder, local attorney Sid Farthing, returning from a hike on a remote section of the Appalachian Trail, notified the police that he had prepared a will for Kammler. He confirmed that Kammler had no living relatives and had named Jerry Kosinsky as the sole heir to his estate. Having recently come into a modest inheritance after his father's death, Kosinsky convinced his skeptical wife that they should refurbish the shop and turn it into what he called a "book lover's paradise." With the school year about to end and no summer school teaching obligations, she acquiesced and they took the plunge.

YEARS EARLIER, JERRY had given up his effort to write a sprawling, picaresque novel in the tradition of the great English writers of the 18th and 19th centuries. He kept the draft in his closet but had hardly glanced at it since he first started writing feverishly each morning at Trowbridge Cottage, the retreat on the Connecticut shore that Cyrus Trowbridge had bequeathed to him in his will. Jerry had even envisioned a broad, sweeping trilogy like Dos Passos' *U.S.A.* He now rationalized that his mistake was in thinking too expansive for his inaugural literary effort. The simple truth was that he had wilted under the daily grind of writing and had gradually stopped retreating to the cottage each morning before the start of school.

After almost two decades of teaching, Jerry realized that he was losing the spark in the classroom as well and wondered if his students noticed. He hoped that he was merely experiencing a mid-life malaise that would somehow self-correct. He remembered that Thoreau had become disillusioned as a teacher and went off to Emerson's pond in Concord to find inspiration. It was there that the famous recluse ended up writing *Walden*. Jerry had no illusion about crafting another transcendental masterpiece but knew that he hungered for a fresh start. While the inspiration provided by Trowbridge Cottage had been fleeting, being the owner of a bookstore, he reasoned, might launch him on a new, creative path.

It was not difficult to like Jerry Kosinsky. There was no false comity in his nature, no manufactured bonhomie. His easy-going, engaging style was authentic and it endeared him to most people. His thick hair still flopped down his forehead but had turned from brown to mostly gray. Whenever anyone asked him a question, he invariably pushed up his tortoise shell glasses and squinted before responding, a tic formed in childhood that had never left him. In recent years, because of his girth and height, he was affectionately known as "The Candyman" at the high school. That comparison to the actor John Candy ended abruptly in 1994 when the comedian died of a heart attack. There wasn't a student in any of his classes who wanted their beloved teacher to suffer a similar fate.

Before beginning renovations of the shop, Jerry decided to sell off the inventory of antiques that cluttered the floor and shelves. He envisioned a bright, airy bookstore offering a broad array of books that would attract an eclectic audience. A colorful sign at the highway exit would beckon travelers who never knew that Kammler's shop even existed.

One evening, walking through the shop, Jerry stopped in front of a sagging floor-to-ceiling bookshelf that had been nailed to the wall. When he pulled on it, it came crashing down. He was surprised to discover that it had covered up a small, closet size room with a key hanging from the lock. The room was barren except for a shelf that held a single bundle in the shape of a book, covered in faded, yellowed newspapers.

Jerry gently pulled back the brittle tape securing the newspapers and noticed that they were in the German language. Underneath, he found several layers of tissue. Jerry's heart raced. He hesitated before slowly unfolding one layer of tissue after another. Once the tortuous process was complete, he was gazing at a burgundy, gold-embossed hardcover book. When he turned the book and looked at the spine, he discovered that he was holding a copy of *Little Dorrit* by Charles Dickens. Jerry's head jerked back and his eyes widened when he opened the book and stared at the inside of the front cover. It was dominated by an ornate bookplate with *Ex Libris* in a ribbon across the top. In the center there was a spread eagle and a swastika surrounded by oak leaf. Along the bottom was the name Adolf Hitler in bold lettering.

Jerry's hands trembled. Was he actually holding a book from Hitler's personal library? Was the bookplate authentic or could it be a forgery, someone's idea of dark humor? He tried to imagine Hitler, one of the most diabolical men in history, sitting in an easy chair in the evening perusing a Victorian novel after spending the day plotting the destruction of Europe.

Flipping ahead to the title page, Jerry saw that the novel was published in 1857 in London by Bradbury & Evans. In the middle of the page was a tiny woman in a dark cape and bonnet standing in a doorway with a surprised look on her face.

On the opposite page was a drawing that depicted a group of Victorians gathered under a chandelier. Jerry wondered if he had stumbled upon a Dickens novel so rare and valuable that Kammler was compelled to hide it. Was it because of the Hitler bookplate? If so, the novel needed to be appraised by an expert not only for insurance purposes but also for potential resale.

Jerry Kosinsky sat down, *Little Dorrit* heavy in his lap, and stared into the empty closet, stupefied by his discovery and pondering its significance. What had prompted old Kammler to hide away this valuable edition of a Dickens novel, making it inaccessible to walk-in customers? Had Kammler been holding the book for someone else who never showed up? Was it possible that the murderer came looking for this very book and, frustrated in his efforts, took his anger out on Kammler? Alternately, Jerry considered that the murderer got what he had come for in the form of an antique figurine like the one that had been used to cave in the shop owner's skull. This second possibility eased Jerry's concerns and it made him feel ashamed.

As he sat mulling various possibilities, Jerry recalled when he first arrived in Graniteville and conducted research on Capt. Kidd and his tenuous connection to the Thimble Islands. To this day, locals found it amusing to watch tourists flock to the area each summer in search of the booty that Capt. Kidd had allegedly buried on one of the islands over three hundred years earlier. "Well, it appears that I hit paydirt by simply knocking down a bookshelf," Jerry mumbled. He tried to laugh but the words stuck in his throat.

He carefully re-wrapped the tissue and the newspapers around *Little Dorrit and* placed the book on the shelf before locking the door and removing the key. He needed to find someone he trusted to validate the book's authenticity. If he was now in possession of a rare collector's item and it did come from Hitler's library, then he had indeed discovered a unique treasure. He tried to imagine the connoisseurs for such a book. Specialized libraries and World War II afficionados came to mind – as did rabid Hitler acolytes.

Jerry had two trusted advisors, close friends in truth, to whom he could turn for counsel. One was now teaching at Thorndyke College, a short ride from Graniteville. Professor Isaac Fensterwald, a German by birth, would be able to translate the newspapers that encased the novel. The other friend, Woody Meacham, his "blood brother" from a small town in Upstate New York called Parlor City, was somewhere in Europe and Jerry would have to track him down.

As the euphoria surrounding his discovery faded, Jerry had a growing fear that Kammler's brutal murder was linked not to a figurine but to the book in the closet. Buried treasure often brought danger with it, right? Jerry had learned that after British royalty turned against Capt. Kidd, deciding that he was no longer useful to them as a privateer, he was adjudged a pirate, thereby sealing his fate. Brought back from America to London, Kidd's ignominious end came at the mouth of the River Thames, his rotting corpse hanging in a gibbet as a warning to other buccaneers.

After locking up, Jerry drove over to Trowbridge Cottage before going home. He pulled the first edition of *Oliver Twist* that Cyrus had bequeathed to him along with his cherished, shorefront getaway. What was it about rare books and Charles Dickens that kept insinuating themselves into his life? If Cyrus were still alive, what counsel would he give?

Well, one thing was clear and indisputable. If old Kammler had been defiant to the end, even as the figurine was smashed into his head, Jerry understood that so vicious a killer would stop at nothing if his purpose was to gain possession of *Little Dorrit*.

CHAPTER FOUR
FINDERS KEEPERS

BEFORE MAKING THE drive north to Thorndyke College to meet with Prof. Fensterwald, Jerry placed a call to Woody Meacham at his home in Tarragona, a town on the Spanish coast near Barcelona. His wife Hannah answered and informed him that his friend was at an Interpol conference in Geneva. Two years earlier, Woody had tracked down two thieves who had purloined rare maps from the Girolamini Library in Naples, Italy. As a consequence of his success, his investigative services were currently in greater demand in Europe than in the states. "You can reach him at the *Hotel d'Alleves*, Jerry. He will never be too busy to speak with you. If he calls here, I will tell him you are trying to reach him."

Interpol was headquartered in Lyon, France and enjoyed an image of daring and intrigue that did not comport with its mission or its capabilities. People who watched too many old movies pictured it as an international FBI but Woody had once explained to Jerry that it was in reality an organization comprised of member countries and served primarily as an international clearinghouse on criminals and their whereabouts. Its investigative capabilities were limited and it possessed no police powers.

Jerry left a message for Woody at the *d'Alleves* and then decided to call the lawyer who had overseen Kammler's estate. After describing in general terms his discovery of an old novel in pristine condition among the shop's inventory, Farthing said, "You're on solid ground, Mr. Kosinsky. You know the old saying, right? Possession is nine-tenths of the law. Not to go into the technicalities of the property statutes but "finders keepers" is the operative rule. Of course, if documentation turns up indicating that Kammler was holding the book for its owner, that would be a different case entirely. We might need to do battle in court. If so, you'll have Clarence Darrow in your corner." Farthing laughed and then asked, "How old is the book, did you say? It's probably best that I examine it right away. If it was stolen from a library or museum and that fact can be proven, things could get dicey. Any markings on it indicating ownership?" Farthing had been flippant in his tone but now sounded lawyerly, sniffing the opportunity for some billable hours.

Jerry deflected his inquiry and said, "I'm going to get the book appraised." He was glad that he had not mentioned that Hitler's bookplate graced the inside cover of *Little Dorrit*. Farthing's shelves were filled with impressive-looking legal tomes and it annoyed Jerry that the lawyer patronized him with trite aphorisms, not bothering to cite any particular section of the law that might assuage his concerns. Jerry could have said, "Sure, Farthing, but what good is possession under the law if someone is willing to commit murder to get their hands on a book from Hitler's library?" It was all well and good that their conversations were protected by attorney/client privilege but Farthing had been too facile with him. He had a mouth as big as his ego. Jerry didn't want the attorney blurting out any details about the novel at his club after a few cocktails.

BACK WHEN JERRY was assisting Woody in his 1985 investigation of a relative who had disappeared at the Ashokan Reservoir in Upstate New York, he had contacted Prof. Fensterwald for information on a pro-Nazi group known as the German-American Bund, prominent in the U.S. during World War II. Fensterwald had confirmed the identity of two German agents affiliated with the Bund who admitted to their co-conspirator that they killed the Meacham relative and buried him close to the reservoir. Solving the decades-old mystery had brought Woody acclaim not only in the U.S. but in Europe. Since then, his investigative services have been in considerable demand on both continents. It was the mark of Woody's character that when he received accolades for unraveling the reservoir mystery, he always mentioned the vital assistance provided by his childhood friend.

Fensterwald was a German Jew whose family escaped to England in the early thirties before Hitler made emigration nearly impossible. Previously at Yale, he had been enticed to Thorndyke with a full professorship and the promise of tenure after his book, *Hitler's Fortune 500*, received high praise not just from academicians and historians but also from the general public. It was a catchy title, insisted on by his publisher, but the research behind it was impeccable and irrefutable.

Fensterwald delved into the history of the corporate titans in Europe, the UK and even America who supported Hitler, some openly like Henry Ford, but many others surreptitiously, as the Fuhrer rebuilt Germany's industrial and military capabilities in violation of the Treaty of Versailles. Many of those same companies today, employing armies of PR hacks to constantly burnish their images, were not happy to have Fensterwald remind the world of their perfidy.

Jerry began by telling Fensterwald about the murder of Kammler and his surprised inheritance of his shop. Before removing the tissues covering *Little Dorrit*, he explained, "The book was hidden in a closet behind a bookshelf, wrapped in these old German newspapers."

Fensterwald had been in America for many years but there was still a reserved, old-world style about him and the vestiges of a German accent lingered in his pronunciation of certain words. He studied the newspapers with a stoic look on his face as Jerry, striving to keep his anticipation of some dramatic pronouncement in check, sat across from him in silence.

When Fensterwald looked up, he saw Jerry's anxious expression and smiled. His face was flush and he started talking rapidly. "It is fascinating to see these old newspapers, especially the Münchner Post. It vas highly critical of the Nazi Party and Hitler, all the vay back to the 1920s. I think it vas 1933 when Hitler's SA troops ransacked the newspaper's offices and hauled every one off to prison. It vas the end of the free press until after the vor.

"Now, may I?" he asked, gesturing at the novel with his other hand. Jerry had enjoyed the suspense of holding back the novel until after Fensterwald had examined the newspapers but now eagerly handed over *Little Dorrit*. He watched intently as Fensterwald opened the cover, his face suddenly ashen.

Jerry was worried that the Hitler bookplate might bring back painful memories for Fensterwald. Years earlier, the professor had revealed to him that some family members, obstinate in their belief that the early Nazi persecutions were temporary, had stayed behind in Germany and, in so doing, had sealed their fates. Jerry resolved not to break the silence and after a few minutes Fensterwald resumed his professorial demeanor.

"Someone vit greater expertise than me vill need to authenticate the details of the bookplate. You are no doubt avare that forgeries have been deployed throughout history to deceive people. The Nazis ver notorious in this regard. Vat you have to go on so far is that this Heinz Kammler hid a book that may have belonged to Adolf Hitler. Everything else is supposition until you learn more.

"Ve can agree, it is quite a mystery and maybe even unsolvable yet certainly vert pursuing. Is your friend, the famous Mr. Meacham, already involved?" he asked.

"I tracked him down in Switzerland and hope to speak with him tonight," Jerry explained. "It crossed my mind that the bookplate might be a forgery, but if real, the novel must have considerable value to someone, certainly more than sentimental."

The professor shook his head and shrugged, then examined the newspapers again. His eyes lit up as he scrutinized them in silence. "After the vor, the allies controlled the press and you had to get a license from the Americans to publish. One explanation vas that newsprint vas scarce but, more importantly, the U.S. vanted to control vat the German people read. Protecting them from Nazi propaganda but still it was censorship, right? Did you notice the date at the top? Look, it is November 5, 1932. Someone who despised Hitler kept old copies of the Münchner Post and vanted to make a political statement by covering the book vit them. It seems clear that this book has been, as you Americans like to say, 'under vraps' for more than fifty years."

Fensterwald chuckled at his little joke and then picked up the novel again. He was deep in thought as he flipped through the pages of *Little Dorrit*, stopping to looking at the detailed caricatures that were sprinkled throughout, rubbing his thumb and forefinger back and forth across his lower lip.

Jerry cleared his throat and Fensterwald looked up, as if surprised, and said, "I know little about Hitler's book collection but there are experts who can help you. I can make discreet inquiries if you vish. The date of the newspaper is a clue vich now makes me think the book probably came from Hitler's library in Berchtesgaden, only a few hours by car from Munich. Did Kammler or someone close to him live in the area at that time? That vood be a good start. I can tell you that Hitler spoke German in the Bavarian dialect vit a distinct Austrian accent. Historians agree that he knew a few English verds but couldn't speak or read the language so it is interesting that he vood possess the English language version of a Dickens novel. Perhaps, he had Eva Braun read it to him. A bedtime story, maybe?" Fensterwald's eyes twinkled at his rare *bon mot* and it made Jerry laugh.

The professor held up one hand and now looked stern. "Some people who like to think that Hitler sprung forth like a mythical, feral beast ignore the family's troubled history."

Fensterwald went on to tell Jerry about Hitler's father, Alois, the bastard child of Maria Schnicklgruber. Alois was eventually adopted by his stepfather after Maria married Julian Hiedler. As an adult, Alois convinced Austrian authorities that he was the biological son of Hiedler and took his name, subsequently changing the spelling to Hitler. Alois was a brute and a tyrant who sired six children – including Adolf – through three marriages.

One son, Alois, Jr., ran away to Dublin and eloped with an Irish girl, eventually ending up in Liverpool, England. Alois, Jr. abandoned his wife and returned to Germany where he opened a watering hole in Berlin popular with Nazi stormtroopers. After the war, he made a meager living by selling autographed pictures of his brother to tourists.

"There is a story told by Alois, Jr's wife that Hitler visited his older half-brother in England around 1912 but many historians dispute it. If true, though, it could have been the occasion to pick up *Little Dorrit*. Alois, Jr. could read and speak English so maybe it vas his copy of the novel vich he gave to the future Fuhrer. Who can know, right?" Fensterwald explained.

The most intriguing part of Fensterwald's narrative was Hitler's relationship with his niece Geli Raubal, 19 years his junior. By all accounts, Hitler was obsessed with Geli, declared that she was his true love, and took complete control of her life, practically keeping her under lock and key in his Munich apartment. In 1931, she was found in a pool of blood in the apartment, an apparent suicide from a pistol shot to the chest. Hitler was allegedly not in Munich at the time but the weapon of death did belong to the leader of the Nazi Party. It was a time when the future Fuhrer was rapidly gaining strength in Germany and no inquiry into Geli's death materialized.

After Fensterwald stopped, the two men sat in silence, looking into each other's eyes. They had both drifted back to 1985, recalling how they had met and how the major events of the reservoir investigation had played out, not just with the discovery of the grave of the long-lost Meacham relative but also with the downfall of a business titan and the murder of his son.

Finally, Fensterwald broke the silence and said, "So, you have chosen to be a man of business. Vat a change from ven ve first met, no? And now, the boys from Parlor City have another mystery to untangle," he said wistfully, looking into Jerry's eyes.

Fensterwald walked from behind his desk and placed his hands firmly on Jerry's shoulders. "And now, I must prepare for a class. Ve vill talk again soon, I trust. I am protected here, cloistered behind ivy-covered valls but you must alvays be careful out there," Fensterwald intoned, waving one arm toward the window.

Shortly after Jerry returned home, Woody Meacham called from Geneva. He had already been told about the murder of Kammler and Jerry's surprise inheritance. Now, he listened intently as his friend described the discovery of the Dickens novel and his visit with Prof. Fensterwald.

"There's always the possibility that the shop owner was killed by someone desperate for cash, a junkie perhaps, who then fled in a panic, grabbing a few figurines without taking the time to look for the cash box," Woody suggested. "Or?" Jerry asked, urging his friend on. "Or, he was after a particular antique vase, found it and escaped. A tale reminiscent of the Maltese falcon, if you want to be dramatic. Now, if

Kammler recognized the intruder, that might explain the murder. The perp felt he had no choice but to eliminate the eyewitness."

"But Kammler was a recluse" Jerry pressed.

"Look, I don't know what to believe yet, Jer. I'll check out the shop owner's name with some sources here and in Germany. In the meantime, move the book to a safe place. Also, the shop's collectibles need to be inventoried and appraised. A great deal of junk is sold in so-called antique shops to gullible buyers, hoping to secure a piece of history on the cheap. If all the figurines and vases are of modest value, that will be telling."

Woody was certain that Jerry had already surmised that if the shop was full of over-priced junk, like the merchandise peddled on those ubiquitous television shows, then the murderer hadn't come looking for an old German figurine. He wished now that he hadn't alluded to the Dashiell Hammett novel and hoped Jerry hadn't caught it. In the *Maltese Falcon*, the search by desperate men for the illusive black statuette had left a trail of murders across several continents. Was there someone out there just as obsessed as the villainous Kasper Gutman in the Hammett novel who would stop at nothing to possess Kammler's copy of *Little Dorrit*? And if so, why?

CHAPTER FIVE
NEAR FINE

────◆────

THE NEXT MORNING, Jerry moved *Little Dorrit*, once again wrapped in tissue and the old Bavarian newspapers, to the basement of the Thimbletown Inn, a short walk from the shore of Long Island Sound. Jerry and his wife, the former Fanny Tulk, had purchased the Inn in the late 1970s from the Trowbridge estate, in part to prevent the property from falling into the hands of an out-of-state developer who planned to build pricey condos with a water view, thereby restricting the enjoyment of the majestic panorama to a privileged few. Jerry referred to himself as Fanny's "aide-de-camp," as it was she who managed the Inn – and him – with benevolent but imperial authority.

"What do I need to know, Jerry?" she asked when her husband approached the front desk after emerging from the basement. Fanny had not yet been told about his meeting with Prof. Fensterwald or his conversation with Woody.

"First, I've got to get the book authenticated and appraised to find out if it has value as a collectable. Fensterwald is going to locate experts who can help. Woody is running a check on Kammler through Interpol and other sources. We're hoping that his background in Germany will provide a clue as to how he came into possession of the Dickens novel. That's where we are now, Hon."

Fanny stared at her husband. A slight smile creased her mouth as her eyes narrowed. Jerry had seen that look before. She was not placated by his mundane summary but he hesitated to elaborate. When the smile disappeared and she cocked her head to one side, he gave up and continued. "Woody thinks there's a possibility that the thief didn't find what he was looking for and might return. If so, one of the figurines or the book could be his target."

"Even if it came from Hitler's library, can the book be that valuable, Jerry? Enough to get an old man killed? I don't understand. Please tell me that we are okay," Fanny implored. Jerry knew she was thinking of their two children, Maude and Cyrus, so he said, "I'll call Fensterwald and give him a nudge. Getting the novel appraised is my top priority, I promise you. If it has minimal value, we can relax and assume the killer got what he was looking for, most likely an antique vase."

Jerry knew Fanny wasn't satisfied with his perfunctory analysis so he shrugged, hoping to avoid further interrogation. "You have to promise me that you will no longer work at the shop alone, day or night, starting now," Fanny demanded, before adding, "Luckily, the kids go off to camp in two days. I'm sure you don't want them returning home as orphans." Jerry nodded his head sheepishly. It hadn't dawned on him until her dark observation that his entire family might be in jeopardy.

IT TOOK ANOTHER day for Fensterwald to identify two experts that had the qualifications to evaluate *Little Dorrit*. He related the news to Jerry in high spirits. The first was an antiquarian book dealer in New

Haven by the name of Harley Grantham who specialized in Victorian literature and ephemera. The second was a curator at the Library of Congress in Washington, DC by the name of Oswald Brenner. Speaking with a former colleague at Yale, Fensterwald confirmed that a sizable portion of Hitler's library had been seized by U.S. troops after the war and was initially sent to a warehouse in Alexandria, VA before ending up at the national library. "Ven I told them that you had come upon a book of potentially significant historical value that might have a connection to Hitler, they both asked for details but I offered nothing. I vas very clever in teasing their curiosity, yes? Vell, they both have your name and know you vill be calling. Good luck, my freund."

That afternoon, Jerry drove to New Haven to meet with Harley Grantham. The store owner was wearing a brown tweed jacket with elbow patches and a red striped bow tie. His spare mustache was neatly trimmed and his thinning hair appeared to have been professionally permed. With his head tilted slightly back, he eyed Jerry through his nose. Jerry held his pique in check and murmured "prig" under his breath as Grantham sniggered and offered him a limp hand, as if to say. "Let's see if you have anything worthy of my time."

Jerry, already regretting that he had entered the shop, removed *Little Dorrit* from his valise. He had left the yellowed newspapers at home and the novel was now encased in layers of bubble wrap. Grantham donned blue latex gloves before picking up the novel. Jerry wondered if Grantham was trying to impress him with his professionalism or was merely a germaphobe. Grantham turned the novel over and back a few times before opening it. After glancing at the Hitler bookplate, he turned to the title page and involuntarily nodded his head. The smirk was gone.

"It was first published in serial format, like most if not all Dickens novels, beginning in 1855. The publisher came out with a hardcopy version in 1857 and, if I'm not mistaken, you are in possession of a first edition in excellent, or what we like to call 'near fine' condition."

Grantham then went silent as he paged through the novel, halting to admire the illustrations by Hablot Browne, popularly known at the time as Phiz. When he got near the end, he looked up at Jerry, pointing to the page where he had stopped. Turning the novel around, he said, "I suspect you didn't notice this, Mr. Kosinsky." Jerry looked nervous when he saw a note that had been bound into page 467. It made Grantham smile.

"Relax. It's what's called an error slip, proving the novel's status as a first edition. Dickens was careless and mis-named a character in this chapter. It wasn't caught until after the first printing but was corrected in later editions. The slip was the publisher's way to acknowledge the error and, for collectors, it proved that a first edition could be authenticated by Dickens' oversight.

"I am not sure how or if the Hitler bookplate adds to or detracts from the novel's market value until it is made available for bid. Of course, I am confident that I can secure you a most advantageous price – less my fee, of course." Grantham's voice was now cloying and Jerry saw through his effort to suddenly sound engaging.

When Jerry didn't respond, Grantham raised one hand in a cautionary way. "Now, it does not appear that anyone has tampered with the bookplate, the frontispiece or the cover page but I must add a note of caution. Book thieves have been known to insert what are known as 'typographical facsimiles" into later, less valuable editions of books in an effort to make them look like first editions. In other words, the frontispiece and cover pages are sometimes copied from or sliced out of first editions that are in very poor condition and meticulously glued into cheaper editions. Some of these con artists are masterful and many collectors and libraries have been swindled by this insidious subversion of art. In other words, a closer examination of the paper used, along with an examination of the bookplate, would certainly be wise. Naturally, that can be expensive. I keep no secrets from my customers, sir. You can take that commitment to the bank any day."

Jerry nodded and then asked, "But since you seem convinced that I am in possession of a first edition, what value would you put on it for insurance purposes?" Grantham frowned and his head once again tilted back. So, you are contemplating keeping it, Mr. Kosinsky? I had not pegged you as a serious collector."

Jerry didn't take the bait and there was an uncomfortable silence, after which Grantham smiled and said, in a saccharine voice, "Why not forego the expense of an appraisal and consignment. It could be a lengthy and time-consuming process. Not to mention that the vulgarity of the Hitler bookplate might present some problems. I am prepared to assume all these risks and take the novel off your hands right now for $600 – in cash. What do you say, Jerry?"

Jerry shook his head, amused by the false geniality of suddenly being on a first name basis and, without looking up, started wrapping *Little Dorrit*. "I may be back in touch, Harley. It has been enlightening and I do appreciate your time today."

Grantham's nostrils flared just enough to reveal his contempt. Both of them understood that it was the last they would see of each other.

WHILE JERRY WAS being tutored by Grantham in New Haven, DeBruycker sauntered into a bookstore off Central Park South featuring rich mahogany, glass-encased bookshelves floor to ceiling with a carpeted staircase leading to the second floor. He scrutinized each set of glass doors to confirm that they were all locked.

On a table in the middle of the room, he picked up a copy of *FIRSTS, The Book Collector's Magazine*. Leafing through it, Theo saw that a rare copy of Bronte's *Jane Eyre* was being offered by a bookseller only a few blocks away.

Casaubon's Bookshop was just off Fifth Avenue on 55th Street. Theo pushed the buzzer and waited for the humming sound to unlock the heavy glass door. He was dressed in an exquisitely tailored charcoal grey suit, complemented by a white shirt and club tie, knotted in classic Windsor style. His neatly trimmed Van Dyke goatee and matching mustache gave him a distinctive aristocratic, old world look. He glanced at the glass case behind the front desk, holding some first editions, noticed it was unlocked, and kept walking. He suspected that *Jane Eyre* would be housed there unless it had already been sold.

He browsed with an insouciant air, waiting to be approached. Within minutes, he was accosted by a man who introduced himself as the manager. No, they did not have a first edition of *Little Dorrit* in the shop, Theo was advised, but it could be secured within a few days. When DeBruycker, deploying his best French accent, explained that he was only interested in an 1857 first edition of the first printing in fine or near fine condition, the manager nodded his head knowingly. "Give me a few moments, sir," he said, practically bowing in retreat.

After the manager disappeared into the back of the shop, DeBruycker returned to the front and glided behind the counter, scanning the books shelved in the unlocked glass case, a surprisingly common error that never ceased to astonish him.

He quickly spotted the leather-bound copy of *Jane Eyre* and slid it from the case. A notation in light pencil on the inside of the board confirmed that it was a first edition of the U.S. printing by Harper and Brothers. It was in very good condition and was printed with Bronte's pen name of Currer Bell on the cover page as "editor," instead of her actual name. It would command a handsome price. In one fluid motion, the novel went into the oversized pocket he had sewn inside his suitcoat. He still had the touch and it felt reassuring after the debacle at Kammler's shop.

The manager returned wearing a triumphant smile as DeBruycker lounged by the entrance, gazing out on W. 55th Street. He knew it was important that he play this little charade to the end. A first edition, first printing of *Little Dorrit* in "like new" condition, he was happy to report, could be acquired for a price of $5000 but the manager cautioned that such a rare find would not be available for long.

"You can certainly find a less expensive first edition, sir, but what makes this one especially unique is that it includes an original watercolor by the bookbinder's granddaughter, Helen R. Haywood, who was herself an exceptional talent. I should add that the rebinding by Riviere circa 1930 is exquisite."

DeBruycker feigned interest and the manager, looking earnest, handed him his card. "I have been advised that the novel will be on display at the International Antiquarian Book Fair in Boston next week. I suspect it will leave there under new ownership, sir," the manager warned.

Theo studied the card and said in a desultory voice, "I am staying at the Hotel Dorset a few blocks away. Call me when you have the novel in hand. I am confident that we can come to terms quickly."

DeBruycker scribbled his name on the back of the manager's card, handed it back and started toward the door. He looked back when he heard the manager say, "We would certainly appreciate your business, Mr. d'Arblay. I will be in touch very soon."

DeBruycker was feeling smugly self-confident as he strolled over to Central Park and looked for a French café at which to celebrate his productive morning. He had secured the information he sought regarding the value of a first edition of *Little Dorrit* and had lifted a valued copy of *Jane Eyre* with ease. It would not dawn on him for a while but in a moment of hubris, he had committed an amateurish sin by giving out his alias without purpose or gain.

Sipping his Campari and soda, he thought back to the incident years earlier when he was approached by an attractive woman in a Bruges restaurant who told him he had an uncanny resemblance to the dashing and handsome archvillain in the movie *Day Of The Jackal*. When he made a play for her, she declined his advances, explaining, "Please don't be offended. See the movie and you will understand why."

Theo did see the movie, more than once, mesmerized by the English actor who played the Jackal. He even took notes while watching Edward Fox assume several disguises while plotting with precision the assassination of French President Charles De Gaulle. He studied his cool and unflappable style, his polished mannerisms, his exquisite wardrobe and his powers of seduction with both sexes. Theo bought the novel by Frederick Forsyth, upon which the movie was based, to get a deeper understanding of the character – and the actor – whose style he began to emulate. It had taken a while but Theo had even learned to like the bitter taste of the Jackal's favorite cocktail.

Theo finished his lunch and was nursing an espresso as he surveyed his surroundings, admiring the large American elms swaying in the park just a short walk away. It seemed almost surreal that a poor orphan boy from Ghent, in the heart of the Flemish Low Country, was here in the land of unlimited opportunity, a jackal in their midst, where pedigree was not essential to success. It was now that his blunder with the Casaubon manager suddenly hit him, turning the taste of the espresso sour. He consoled himself with the fact that very soon he would look nothing like the suave Frenchman.

Theo decided it would now be best to pawn *Jane Eyre* off on another New York dealer further downtown for half the inflated retail price. He could walk away with cash to pad his bankroll and eliminate the evidence of his presence in the Casaubon shop. More importantly to Theo, he had learned that the fee he was being paid to steal Kammler's copy of *Little Dorrit* wildly exceeded the value of a rare first edition of the novel. It was clear now that Kammler's copy was important to the German buyer beyond its intrinsic value. Was it reckless to think that if he could find out why, he might be able to up the ante or even start a bidding war? Would Von Paulus be receptive to such a bold move, he wondered?

Next, his thoughts turned to the upcoming Boston book fair. Rare book dealers from around the world, supercilious to a man, would converge on that city, offering their most precious possessions with a languid air that made Theo think they were just there to strut, pose and tell fantastic tales about their collections. Well, if he could complete his work in Connecticut in a timely manner, he might just head up to Boston and try his luck with these insufferable humbugs before flying to Hamburg to deliver *Little Dorrit*.

CHAPTER SIX
An Education
In Antwerp

It was the early 1950s when Jules DeBruycker opened a small bookstore in Ghent, one of the larger cities in Belgium's northern region known as Flanders, where a majority of the population spoke a Dutch dialect known as Flemish. French was the predominant language in the southern part of the country, a region commonly known as Wallonia.

The DeBruycker shop was close by the university where Jules hoped that his son Theo would eventually study. The father was known as a humble, benevolent man who had no practical business sense, that talent having resided in his wife. When she died unexpectedly, and to the amazement of many, Jules kept the shop afloat without her, even though sales were meagre. And inexplicably, in the judgment of his rival dealers, he lent books out on credit to university students and others who pled poverty. It was the considered opinion of other booksellers in Ghent that Jules DeBruycker was not only an easy touch but also an irredeemable coxcomb.

After his mother's death, four-year-old Theo turned sullen and taciturn, defying the urge of most children to seek companionship. Friends warned Jules that little Theo, with his nightmarish dreams, was suppressing an anger and a rage that would burst forth one day and be the boy's undoing.

Jules felt helpless to remedy the situation and often joked, ruefully, that Theo was his little "night watchman" who preferred the solitude of the shop floor over his bed. After his father retired for the evening, the lad would creep out from the family sleeping quarters upstairs, toting a pillow and dragging a blanket behind him. Theo would choose a different aisle each night and ensconce himself beneath the rows of books that towered above him. With a flashlight, he recited the authors' names aloud before falling off to sleep.

Jules offered a broad array of cheap, modern editions of the world's great novels published over the last two centuries. It was this literature section of the shop where the precocious Theo gravitated. With a special affinity for the English writers, he eventually devoured the Dutch and German translations of the works of Smollett, Fielding, Swift and Defoe. But, above all, he revered Charles Dickens.

As he grew, young Theo had free rein in the shop when not in school – all except for a locked room in the back. When he asked his father about it, he received a bemused smile and a wag of the finger in return.

On his twelfth birthday, Theo was taken by Jules to the *Boekentoren*, the book tower at Ghent University that its architect had proclaimed "a mighty bookcase built up high." The tower stood over two hundred feet tall, with twenty-four floors holding more than three million books, manuscripts, maps and other rare documents.

It was at the *Boekentoren* that wide-eyed Theo first saw behind the locked glass cases the treasures that would change his life. He gazed in wonder at the *Waverly* novels of Sir Walter Scott, Goldsmith's *Vicar of Wakefield*, Smollett's *Peregrine Pickle* and, in all its magnificent, leather-bound glory, a signed first edition of Charles Dickens final, completed novel, *Our Mutual Friend.*

It was shortly after this visit to the *Boekentoren* that Theo announced that he would one day assemble a grand library of the world's great literature, first editions of the rarest kind. His father was amused and said, "And how do you intend to start, Son, by stealing them from the Boekentoren?" He explained to Theo that such a collection was beyond the means of only a privileged few, the well-endowed libraries and the richest aesthetes of the world. "Bibliomania is a curse if you let it dominate your life, my boy," Jules warned. Theo was angered by his father's admonition but said nothing.

At school, Theo discovered that he was a gifted linguist. He mastered English by his early teens, adding it along with French to his native Dutch and German. One of his teachers told him he was a polyglot. It caused Theo to lower his eyebrows and smile sardonically, explaining that hyperpolyglot was a more apt description of his talents.

And then tragedy struck the DeBruyckers again one afternoon when Jules fell from a ladder while stacking books and broke his neck. That evening, Uncle Luc arrived. Within a week, the bookshop was closed and Theo, now 15-years old, was taken away to the Belgian seaport city of Antwerp, where Luc DeBruycker operated a scrap metals yard near the docks. Unlike his brother Jules, Luc was a gruff, vulgar man with crude habits and a nasty temper. He was squat and barrel-chested and favored tight shirts unbuttoned halfway to his navel, revealing a thick forest of black hair. Theo found his uncle repulsive.

Luc never missed an opportunity to ridicule the boy's naivete and scoff at Theo's grandiose plan to assemble a library of rare books. He decided to teach his nephew a lesson and gave him an early edition of Dickens' *Hard Times* for his next birthday. The boy was elated until his uncle explained that it came from the locked room in the back of his father's shop, a room that had mystified Theo while growing up.

Theo learned from Uncle Luc how his father had operated a black market in rare books, using a team of scouts and thieves to steal, by special request, prized tomes from rival booksellers and libraries in Belgium's major cities. Even the prestigious *Boekentoren* in Ghent had been a target.

Luc seemed determined to destroy all vestiges of Theo's life in Ghent by also revealing how his father also dealt in the black market for Christian erotica, then outlawed in most if not all European countries. Luc showed Theo a book which, when closed, revealed decorative coloring on the edges of the pages. When the pages of the book were fanned, however, the image of a nude woman in a sensual pose magically appeared. This artistic process of concealment was known as "fore-edging" and was very popular among Jules' wealthy clients, Luc explained. These latest revelations about his father sent Theo spiraling into a prolonged depression.

To further Theo's indoctrination into his world, Luc demanded that his nephew accompany him on a drive to Brussels one afternoon. They cruised the neighborhoods surrounding the *Gare du Midi*, the train station near the *Boulevard Maurice Lemmonier,* known by locals as Kandahar Lane because of its predominant Middle Eastern population. At a few shops, Luc would pull up and someone would come out to greet him at the trunk of his car where boxes were quickly unloaded and money was exchanged.

Luc drove on to the *Anderlecht* district, heavily populated by Eastern Europeans and dominated by Albanian gangs, well-known to the Belgian police for human trafficking and the sale of fake identity documents. Again, the ritual at the trunk was repeated, this time at a few seedy-looking taverns as Theo watched the transactions completed in the side mirror of the car. "If you ever want a new identity, boy, come here and seek out the Albanians," Luc explained, laughing while he cuffed Theo behind the head.

BITTER AND DISCONSOLATE, Theo dropped out of school and started working at Luc's other business, a used appliance store in the downtown Antwerp neighborhood known as the *Borgerhaut*, heavily populated by Moroccan immigrants. In his spare time, he wandered the streets of the city. One day, he found himself on the steps of the Hendrik Conscience Heritage Library, adorned in front with a statue of the revered Belgian writer by that name. No longer the innocent dreamer from Ghent who imagined that he would somehow magically assemble a library of famous novels, Theo was now a cynical young man. As he strolled through the rooms of the Heritage Library, he became angry as he fantasized about stealing treasures from its rare book rooms. Why not follow my destiny, he thought to himself.

As chance often intervenes, Theo was befriended by an elderly female librarian by the name of Renata Peeters. Affecting a shy and self-effacing manner while standing outside the rare book room, Peeters felt compassion for Theo and invited him in. When he returned to the Henrik a few days later, Theo came with the copy of *Hard Times* that Luc had given him for his birthday. Theo's father had scrubbed the novel clean of any markings that would have identified it as coming from the private collection of a wealthy Ghent businessman. It was a first edition, she exclaimed enthusiastically, marveling how this young man came to possess such a valuable book.

Thus began the tutelage of Theo at the knee of Renata Peeters. She taught him the difference between "fine," a book in almost pristine condition and a book classified as "good," still valuable but with imperfections.

Theo was an avid student, receiving the education from a stranger that his father should have provided. He didn't mind when Renata gently chided him if he referred to the "cover" of a rare, hardcover book. She smiled and explained that to establish his credentials, he must master and then deploy the vocabulary of a collector. Use the word "boards" instead of cover, she insisted. During the binding process, she pointed out, the boards would be covered with cloth to enhance the quality and beauty of the book.

"Bumping," she explained, was minor damage to the corner of the boards. Renata taught Theo about the other categories of damage that would reduce the value of an otherwise priceless book. Referring to the inside of the book, she taught him about "foxing" and "yellowing" which would signify the aging of the paper, often caused by excessive exposure to sunlight or humidity. Then, there was the "smell" test. A seasoned collector can detect the scent of incipient mildew, a condition that will ruin the book and its collectable value.

Upon returning from a Brussels book fair, Renata almost wept as she described to Theo the copy of *Dracula* that she had seen there. It was a rare "first edition" that had been authenticated by several antiquarians as coming from the first ever printing – or "first impression" of the novel. She referred to *Dracula* as her "black tulip," a book so rare, like the flower, that eager collectors vied for the occasional copy that came on the market.

Renata warned Theo that amateur collectors could be fooled, even conned at times, when they purchased a "first edition thus," not comprehending that it was merely a way to define the first printing of the novel by that particular publisher, months or even years after the authenticated and true "first edition" by the inaugural publisher. She pointed out to Theo that the collectable value of two "first editions" of the same novel could therefore be widely disparate. Theo drank in all the training that Renata could offer and, in the process, developed an intense dislike for what he perceived as the elitist collectors and dealers who could use obscure and confusing terminology to deceive and even take advantage of the novice collector.

ONE DAY, AFTER spending the morning at the Hendrik Library, Theo showed up for work at Luc's appliance store and found it was closed. Returning home, he discovered that his uncle wasn't there.

The next morning, Theo went to the scrap metal yard and saw it swarming with police and custom agents. A crowd had formed around the cordoned off area and Theo spotted one of Luc's workers on the edge of it. The worker made a grimacing face and warned Theo to stay away with a violent movement of his arm.

It would be a few days before Theo learned that the appliance store and scrap metal yard had served as fronts to "wash" the money Luc earned from his smuggling operation. Antwerp had the best cigarette warehousing facilities on the continent and was a major port of entry for U.S. companies like R. J. Reynolds and Philip Morris. Through his connections with a few corrupt customs agents, Luc had established a highly profitable operation, siphoning off just enough boxes of cigarettes each month to escape notice. Avoiding import duties and other taxes, contraband Winstons and Marlboros from the U.S. could be sold cheaply. Steal them outright, as Luc and his partners did, and one could garner enormous profits.

To expand his cigarette smuggling enterprise, Luc went into partnership with a ruthless gang from the *Borgerhaut* known as the "mocro-maffio," a group of Moroccans with a thriving drug operation. Word spread quickly that Luc had short-changed his new partner and, as a warning to others, had been dismembered and fed to the fish in the North Sea. It was enough to send Theo packing.

CHAPTER SEVEN
THE MAKING OF A BIBLIOKLEPT

THEO SCOURED HIS uncle's house and found cash taped behind pictures and mirrors, enough to live on for several weeks. He boxed up the books that had been removed from the locked room in his father's bookstore and took the train to Ghent, where he found a cheap apartment near the University. Out his window, he could glimpse the top of the *Boekentoren* that had inspired him as a young boy. Now, he gazed on it as a symbol of greed, and a target for exploitation.

When he contacted the Von Paulus and Reinhold auction houses in Germany, he was pleased to learn that they would be happy to do business with Jules DeBruycker's son. Next, he recruited a few thieves and scouts. Before long, he had a small network lifting books by special request from shops and libraries in and around Ghent. As the months went by, Theo's enterprise achieved modest success.

One day, Theo received a call from a bookdealer in Ghent with whom he had established a working relationship, alerting him that someone had called him, offering to sell a Georges Simenon novel that the dealer was almost certain had been stolen by Theo's team expressly for one of the auction houses in Germany. Theo instructed the book dealer to show interest in acquiring the book and to set a time for the next day to complete the transaction.

Arriving early, Theo positioned himself in a back room with the door ajar so that he could observe the meeting. He watched as a feeble-looking, white-haired old man presented a first edition, first issue of *Maigret Abroad*. It was the first English language edition of the Simenon novel, published in London in 1940. Theo had never seen the old man before and wondered how he had come into possession of the book.

When the old man started talking, Theo's ears perked up. He was amazed to hear the distinctive voice of the part-time student and actor on his team.

Theo walked out and calmly confronted the man before erupting in rage, thrashing him until he crumbled to the floor. After this incident, Theo couldn't stop thinking about the impressive disguise that would have beguiled him in any other setting.

By nature a loner, Theo concluded that he could better operate solo, accountable to and dependent on no one else. To start anew, he decided that he must leave his hometown of Ghent. Within a month he had moved to the city of Bruges.

It was shortly after moving to Bruges that Theo encountered the woman at the restaurant who educated him about the Jackal. He marveled at how the English assassin, with disguises and false identities, constantly thwarted the police in their manic, nationwide hunt to track him down. Theo had no ambition to be a killer for hire but, in all other respects, was determined to imitate the prowess of the Jackal.

Theo devoted hours to reading stories of the thefts of antiquities, often inside jobs by archivists and librarians. He was fascinated by the legend of the fanatical Don Vicente who allegedly committed arson and murder to obtain coveted rare books in Barcelona during the 1830s. He read with admiration about the exploits of the German theologian Elois Pichler who, over a century earlier, had stolen thousands of books, many of them rare, while working as a librarian at the Russian Imperial Library in St. Petersburg. The ingenuity of Pilcher impressed Theo. The German had sewn a large, deep pocket on the inside of his coat where he could secrete rare documents in its deep recesses, giving him the ability to stroll out of bookstores and libraries unchallenged. Theo's respect for Pichler had not abated when he learned that the German was eventually caught and sent to Siberia to serve his prison sentence.

Awed by the Jackal's meticulous preparation, Theo spent hours studying various disguises. He collected items from costume shops and second-hand vintage clothing stores and experimented with make-up, wigs of various shades and facial hair. He accumulated a collection of emollients, salves, creams, hair dyes and tints along with spectacles of various styles and colors, all with clear lenses. He found out that he enjoyed his talent for disappearing into another world, to be the only one who knew that there was another person beneath the façade.

Over the next several months, Theo would go out in the guise of a beggar, priest, policeman and an old man. He practiced at home being the one-legged soldier in the jackal movie but strapping his leg tightly behind him was too painful to endure for more than a few minutes. Wherever he ventured, Theo wore one of the coats into which he had sewed what he called his "Pichler pocket."

As the years passed, there was talk among book dealers, librarians, museum directors and reputable private collectors about the proliferation of rare book thefts throughout Belgium. At their regular conclaves, while sipping wine and bemoaning their losses, each one had a unique story to tell but there was no consistent, reliable description of a suspect. They reached the conclusion that a loose, criminal network, a gang of rare book thieves, had decided to go on a plundering spree. Amidst the growing complaints, the police felt helpless to react and the pilfering went on unabated.

THEO HAD DEVELOPED a compulsion to steal and viewed books like a mortician surveys a cadaver. He had learned to be cool and calculating like the Jackal and appreciated the utility of being charming and urbane toward women, beyond the power to merely seduce. Unknowingly, Renata Peeters had taught him its value at the Henrik.

Theo considered the antiquarian book industry a club of elitists who conversed in their own unique vocabulary. He despised these "blue bloods" with a fierce passion. For all he knew, they had a secret handshake like the Knights Templar or Freemasons. What he was sure of was that some of these people had disdain for the amateur collectors, the dilettantes who were only too eager to overpay for what they assumed were rare first editions.

Renata thought that she had been mentoring a future rare book librarian or collector. Before he disappeared from Antwerp, she had arranged a scholarship for Theo at the prestigious Katholieke Universiteit Leuven, not far from Brussels.

Weeks after Theo's departure for Ghent, the Henrik discovered that a rare copy of *Paradise Lost* printed in 1666, with illustrations by Gustave Dore, was missing from the library's rare book collection. John Milton's epic poem brought DeBruycker a handsome fee from the Von Paulus auction house in Hamburg and set him on the path that would eventually bring him to the United States.

CHAPTER EIGHT
SLEIGHT OF HAND

THE EVENING OF DeBruycker's visit, the manager of Casaubon's shop was preparing to close and went to lock the glass case behind the front counter when he noticed that *Jane Eyre* was missing. He searched frantically, hoping it had slipped behind another book. He reviewed his day's activities and recollected the customers with whom he had personally engaged during the day. His heart began to thump violently when he thought of the well-dressed Frenchman with the Van Dyke goatee. He pulled the card from his pocket, his hand trembling, as he mouthed the name Alexandre d'Arblay. When he called the Hotel Dorset and learned that no guest by that name was registered there, he felt weak in the knees. The vision of a handsome commission on the Dickens novel quickly faded away. What made him fear for his job was when Edward Casaubon, the dour and unforgiving owner, learned that he had been victimized by a careless manager and a master book thief.

DeBruycker spent a few days in New York City scoping out bookstores, wandering around Times Square and rummaging through the costume shops in the theater district. In the evenings, he watched the incessant coverage of the O.J. Simpson trial on all the news channels, then tried unsuccessfully to enjoy the canned humor of *Friends* and *Roseanne*. One night, he went out to see the recently released *Batman Forever* and decided that Nicole Kidman would be a worthy conquest for the Jackal.

DeBruycker concluded that he could no longer wait to confirm Heinz Kammler's death or hospitalization. The fate of *Little Dorrit* weighed heavily on him and he considered – as he always did – the worst case scenario. There was the danger that the novel could be swept up in an inventory remainder sale before he could retrieve it, forcing him to begin anew. Returning to Europe without *Little Dorrit* was not an option.

If Kammler had somehow miraculously survived, in other than a vegetative state, it was possible that his shop would simply be closed up, pending his recovery. In short, he needed to return to Graniteville, in a new disguise, assess the situation and then formulate a plan to secure the novel. Theo was also mindful of the assignment he had undertaken at the Yale library and knew he could no longer delay his return to Connecticut.

Ever cautious, DeBruycker had changed hotels and removed the Van Dyke disguise. The manager of the Casaubon bookshop had assuredly discovered the heist and sent the police looking for d'Arblay at the Dorset. Even if the store did not have security camera footage, he felt certain that his distinctive, old-world look had been described to authorities, who would then be looking for a Frenchman who had vanished into thin air.

Theo carefully removed the markings which identified Casaubon's ownership of *Jane Eyre*. Even a dishonest collector would be demanding enough to require a "clean" copy of the novel, critical to supporting plausible deniability should the novel's true ownership ever be established. He then called Simon Wegg, the proprietor of a used book shop on Lower Broadway, near the infamous Book Row of dealers that dominated the neighborhood decades earlier. Theo was reminded of the story of the Romm Gang, allegedly led by the antiquarian Charles Romm. In the 1930s, the gang thrived by selling stolen books to dealers in the area where Wegg's shop, opened by his father, could still be found. Dealers of questionable ethics, with a wink and a nod, gobbled up every book that Romm's boys brought to them.

It was well known among book thieves that Wegg was as unscrupulous as they came and had for years trafficked in books stolen from libraries – as well as from his competitors – up and down the East Coast. It made Theo wonder about those victimized by his father but he quickly pushed that unpleasant thought aside. There would be some haggling over *Jane Eyre* but DeBruycker and Wegg would come to terms.

BEFORE BOARDING THE New Haven-bound train the next morning, Theo found a travel agency off 37th Street with self-service storage lockers. He put his larger suitcase in one of the lockers, dropped four quarters in the coin slot and extracted the key after shutting the door. Before walking out, he slid open the hollowed out heel of his right shoe and inserted the keys for his suitcase and locker.

Today, a clean-shaven DeBruycker was outfitted in a blue blazer, white shirt and a tie adorned with the Belgian coat of arms. He had dyed his thick hair grey, with flecks of white, and combed it straight back. He donned rimless eyeglasses with small, clear lenses that gave him the older look that he desired.

He was a bit out of sorts since Wegg had "jewed him down" on the price for *Jane Eyre*. It was a slur he picked up from his Uncle Luc and he felt dirty just for recalling it. Still, Wegg must have sensed that Theo wanted the cash and he resented the book dealer's ability to read the situation correctly.

When he arrived in New Haven, Theo put his suitcase in storage and made the short walk to the public library. It had a section housing a collection of newspapers from towns in the region. It had morphed into a gathering spot for elderly, idle men who lounged in overstuffed chairs as casually as if they were in their own dens, some dozing with papers draped across their distended stomachs, the pages rising and falling in synchronization with their breathing.

Theo was conflicted when he read in one newspaper that Kammler was on ice in the morgue. The article went on to say that the police admitted they had few leads and no suspects. There was no mention of an old man with white hair and a mustache spotted at the train station. It was good news but wasn't particularly surprising. When he found a copy of the *Graniteville Gazette*, he learned about Kammler's will, designating a local man by the name of Jerry Kosinsky as his sole heir. The article went on to describe the bookstore as the decedent's only known asset and quoted Kosinsky as saying he had every intention of re-opening the shop as soon as possible.

DeBruycker was elated by the Graniteville news and now turned his attention to the unfinished business in New Haven that had been postponed because of his brutal reaction to Kammler's intransigence. The assignment at Yale required finesse and also carried considerable risk that would put his iron will and talents to a rigorous test.

JERRY LOCATED TWO antique dealers in a nearby town who agreed to evaluate the figurines, lamps, candle holders, steins and other collectables that, awaiting their fate, had been covered with a sheet and crowded into a corner of the shop. Before the sale, Jerry's wife came by and picked out an assortment of Hummel figurines to adorn the shelf behind the front desk at the Thimbletown Inn.

Fanny had done a superb job of revitalizing the Inn, which had fallen into disrepair at the end of the Trowbridge era of ownership. As she walked around the shop, her eyes darted constantly and Jerry smiled, knowing that he would yield to her vision of what needed to be done to attract customers, an objective that seemed never to have crossed Heinz Kammler's mind.

Kammler's prized possession, *Little Dorrit*, sat shrouded in layers of newspapers, tissue and bubble wrap in the basement of the Thimbletown Inn while Theo DeBruycker was plying his unique skills less than ten miles away.

THAT EVENING, WOODY was back home in Spain and called Jerry with news about Heinz Kammler. "I learned that his mother was the sister of Karl Schuster, the owner of the Hotel zum Tuerken in the town of Berchtesgaden, just down the mountain from Hitler's retreat. The Fuhrer named his mountain chalet The Berghof. Kammler must have been a boy or young man in the early 1930s. In any event, Schuster refused to sell his property to the Nazis but after they threw him into prison at Dachau, he had a change of heart. After the coerced sale, the hotel was used as a guard house and communication center.

"I'm just speculating but maybe Kammler's mother got employed at The Berghof when the hotel was forced to close. Someone is checking the passenger lists for ships that departed Germany before the war. Maybe Kammler's name will appear on one of them. Local records indicate that a number of families from Berchtesgaden emigrated to America before the war and settled in Baltimore where there was already a strong German community.

"And get this, Jer. As the war was ending, our soldiers found thousands of books from Hitler's library boxed up in schnapps crates and hidden in the Berchtesgaden salt mines. They were eventually catalogued and sent to the States, ending up at the Library of Congress. The consensus is that not all the books were retrieved by our boys from either the salt mines or Hitler's mountain retreat and that many ended up in private hands. It's circumstantial, I know, but the book you found in Kammler's closet could very well have been removed from Hitler's library – if not by his mother then by someone with connections to the Schuster family – before our doughboys showed up. I checked with the antique and rare art units at Interpol. Their databases are fairly current and none of them show a theft of *Little Dorrit*."

When Woody didn't get a reaction, he paused for a few seconds and his voice lowered. "You still there, my friend?" There was a cough on the other end of the line as Jerry cleared his throat. "I've been shaking my head the whole time you were talking, Woody. Fensterwald gave me the name of someone who oversees the Hitler archives at the Library of Congress. I'm guessing it includes the cache of books that came from the Berchtesgaden salt mines. I plan to meet with this man if he'll just return my damn call. All I want him to do is examine *Little Dorrit* and verify its authenticity."

Jerry's voice sounded shaky and Woody noticed. "Listen, I'm flying back to the states in a few days. Let me see what else I can find out on Kammler and the books discovered in the salt mine, okay? If you don't object, I'll go with you to the Library of Congress. Might even be able to smooth the way for the meeting, especially since your contact seems reluctant to cooperate. You worried about Kammler's murderer coming back, looking for the Dickens novel?"

"The book's in a locked utility closet in the basement of the Inn so he's not going to find it at the shop if he does come back. Of course, if he learns that I inherited the shop, that changes everything, doesn't it?" Jerry suggested.

"No harm in being cautious. Watch for strangers and keep the doors locked. I'll be on your doorstep soon," Woody said, hoping he sounded reassuring.

DeBruycker was deep in thought as he made his way to Yale's Beinecke Rare Book and Manuscript Library. Today's work would be neither quick nor so easy as lifting *Jane Eyre* from the inattentive Casaubon shop manager. There would be protocols to follow at Beinecke as well as surveillance, not to mention the scholars who would populate the reading room, any one of whom might decide to scrutinize him.

DeBruycker stopped in front of the imposing stone structure and took a deep breath as he gazed up at the rows of windows. After walking through the revolving doors, he stepped back involuntarily and stared at the central tower which housed tens of thousands of rare books and manuscripts. He felt a pang when he thought back to that day when he was only twelve years old and first entered the book tower at Ghent University with his father. Those days of innocence were long past.

He checked in at the registration desk and produced the requisite identification, using the forged credentials of a Professor Frans van Duyse from Katholieke *Universiteit Leuven, a school not far from Brussels.* He smiled involuntarily when he remembered that Renata Peeters had wanted him to attend school there. Ostensibly, he had visited the campus to please her but his motive was to case their library for its prized holdings.

Theo submitted his request for two rare items – the world atlas compiled by Gerard de Jode, published in Antwerp in 1578 and a Mercator atlas by Ortelius.

While waiting for the attendant to deliver the atlases, DeBruycker looked around for surveillance cameras before stuffing a two foot long piece of cotton string into his mouth, maneuvering it to the corner of his jaw like a slug of chewing tobacco. He found a long table in the corner occupied by two men sitting across from each other, both of them hunched forward as they inspected ancient tomes. When DeBruycker took a seat at the far end of the table, one of the men looked up and stared off into space, transfixed, as if transported back centuries in time. It was as if DeBruycker wasn't even there and it made the Belgian relax.

When the atlases were deposited in front of him, along with two weight bags to hold them open, DeBruycker searched the index for the de Jode map. There it was, the antique map encompassing part of Bavaria and Wurttemberg. DeBruycker worked the cotton string in his jaw as he scoured the room. There was never an absolutely perfect time to make the move he was contemplating but in every direction he looked, readers at the various tables were preoccupied with their research. After positioning the weight bags on the pages opened to the German map, he casually moved his fist up to his chin and coughed up the damp ball of string into his hand. He scanned the room again, then carefully laid the string along the inside of the page before closing the atlas and pressing his forearm down on the cover. He checked his watch and marked the time. He would wait 15 minutes and then complete the decisive step.

Theo cleared his throat and looked around to gauge any reaction that might suggest he was being watched. Excepting for a muffled cough, the room was silent. Theo felt as if he was invisible, a phantom, and it made him smile faintly for the first time since he walked into the Beinecke. He leafed through the Ortelius atlas, trying to look studious as he bided his time.

Safety precautions had been put in place due to a rash of thefts over the years that eventually came to light not because of the library's diligence but because the thieves had tried to pawn their booty off on reputable and knowledgeable dealers. He almost chuckled when he thought of the two Byzantine priests from a monastery in New York City who had stolen rare atlases from Yale's other library – the Sterling – by hiding them in their cassocks. Even if he was reckless enough to try, there was no chance in hell that DeBruycker would attempt to insert the bulky de Jode atlas into his coat. Even his "Pichler pocket" could not accommodate it. In any case, all he was hired to secure was a single map that some collector in Germany coveted.

DeBruycker checked his watch and was surprised to see that 20 minutes had elapsed. He opened up the de Jode atlas to where he had inserted the moistened string. Gripping the outer edge of the page, he gently pulled it away from the spine in almost imperceptible movements and felt it give way. Finally, he sensed that the map was entirely free of the binding, ready to be slid out.

He surveyed the room once more before turning the atlas so that the spine was facing away from him. In this way, he was able to drop the map into his lap. Once there, he carefully rolled it into a cylinder and slipped it into the deep pocket of his blazer. He felt his arm muscles tense up and noticed that his armpits were damp. For some reason, it made him relax. It had been a daring maneuver and DeBruycker was enjoying the adrenalin rush. He sat quietly, waiting to see if anyone approached him. Ten minutes later, he walked out the front door of the library unmolested and considerably richer then when he came in.

As HE WALKED back to the train station, DeBruycker reviewed his recent efforts. After the debacle at Kammler's shop, he had lifted and then pawned off *Jane Eyre* for a cool two grand and now had the de Jode map in his possession. Next, he would purchase an aluminum tube and ship the map via an overnight courier service to Dresden then wire his contact at the auction house that the prized map was on its way. A handsome fee would await him on his return to Europe.

DeBruycker sat on one of the wooden benches at the train station and looked up at the giant screen on the wall that listed arrivals and departures. He should have been elated but found himself fretting again about the complications caused by the death of Heinz Kammler. Murder was not DeBruycker's game and, unlike the Jackal, it bothered him that he had taken a step into a darker world that might not be reversible. When he got possession of *Little Dorrit* – as he knew he must – would it turn out to be a curse because of what he had done to secure it?

The next train to New York City was announced over the loudspeaker and, for a moment, it weakened Theo's resolve. Heading south would be tantamount to surrender and word would inevitably get out that he had blown an assignment and simply walked away. How could he return to Belgium with such a stain on his reputation? Von Paulus and Reinhold would never deal with him again. He looked at the giant screen again and saw that the northbound commuter train that made a stop in Graniteville left in one hour. That was the signal he needed.

After mailing the de Jode map to Dresden, he returned to the train station, retrieved his luggage and entered a bathroom stall. He put away the rimless eyeglasses and tinted his hair a medium brown. After checking himself in his handheld mirror, he was now ready to return to the scene of the crime.

CHAPTER NINE
OLD FRIENDS UNITED

———◆———

A FTER WOODY MEACHAM'S flight from Madrid landed in New York, he hired a car service for the trip to Connecticut. When they reached Graniteville, he had the driver go past the former Kammler shop and noticed that the lights were on. A van was backed up to the front door and on the side panels the name Dick Swiveller's Olde Curiosity Shoppe was stenciled.

Jerry emerged from the shop and was shaking hands with the van driver when he caught sight of his old friend walking toward him. He rushed over and wrapped Woody in a bear hug.

"Damn, you're a sight for sore eyes, pal," Jerry blurted out, his eyes glistening as he pulled back and beamed at Woody. "Still can't believe you found time to come up here. Is it just my luck that you have business in the states, some big case that brought you back?"

Woody chuckled and patted Jerry's arm. "In between cases, Jer, and that's the truth. I have a few courtesy meetings in DC and some family business in Parlor City but that's it. What's the verdict on the collectables – vintage or junk?" he asked, pointing to the van as it pulled away.

Jerry laughed and shook his head. "Just as we expected. Two bidders gave me the same estimate for the whole shebang but Swiveller was the only one willing to haul it away. The kind of stuff you pick up at a yard sale, Swiveller told me. Hell, I was at the point where I was ready to pay someone to cart the whole shooting match away. Might be a diamond in the rough but I don't give a damn. I've already got my gem, right?" Jerry didn't need to mention the Dickens novel when he saw Woody nod knowingly.

Woody paid the driver while Jerry grabbed his luggage from the trunk. "C'mon inside and look around before I lock up. The book inventory is in storage while we renovate so there's not much to see, other than the mystery room."

The two men walked around the cavernous shop, then gravitated to the closet that had housed *Little Dorrit*. "Wonder how long it was in there?" Jerry finally said, turning to look at his friend. "And why?" Woody added, sounding unintentionally ominous and wishing he had said nothing.

Jerry laughed nervously and draped his arm over Woody's shoulder. "Fanny's waiting dinner for us back at the house. We won't mention the novel unless she does, okay?" Woody nodded in acknowledgement. "I brought a couple of bottles of El Grajo Viejo. If you haven't tasted Barcelona red wine, you're in for a treat."

DeBruycker hailed a taxi at the Graniteville train station for the short ride to the town center. He could have easily walked but he was seeking information more than transportation. He fought off the temptation to send the cab past Kammler's shop and risk drawing unwelcome scrutiny.

"Came to town on short notice. Can you recommend a place to stay?" Theo asked, affecting a French accent. The driver looked in the rear view mirror and surveyed the well-dressed stranger. "There's a motel on the edge of town near the highway. One of those cookie-cutter, prefab operations. I'd recommend the Thimbletown Inn down by the water instead. It's run by the couple that just inherited the bookshop where the owner was murdered a few weeks ago. Doubt you heard about it but it was the biggest news hereabouts since a severed finger washed ashore some 20 years ago. Now, that's a story for the ages. The Inn seems like your style. It's quaint and charming plus it offers a helluva view of Long Island Sound."

The sun was setting as the taxi pulled up in front of the Thimbletown Inn. Theo was taken by the reddish orange hue that suffused the glistening water. The driver turned half-way around as he pointed out through the windshield, unable to resist the opportunity to be a tour guide. "Thimble Islands right out there," he said, still gesturing. Theo squinted and was able to make out a few protrusions visible on the horizon. "They're worth a look if you have the time and the inclination. There's a long history of the Thimbles, all 365 of them. Of course, most of them are underwater. My family lived out here for about a year when my dad worked on one of them. Quarry Island is its name. Those days of excavating pink granite here are long past." The driver caught himself expounding, dreamily, about an ideal past that never existed and added, "Hey, I'll wait here to make sure you can get a room."

A few minutes later, Theo was back, leaning into the driver's window. "I'm all set for the night. You're right, by the way. I'm quite sure this place will suit me perfectly."

THERE WAS NO mention of *Little Dorrit* during dinner but with the encouragement of Fanny, there was a great deal of reminiscing about the old days in Parlor City and the endless adventures to which the two friends were preternaturally drawn – commencing with Woody's discovery of a gun in a park when they were only ten years old. That memorable occasion brought Det. Billy Meacham, Jr. into both their lives after the weapon was eventually linked to a series of crimes, including a gruesome murder. The exploits of Billy Meacham were legendary. He became known as the "wonder boy" detective throughout the state for his uncanny ability to solve the most complex and bewildering criminal cases.

When Meacham married Woody's widowed mother and subsequently adopted him, it served as a sort of prelude to the two friends' involvement in a series of investigations spanning the next forty years.

With all this history between them, Woody and Jerry had difficulty accepting the theory that Heinz Kammler's murder had been the result of a random robbery gone bad. Happenstance just wasn't in the cards for them. Woody never forgot his stepfather's advice when he quit the police force to open his own private investigative agency. "When you get rid of the improbables in a case, Son, you are left with the possibles. That's where you need to focus your energies."

If it hadn't been for what they had already learned about the history of Kammler's copy of *Little Dorrit*, and the fact that it had been hidden away behind a bookshelf, they might have concluded that the perpetrator had either got what he wanted or was so horrified by the deadly outcome that he would never return to the scene of the crime.

Fanny was the first to allude to the novel, if only obliquely, as Woody refilled glasses from the second bottle of El Grajo Viejo. "My uncle arrives in the morning so you two Sam Spades can head down to DC with a clear conscience," she announced, tipping her glass in salute to both of them. "Uncle Homer relishes the idea of being my bodyguard while you're gone. I appreciate that his presence will calm you two worrywarts," she added.

Homer Tulk was the retired chief constable of Graniteville, serving in that capacity before the town had grown in size enough to justify its own police force. He was near eighty but as fit as any 50-year-old and an expert marksman to boot. Tulk still packed the Ruger Service Six, a blue steel revolver he had purchased in the sixties. It would be on his hip until Jerry returned home.

"We're catching one of those early bird prop planes out of New Haven and I'll be back the next day, Babe," Jerry explained. He was pleased that Tulk would be present but wasn't going to make a big deal out of it.

Fanny laughed and her face glowed from the wine. She was a handsome woman who rarely got ruffled, taking life's vicissitudes in stride and functioning as a calming influence on her excitable husband. "Uncle Homer will be shadowing me like a Secret Service detail not just here but over at the Inn as well. Which reminds me; I'd better check in with my night manager before I start slurring my words."

When Fanny left, Jerry said, "Thanks for setting up the meeting at the Library of Congress. This Brenner character never had any intention of calling me back. Tell me, if the novel really is from Hitler's library, can they seize it as government property?"

"First they'd have to prove it and even then, it's doubtful. Don't forget, a lot of our soldiers walked away with souvenirs from the war more valuable than an English novel. Things like oil paintings, badges, Nazi hats and revolvers. We'll know more after tomorrow's meeting. Keep in mind, Jer, that the purpose of this visit to DC is to authenticate the book. If the Hitler bookplate is a forgery, then it raises a number of questions. For one, why would someone defile an early edition of a novel and reduce its value? I'm for holding off on further speculation until we meet with the expert."

Jerry's head was bent down and he was rubbing his nose with his thumb and trigger finger while peering at Woody over the top of his tortoise shell glasses. "I'm trying hard to convince myself that whoever killed Kammler got what he came for and is far away by now, never to be seen in these parts again. Then, I think of all the things we've been through together over all these years and my rationalizing is just not working."

The men heard footsteps and perked up as Fanny walked back in. "Everything's copasetic. A well-dressed and very suave French gentleman, a visiting professor at Yale according to Maddie, checked in a few hours ago so we're full up for the night. Did you boys get all your conspiratorial talk out of the way while I was gone?"

———◆———

OVER AT THE Inn, DeBruycker fiddled with his pipe, a useful professorial prop, in the small lounge off the lobby. He had stopped at the front desk after dinner and chatted with the attractive night manager, instantly sensing that she was a vulnerable woman who could be easily charmed. She had already revealed what Fanny had told her about the plans for the Kammler shop – including the fact that the collectables were being sold off and that the book inventory was in storage while renovations took place. Had she been making eyes at him, he wondered? She was slim with a winsome smile that he found captivating but he had no experience with American women and wondered if she was just being indulgent because he was a guest.

Before heading up to his room, he would stop by the front desk again to see if his intuition about her had been correct. It had been some time since his last conquest and Theo DeBruycker, like the Jackal, was not a man to pass up the chance for a romantic interlude, especially if there was a chance it might further his objectives.

Theo would be careful not to press Maddie too hard for information. He felt confident that in a town as small as Graniteville, he would have little trouble finding out where the books were stored. He just hoped that *Little Dorrit* was among them. He wondered if Kosinsky had any clue as to the value of the Dickens novel. It amused him to think that even he didn't know why *Little Dorrit* was prized so highly by Von Paulus' secretive client back in Germany.

CHAPTER TEN
The Temptation

——◆——

After dinner, Jerry walked over to the Thimbletown Inn to retrieve *Little Dorrit* for the trip to Washington, DC. The novel was on a shelf in a locked utility closet in the corner of the basement. It wasn't until he got close to the Inn that he had a fearful vision of the closet door wide open and the novel gone.

Perhaps influenced by the arrival of his friend, Jerry looked around furtively as he came in the side entrance. He hesitated for a moment when he glimpsed a man leaning into the front desk, most likely a guest trying to make time with Maddie Lever. He quickly descended to the basement through a door marked EMPLOYEES ONLY and laughed at his "cloak and dagger" antics as he unlocked the closet and retrieved the novel.

His curiosity aroused by the man at the front desk and feeling foolish about his own surreptitious movements, Jerry came up the front stairwell into the lobby. Maddie waved Jerry over and introduced him to Prof. d'Arblay. "He checked in tonight, Jerry, and has been regaling me with stories about Belgium culture and its old world beauty. He was attending a conference down at Yale and someone remarked that he should visit the charming Thimble Islands before returning to Europe. So, here he is." Jerry had never seen Maddie so vibrant and thought she was acting giddy in front of the good-looking foreigner. "You'd think she was a college freshman smitten by her professor," Jerry said to himself.

DeBruycker smiled and, bowing his head imperceptibly, turned toward Jerry and said, "I was explaining to Ms. Lever that French is spoken with a distinctive accent in the south of Belgium, where my parents are from, whereas Flemish Dutch predominates in the northern part of the country – Flanders, as it is generally known. I find in my travels that my country is the stepchild to France, Italy and Germany when Americans visit the continent. We are trying to attract more tourists, as I explained to the young lady, but it is a challenging task."

Jerry had shifted his body so that he was standing almost sideways, with his bubble-wrapped bundle positioned away from DeBruycker. It was an instinctive, protective maneuver, duly noted by the Belgian.

After an awkward silence, DeBruycker said, "I understand that you inherited the bookshop after the elderly owner was killed. Such a sad, senseless tragedy. Have you decided when you will reopen?"

Jerry shrugged and said, "Nothing finalized yet, I'm afraid. Well, I must be off. Company at the house. Enjoy your stay, Professor." He was anxious to get away from this suave poseur with the French accent and only wished he could have pulled Maddie aside and warned her not to fall under his spell.

"I'M SURE YOU'RE exaggerating but, even so, she deserves a little excitement, Jerry, even if it is fleeting." They were lying in bed in the dark and Fanny had listened to her husband tell the story of the debonair, French-speaking professor. She stifled a laugh when she heard her husband say that Maddie was fawning over him, practically throwing herself at his feet. "He referred to her as a young lady and she practically swooned," he explained.

"She's been a widow going on five years now, and she's not even forty yet," Fanny explained. "And you have to admit, she's quite attractive, in an innocent Natalie Wood sort of way. Let her enjoy her little flirtation. He'll be gone in a few days."

Jerry grunted something unintelligible, a sign that he had hoisted the white flag. Fanny smiled and rubbed his back when he rolled onto his side. She had prevailed and was not one to persist when victory was in hand.

THEO REALIZED THAT staying in Graniteville more than a few days and asking too many questions about Kammler would look odd, might even generate suspicion. This Kosinsky character struck him as an intellectual lightweight. Accidentally possessing *Little Dorrit*, did he even comprehend its value? And what was that bundle under his arm that he so indiscreetly tried to hide? Was it conceivable that he had been standing only a few feet from the treasured novel?

DeBruycker lingered another 30 minutes talking to Maddie after Jerry departed. He learned that the Graniteville police remained baffled by Kammler's murder and, along with most locals, settled on the "smash and grab" theory, envisioning a desperate, crazed druggie pulling off the highway, hitting the first shop he saw and fleeing back into the outer world. Certainly, it was ridiculous to consider that a resident of Graniteville had committed such a heinous crime, Maddie explained. In truth, Heinz Kammler had been pushed down the memory hole and, with the summer tourist season approaching, it was difficult to find anyone in Graniteville who wanted to talk about the murder.

Before heading upstairs to his room, Theo mentioned to Maddie the taxi driver's suggestion that he visit at least a few of the Thimble Islands and asked if the Inn could provide a tour guide. "I'd be delighted to show you around if you can wait until tomorrow afternoon. I'm off at six in the morning but won't be much of a guide if I don't get some rest first." Maddie offered, her cheeks blushing. "You get your beauty rest, Maddie Lever, and I will be waiting for you in the lobby right after lunch." Her hands were on the front desk and Theo slowly raised them to his mouth. She didn't resist as he gently brushed his lips across her fingertips before strolling to the stairs.

A NARROW BAND of sun was streaming through the curtains when Theo awoke the next morning. He walked to the window and looked out on what he would later learn was DeCourcy Island, one of the larger Thimbles and the scene of the mysterious severed finger that washed ashore some twenty years earlier. The residents of Graniteville had, as Maddie suggested, already put the Kammler murder behind them but it would be resurrected when Theo completed his mission.

Maddie had mentioned that the Graniteville Library was a short stroll from the Inn so Theo decided to educate himself about the area – especially the Thimble Islands – before they met that afternoon. It pleased Theo that he could walk into a library in a strange town without the desire to scout for rare books. He liked Maddie's innocent charm and knew she was susceptible to subtle manipulation. On the off chance that he spotted a rare edition, he would do nothing to jeopardize his mission.

FANNY WAS AT the front desk, chatting with a guest, when Theo walked by on his way to breakfast. She glanced up and immediately guessed that he was the handsome foreigner that Maddie had described before leaving that morning. Jerry had been right. Her night manager was understandably enthralled and Fanny was relieved that this courtly charmer would not be in Graniteville long enough to break her heart.

Uncle Homer was sitting in a large leather chair across from the front desk reading the *Graniteville Gazette*, his revolver in a leather hip holster, covered by his jacket. He watched DeBruycker strut by and scowled from behind his newspaper.

THE GRANITEVILLE LIBRARY did have a few rare books on the history of the Thimble Islands. They were in fragile, tattered condition and sat in a glass case behind the librarian's desk. The sight of them made Theo's heart beat a little faster but it was a simple reflex upon which he had no intention of acting. No, he would do nothing so foolish. He thought of Maddie Lever and smiled. He had decided that it would be unlike the Jackal to neglect fruit hanging before him, especially when it was ripe for the plucking. Maddie would be a fount of information – and much more – before he left Graniteville or Theo DeBruycker was losing his touch.

CHAPTER ELEVEN
HITLERIAN OBSESSION

As Theo was visiting the Graniteville Library, Woody and Jerry walked into the Library of Congress, located in the Capitol Hill neighborhood of Washington, DC. The original library was burned to the ground by the British during the War of 1812, incinerating at least a portion of its modest collection of three thousand books before the remainder could be evacuated. Not satisfied, the invading Brits also set fire to the US Treasury building, the Capitol and the White House.

After the war and to replace the lost volumes, former President Jefferson offered to sell his library of over six thousand books, an opportunity readily accepted by Congress. The library today, housing more than 167 million items – including thirty-nine million books – is the largest in the world. It is now comprised of a three-building complex in different architectural structures and named after three successive presidents – Adams, Jefferson and Madison.

The Third Reich Collection, as it is called, consists of books, photographs, maps and other materials, including a braille edition of *Mein Kampf,* which were confiscated from the Berlin library as well as several other locations throughout Germany – including the salt mines outside of Berchtesgaden. The Collection is maintained in the library's Rare Books and Special Collections Division in the Jefferson building. Through his contacts in the FBI, Woody had made certain that Oswald Brenner would meet with them.

The curator was a pale, diminutive man with a high forehead topped off by tufts of unruly grey hair. He was outfitted in a brown suit and matching vest, with a dark tie that was knotted so tightly it caused his chicken-like neck to bulge in a cascade of wrinkles above his starched, white collar. Wire-rimmed glasses blended into his face and rested on a narrow nose that sloped down to an overlong, perspiring upper lip. While someone high up had directed Brenner to meet with and provide expert advice to what he considered two interlopers, he had not been instructed to be pleasant. His pinched mouth could not hide his annoyance.

"I am never happy to hear that another item that rightfully belongs in our collection eluded our military's grasp after the war," Brenner announced after handshakes were exchanged. Woody and Jerry struggled to look sympathetic as the curator frowned and continued. "Not that I fault you gentlemen, you understand, but it is a frequent irritant with which we must deal. Now then, what have you brought for me to examine?"

Jerry skipped over Kammler's murder and described the discovery of *Little Dorrit* in a shop that he had inherited. He then unwrapped the novel and handed it to Brenner. The curator's languid expression disappeared when he opened the book and saw the Hitler bookplate. He then flipped ahead to the title page before pulling a small, black magnifier loupe from his coat pocket. Returning to the bookplate, Brenner brought his head in close until the loupe was flush with his eye socket. Woody and Jerry stared at his mottled scalp in silence while they waited for the oracle to render judgment.

When he finally looked up, Brenner sighed and said, "First time

I've seen a novel in English from the Fuhrer's collection, assuming that it came from one of the locations where we know he maintained a library. He had a complete set of Shakespeare's plays, you know, but they were naturally in a German translation. Had the effrontery to have some lackey engrave his own initials on the spine instead of The Bard's. Odd that he had a fascination with the *Merchant Of Venice*, isn't it? He was also an enthusiastic fan of *Gulliver's Travels*, *Robinson Crusoe* and *Don Quixote* – again in the German translations.

"People want to believe that Hitler was merely a dim-witted demagogue, a crazed, messianic figure to a very receptive and idolatrous nation but the truth is that the man read voraciously, books of all kinds. He was known to read half the night and could recite long passages the next day verbatim. Some people, you can imagine the type, actually believe he was a genius.

"Look at the people who visited him and came away praising his vision and leadership. Of course, everyone has heard the story of Neville Chamberlain making a fool of himself but did you know that a former British Prime Minister, David Lloyd George, went to see Hitler two years before Chamberlain's infamous visit and came away praising the Fuhrer as the 'George Washington of Germany?' There was a steady stream of famous people at Hitler's doorstep heaping accolades on the man.

"With the equivalent of an elementary school education, Hitler was an autodidact, particularly on the topics of history and military science. Of course, he had his oddities, one of which was the extensive study of hands. If he approved of your hands, you might get a promotion. Like Napoleon, he considered his hands a gift from God."

Brenner was animated, lost in his own rhetoric, when he realized he had gone on too long. He tapped the book, cleared his throat and continued. "I always approach these situations with a great deal of skepticism, expecting a forgery, except that –. "Brenner stopped abruptly and wagged a finger to dissuade any interruption before going on. "Except that, the bookplate, in my judgment, is authentic and I've seen my share of forgeries. Still, very odd, I must say, the English language version of the novel, I mean."

Brenner listened impatiently as Jerry related Prof. Fensterwald's speculation regarding Hitler's possible acquisition of the novel during an alleged trip to London in 1912 to visit his half-brother. "I suppose it's as plausible as any other theory," the curator remarked tartly, not entirely happy that another expert was intruding on his authority. "You just reminded me of Prof. Weinberg's research in the late 'fifties. He was scrounging around over at the old torpedo factory across the Potomac River. We initially kept the German war records there after they were shipped back from Europe."

Before he could continue, Woody interrupted. "You mean Old Town Alexandria, Virginia, right? I lived there briefly back in the seventies when a few compromising German photographs were stolen from a torpedo factory file and it created a big scandal for a prominent local family. Resulted in a couple of murders, too. Do you recall it?" Jerry glanced at his friend and started to say something but got a hand signal and clammed up.

Brenner looked thoughtful and scratched his scalp, releasing white flakes which fluttered down to his shoulder. "Must have been around the time when the Nazi collection was being moved temporarily to a more secure location in Maryland before it was eventually brought here. Doesn't ring a bell. Anyway, Weinberg found a draft copy of *Mein Kampf* while going through storage boxes in the basement of the torpedo factory. None of the so-called experts wanted to believe it at the time but eventually other historians validated Weinberg's discovery. After that, the professor enjoyed considerable acclaim."

Brenner couldn't resist the temptation to continue his tutorial and went on. "Hitler had visions of a cultural center in his hometown of Linz, Austria after Germany won the war, the centerpieces being the Fuhrermuseum and the Adolf Hitler Bibliothek. The museum would be populated with looted artwork from across Europe and England, including priceless pieces by Vermeer, Michelangelo and Van Eyck. We assume that his own personal libraries would be consolidated at the Bibliothek, 16,000 volumes in all, plus whatever books could be stolen by his henchmen. We have only 1200 volumes here whereas the Soviets carted away thousands. No one has a complete inventory." The archivist looked dejected as if he had been personally victimized by some vast conspiracy to keep Hitler memorabilia from its rightful home.

"So, it's incorrect to assume that except for the Soviet cache, most of his library has been consolidated here?" Woody asked. Brenner scoffed and turned sullen. "Seems like everyone wants a piece of the Hitler pie. Fort Belvoir over in Virginia has statues, Nazi propaganda literature and what they term "wartime art" – including watercolors by Hitler himself, some of it so vile that no one is allowed to view it.

"Brown University has its own collection of roughly fifty books, a donation by the relative of a soldier who somehow smuggled a cache out of Germany after the war. There are volumes from the Reich Chancellery in the archives at the Hoover Institution in California, including the diaries of Goebbels, Himmler and von Ribbentrop. Then, you have soldiers and ordinary citizens who spirited away untold volumes. Seeking a piece of history, I guess. Go into the attics of soldiers who fought in Germany and you're bound to find some item that belongs in a museum or a library. I could go on but you get the idea. Valuable items continue to elude us that should be here," he concluded, fingering *Little Dorrit.*

Jerry reached for the novel and Brenner tugged back before frowning and releasing his hold. "If you decide to donate it, we'd be much obliged. The novel really does belong here and will have a secure home," Brenner said in a low, squeaky voice. The curator tried to smile but the muscles regulating his mouth had atrophied and wouldn't cooperate. Brenner failed to mention that only three years earlier, the

Library had closed its stacks to readers after it was discovered that several thousand volumes had gone missing.

"It's something to consider," Jerry finally said, his tone unconvincing. Brenner stood up and watched as Jerry re-wrapped *Little Dorrit*. "If you're going to keep it, I strongly urge you to purchase a clamshell archival box to protect it. Humidity and exposure to light will eventually destroy it if you don't take some basic precautions. Putting a prized book on the shelf at home is the kind of mistake amateur collectors make all the time." Oswald Brenner was a sore loser and couldn't resist the chance to make a few insinuating allusions before walking away.

"I'D LIKE TO stuff that little weasel into a clamshell box. It would be a tight squeeze but I'd manage it somehow. Hey, why didn't you tell him your torpedo factory story, Woody? It's as good as the plot of a Grisham or Connelly novel if you ask me," Jerry exclaimed as they stood on the steps of the library.

Woody laughed. "That man only wanted to hear the sound of his own voice, Jer. I must say, though, that my amateur sleuthing back in the seventies, just out of the Army and drifting, led to my joining the Parlor City police force which, in turn, got me where I am today. I still think of Det. Willoughby from time to time, wondering what he would do in a perplexing situation. He was brilliant in solving one of the two Old Town murder cases and taught me a great deal that summer. He was a classic, old school gumshoe if there ever was one."

"Someone needs to dust Brenner off and bring him outside before he crumbles. The man has a serious Vitamin D deficiency. Can you believe how that weasel tried to warm up at the end and get his wrinkly paws on *Little Dorrit*? That's twice in one week that someone wanted to con the novel from me," Jerry said, thinking of shop owner

Harley Grantham up in New Haven. "It amazes me that guys like Brenner covet history like they own it yet disdain the average person who rarely gets to see inside their precious clamshell boxes."

Woody smiled vacantly as Jerry was talking, still reminiscing about the torpedo factory escapade that helped shape his life. In a brief timespan while living in Alexandria, Det. Hank Willoughby had befriended him, a budding romance petered out before the flame was even lit, and he met one of the most endearing characters in his life, an Irish saloon keeper by the name of Pudge McFadden.

"What's next?" Woody heard, followed by a nudge from his friend. "Oh, I've got that lunch meeting with the Art Crime Team over at FBI headquarters. I'll ask if *Little Dorrit* is on the list of any recent rare book thefts but your copy won't be mentioned until we decide the time is right. Let's check in to the hotel before we go our separate ways. Going to do a little site-seeing?" Woody asked.

"First stop is the most storied saloon in DC, the Old Ebbitt Grill. It's a tourist trap now but goes back to the Civil War days if I'm not mistaken. I read where Ulysses Grant and Teddy Roosevelt bellied up to its bar over the years, so if it's good enough for those two presidents, then it's good enough for me. Plus, they're rumored to serve great fried calamari. Afterwards, I'm going to walk around by the monuments, arouse my slumbering patriotism and then head over to Old Town Alexandria. It's about time I saw that damn torpedo factory that changed your life."

"It was purchased by the city and converted into an art colony cooperative, Jerry, after the government moved all their World War II files out in the seventies. Quite a tourist attraction now but definitely worth a visit. Hey, Pudge McFadden's original saloon is up the street from the factory. I'll meet you there around five. I'm envious that you'll be hitting two first class saloons in a single day!"

LATER THAT AFTERNOON, before catching the Metro to Old Town Alexandria, Jerry walked by a stationary store, stopped a few yards past it and circled back. A few minutes later, he walked out with *Little Dorrit* in a clamshell box.

CHAPTER TWELVE
The Seduction

Maddie had hardly slept that morning, thinking about her afternoon rendezvous with the professor. Had he been sincere when he offered to squire her around Belgium? Lying in bed, she tried to imagine letting go after all these years, throwing caution to the wind with a complete stranger who she might never see again. Was that what made it so alluring? It startled and thrilled her at the same time, making her think of Joan Fontaine in the movie *Rebecca* when she succumbed to the charms of Laurence Olivier.

When she looked in the mirror, she fretted. She had worn no make-up the night before, as was her custom at the Inn, and he didn't seem to mind. To "doll up," as her mother used to say in that persistently disparaging tone, would be overdoing it. Still, they would be exposed to the sun and wind for a considerable time and her fair skin needed some protection.

She was still a slender 5'6" tall with a pure, girlish complexion and a button nose. Her thick chestnut hair was styled in a layered, pixie style, making her look younger than her 37 years, despite the anguish of five years of widowhood. In her khaki shorts and blue sleeveless top, she was oblivious to the turning heads as she skipped buoyantly over to the Inn.

FANNY WATCHED AS Maddie met the professor near the front door and immediately noticed the unfamiliar yet striking glow emanating from her night manager. It was, of course, against all protocol for an employee to establish a relationship with a guest, but Maddie had been forthright about an innocent boat ride around the islands and Fanny had acceded to her request. "Even if it's for a day, she deserves this interlude of pure enjoyment," Fanny said to herself, looking down to avoid eye contact. She busied herself with some papers and when she looked up, they were gone.

AS THE SKIFF angled away from the dock, Maddie directed the boatsman to steer toward DeCourcy Island, the nature preserve managed by the DeCourcy family trust. She was anxious to calm her nerves and decided to tell the decades-old story of what happened after a schoolgirl spotted a severed finger in her netting during a class outing, setting off a manhunt for a business owner who had disappeared.

"It turned out to be an elaborate hoax to cover up an insurance swindle. The missing man showed up in town a few weeks later, with all ten fingers, right after his wife was found murdered in a nearby motel. It was such a convoluted mystery that it would take forever to relate all the twists and turns. However, what you might find interesting is that the person who helped the police unravel it back then is the person you met last night. Mr. Kosinsky's a teacher up at the high school but a lot of folks think of him as an amateur sleuth."

Maddie was rambling on excitedly when she stopped abruptly, putting a hand up to her face as she felt her cheeks turn hot. "I'm running on like a nervous schoolgirl when I should be letting you talk."

Theo smiled benignly and shook his head. "Students hear me lecture all the time and it creates a danger that we, as professors, must all confront – falling in love with the authoritative sound of our own voices. I'd much rather listen to your lilting voice. A 'phantom of delight,' as Wordsworth wrote in one poem, purportedly describing his own wife." Theo laughed softly and looked away, not wanting to seem too importunate. He waited for the moment to pass, then sounded almost business-like when he asked, "I'm curious. One of my great pleasures is to browse in a well-stocked bookstore. And you, are you hoping that the new owner will reopen the shop soon?"

Maddie leaned forward and lowered her voice, just above a whisper. "Fanny, that's the wife, told me they just got rid of all the so-called antiques. Cheap collectables she called them. They put all the books in storage until they complete the renovation. Oh, but I told you all this last night, didn't I? Anyway, the two of them have been acting mysterious lately. The husband has been over at the Inn more than usual and, for whatever reason, goes down to the basement. And when Fanny came in this morning, her uncle was with her, plopping down in a lobby chair right across from the front desk. He's the retired constable here in town and it struck me that he was here to watch over her while her husband is out of town."

Theo had his opening and took advantage of it. "Your Mr. Kosinsky seemed rather anxious when we met last night, Perhaps, the inheritance of the bookshop and the tragedy connected with it has disturbed him more than he realizes," he said, hoping he sounded sympathetic.

It was enough to get Maddie to continue talking. "Fanny mentioned this morning that Jerry's boyhood friend was visiting from Spain and the two of them had flown to Washington, DC." Theo had a quizzical look on his face and Maddie continued. "She said they were going to the Library of Congress but then stopped short, as if she had said something inappropriate. Of course, it struck me as odd but I didn't want to probe," Maddie explained, shrugging her shoulders.

Theo appeared passive but was now convinced that the men had taken *Little Dorrit* with them. But why the Library of Congress? Had Kosinsky seen something in the novel, a coded message or even a dedication to a famous person, which made him curious about its meaning? Perhaps, this man wasn't such a fool after all. Theo had a sudden fear that experts at the Library might figure out why the novel was so valuable, in which case it might never leave the government's possession. Everything now depended on Kosinsky returning to Graniteville with *Little Dorrit*. It made sense now that the novel never went into storage with the rest of the store's inventory. Was it possible that Kosinsky had hidden it in the basement of the Inn?

Maddie waved her arm and laughed, ending Theo's speculations. "Don't listen to me. I'm just chattering away to hide my nervousness," she said.

Theo reached up and brought her hand down close to his lap without saying a word as they skimmed over the water in silence. The old boatsman was ready and willing to tell a hundred stories about the Thimbles, some real and others dubious, but when he looked at the happy couple, he decided to maneuver the skiff between the islands without saying a word.

———

MADDIE PUT HER arm through Theo's as they strolled away from the dock, subtly urging him forward with gentle pressure. "I'll make you something to eat and you can tell me all about the university and how the pretty young girls throw themselves at your feet. Truly, though,

I have been very intrigued by Belgium since we talked last night. I know nothing of its history but you will educate me."

She lived in a cottage a few blocks from the shore that had been in the family for generations. On the gravel driveway, a bright blue vintage Fiat 124 Sport Spider was parked. "My pride and joy," she exclaimed. "Maybe we should put the top down and take a ride up the coast."

———

As THEY RAVISHED plates of scrambled eggs, Maddie sat transfixed as Theo described the central square in Brussels known as the Grand Place, a collection of structures that include the ornate guildhalls, the 315' tall Gothic Town Hall dating back to the 15th century and the city's museum known as the Breadhouse.

In Antwerp, he promised to take her to the Reubens House where she would be mesmerized by the works of the great Baroque artists. "Then, a short train ride to Ghent where we will take a leisurely boat ride along one of the many canals of the city, as delightful as anything you will experience in Venice. Naturally, you will want to visit the Belfry, the famous bell tower built in the 14th century. Finally, at Ghent University, you will visit another tower known as The Boekentoren, twenty stories high with more than three million books and manuscripts.

"Another short train ride will bring us to Bruges with its world famous chocolate shops, its charming canals, the church that houses a Michelangelo sculpture and the famous belfry in the market square. Have you have heard enough to entice you?"

Maddie bounced up and disappeared into the kitchen. She was floating on air when she brought glasses of iced tea back to the couch. She wasn't sure she believed everything that was happening, and all so fast, but the moment was too delicious for her to entertain doubts.

Her eyes were fluttering as she folded her legs underneath and turned toward him. Theo had been picking up encouraging signals since the night before. If they were faint then, open to misinterpretation, all doubts had now been removed and he knew it was incumbent upon him to make the ultimate overture. He took a sip of tea then put his glass on the low table in front of them and slid over next to her, removing the glass from her hands without resistance. After he put it down and turned back, Maddie's radiant face was within inches of his own. She slid her body even closer and interlocked her hands at the back of his neck before parting her lips ever so slightly.

MADDIE WAS NESTLED into Theo's chest when he stirred, causing her to look up dreamily. It was late afternoon and he had listened to her breathing, pretending to be asleep, trying to decide what he would say when she awoke. He was past having any interest in lovemaking and needed information, starting with the location of the warehouse where Kammler's books were stored, if only to eliminate the possibility that *Little Dorrit* was there. Having pondered the awkward conduct of Kosinsky the night before, attempting to shield the bundle under his arm, he had decided to search the basement at the Inn as a possible hiding place. He needed to understand the basement's layout for his inevitable return. But first, he must be certain that Maddie had revealed all she knew. So, he would probe gently until he was confident that he had lured her in.

"You really should come to Europe. The Fall is best when the overbearing tourists and the bothersome schoolchildren fade away. You can make the grand tour like an American lady from the Gilded Age, saving my country for last."

Maddie pretended to pout when she heard the word last and then smiled mischievously. "So, you would leave me to venture on my own across Europe and be swept off my feet before I made it to Brussels? How ungallant of you," she said laughingly, gazing into his liquid blue eyes before leaning up to peck him on the chin. She had given in completely to their lovemaking and any lingering inhibitions had been cast to the winds.

"You're right," he retorted. "I am properly and justifiably chastised. It is not a risk worth taking and I hereby vow that I will be your knight errant the moment you set foot on the continent."

Maddie moved in closer then shot a glance at the clock, instinctively pulling the sheet up to cover herself. When she looked back at Theo, she laughed and let the sheet drop. "I've got to get ready or I'll be late to work. You can lounge here as long as you like then stroll around town. I will conjure up a European itinerary and share it with you tonight for your approval."

Theo watched with bemusement as she pranced into the bathroom. He was certainly fond of Maddie and, circumstances permitting, would have enjoyed extending this dalliance a few days longer if there weren't risks involved. He thought of the Jackal's stay at an estate in the French countryside where he cuckolded the husband by seducing his love-deprived wife. It had ended badly for the lady in the movie, he recalled.

———◆———

THEO STAYED AWAY from the Inn until he felt it likely that Fanny and her uncle had departed. He learned that there was a self-service storage facility near the highway interchange and assumed that Kammler's book inventory was stored in one of the units. He doubted that *Little Dorrit* was there but would find the means to break in if the novel wasn't found at the Inn.

He called up the image of Jerry Kosinsky standing in front of him the previous night, attempting unsuccessfully to shield the package shaped like a book. If *Little Dorrit* had been hidden in the basement but was now missing, wasn't it probable that Kosinsky had taken it with him to Washington, DC and would place it there again upon his return?

DeBruycker entered the Inn through the side door and descended to the basement where he saw a utility closet in the far corner. The door was half open and a key was dangling from the lock. He looked inside and saw paint buckets and pails on the floor. The shelving on the back wall was piled with cleaning rags and solvents. It did not strike Theo as the kind of room that someone would bother to lock – unless some object of value was, or had been, hidden inside. "When I return," he said to himself, "If this door is locked, I will have my answer."

The lobby was empty when Theo ascended the back staircase. He quickly exited through the side door and walked around to the main entrance. When he opened the front door, he was greeted by the beaming face of Maddie Lever.

That evening, Theo and Maddie made tentative plans to meet in Paris in October, the only caveat being his ability to assign his classes to another professor. Maddie felt reassured, having suffered some doubts after their afternoon tryst, wondering if she had surrendered too soon and was living in a one-sided fantasy world.

The lovebirds said their goodbyes at the front desk. Maddie offered to come by in the morning and drive him to the train station but he insisted that she get her beauty rest. When they parted, she was under the delusion that she would see him in Europe in a few months but he knew that if they met again, it would be soon, right here in Graniteville and purely by accident. He would not be Professor d'Arblay or Theo DeBruycker when he returned. She could walk past him on the street and never recognize him, of that he felt certain.

CHAPTER THIRTEEN
DOWN MEMORY LANE

"Walking into this saloon in the late 70s, a naïve soldier just out of the service, still getting used to wearing civvies all the time, it changed my life, Jer," Woody reflected, after a hardy gulp of his Guinness.

The two old friends were leaning against the bar rail at Pudge McFadden's in Old Town Alexandria, just across the Potomac River from the Capitol. Woody sighed and Jerry punched his friend's arm before saying, "Keep going. It's been a long time since I heard you talk about this most excellent adventure."

Woody winced as if in pain then laughed softly as he pointed to the picture of the shebeen that still hung over the bar, in homage to the original owner who had died almost five years ago. It caused him to recollect the time when he walked into Maude's Shebeen in New York City in 1985 and saw an almost identical picture of a makeshift Irish saloon hanging behind that bar. By then, Woody knew the history of the shebeen, an illicit, unlicensed pub set up in a house, a barn or shanty where poor Irish would secretly congregate to imbibe. Back in Ireland, the "Old Sod" some still called it affectionately, Woody learned from Pudge McFadden and others how life had been a century earlier. It was a constant struggle for the operator of a shebeen to avoid detection by police and local taxing authorities.

"You can start anytime," Woody heard and realized he had been daydreaming. "It was here that Pudge introduced me to Det. Hank Willoughby. He solved the murder over at the torpedo factory and, without knowing it, taught me a lot about the true nature of detective work. For a brief time, we were like the three amigos. Willoughby, if you by chance recall, was the spitting image of the actor William Conrad who played Det. Frank Cannon on the tv series. If you saw pictures, you would agree that both of them were the most unlikely looking gumshoes. But Willoughby was the real deal.

"Anyway, it took me a while to appreciate that after watching Willoughby operate, in his low-key, unassuming but dogged style, that going back to earn my master's degree in history at Thorndyke was not my destiny. Instead, as you know, I headed home to Parlor City and eventually joined the police force," Woody concluded, lifting his pint in salute, prompting Jerry to do the same.

Jerry had a vague recollection that two murders had been committed in the torpedo factory case, with only one of them solved. There was also a rekindled romance back then that flamed out quickly and haunted Woody for years until he met and married Hannah Cavendish. Woody was drifting back again and Jerry decided not to probe further, instead turning the conversation to Woody's meeting with the FBI.

Woody brightened up and said, "I met with the Art Crimes Team. They deal with thefts of art and artifacts but handle the disappearance of rare books as well. They pointed out what should have been obvious to me, namely that a missing painting is spotted and reported quickly. It's hard to miss a blank space on a wall. With a rare book taken from a shelf, it may go unnoticed for week or months – even years. When the loss is finally detected, some libraries don't even report the theft. They're embarrassed or simply don't want the negative publicity."

Jerry scratched his head and asked, "You mentioned *Little Dorrit*, right, without bringing my copy into the conversation?"

"Correct. Told them it was a private matter I was investigating and no one pressed me for details. Then, as if on signal, one of the agents excused himself and came back ten minutes later to announce that a stolen Dickens novel with that title wasn't in the FBI database. That's good news. What happened next will interest if not encourage you. There are several other databases out there run by groups that track the theft of rare books. Take a look at this list they printed out."

Jerry's eyes blurred as he studied the names: Antiquarian Booksellers' Association of America, the International League of Antiquarian Booksellers, the American Library Association, Scotland Yard and the Museum Security Network.

When Jerry looked up, shaking his head, Woody said, "Before I left, my contact sent messages to each of these organizations inquiring about *Little Dorrit*. It'll take a few days but if someone stole the novel from a library or a reputable dealer – or tried to peddle it to members of any of these groups – we'll know soon enough. If we eliminate all or most of the other possibilities, there's a good chance that your copy did come from Berchtesgaden, either through an intermediary or directly into Kammler's hands."

Jerry didn't respond and Woody signaled the bartender by holding up two fingers. The two reminisced about their childhood years in Parlor City, including confrontations with their archnemesis Rudy Gantz and his twin enforcers, the Clintock brothers. Not mentioned but never far from their thoughts was the renowned Det. Billy Meacham, Jr. who most impacted their lives growing up.

"Knock that down, Jer," Woody urged, pointing to his friend's half-finished pint. "There's a great seafood place a few blocks away, with a patio overlooking the river. If I remember correctly, Prawns on the Potomac serves up the best blue crab, shrimp and oysters in Old Town, fresh daily from the Chesapeake Bay."

———

As THEY WERE finishing dinner, Woody informed Jerry that he had arranged a meeting in downtown DC the next morning before they went their separate ways.

"Ever heard of the National Central Bureau?" Woody asked, with a bemused look on his face. "Sounds like something out of Huxley's *Brave New World* or maybe *1984*," Jerry responded, adding, "Is this a joke and I'm supposed to guess the punchline?"

"Yeah, it does have a nebulous, bureaucratic ring to it, doesn't it? In reality, it's the Washington, DC office for Interpol. You could say they like their intrigue. Anyway, I was put in touch with someone there before leaving my Interpol meeting in Geneva and just found out this afternoon that he is willing to meet with us. I figured we should touch all the bases as long as we're down here. Technically, NCB is a part of the Department of Justice and helps coordinate international investigations that involve member countries. Our tax dollars at work around the world, you could say.

"Now, it just so happens that an individual from the German Federal Police has been detailed to the NCB here for a year. His name is Jurgen Eggebrecht and his family has an interesting history. He's related on his mother's side to Hans Scholl, who was one of the leaders of the university resistance movement in Munich where brave students distributed leaflets and painted anti-Nazi slogans on buildings after membership in the Hitler Youth organization was mandated. Scholl and his sister were arrested, quickly convicted in a show trial and beheaded. Just two examples of courageous, unsung heroes that don't make it into most history books, right?

"Anyway, I'm thinking that if Eggebrecht is a student of German history, he might have some valuable insight into what was happening as the Third Reich crumbled and, in particular, who was at Berchtesgaden at the time our soldiers arrived and hauled books out of the salt mines."

Jerry had a troubled look on his face when Woody finished. "You cross the Nazis, even if you are only an idealistic college student, and you die a heinous death. Now, there's some damn sicko on the loose who wants my novel bad enough to smash someone's head in. Some Hitler fanatic? Every once in a while, there's an article in the newspaper or a segment on tv about some Nazi living here in the states, the neighbor next door who seems like an okay guy but turns out to be a sadistic guard from a Nazi concentration camp. Is that who we're dealing with, Woody? Some war criminal who knew Kammler back in Germany and had a grudge against him or, worse yet, knew that Kammler left Germany with the novel?"

Woody sipped his wine and said nothing, giving Jerry a chance to cool down. On the taxi ride back downtown to their hotel, Woody finally said, "If Eggebrecht gives us the slightest clue that leads us to Kammler's killer, Jerry, we're one step closer to solving this mystery. Stay positive and let's see what we learn tomorrow morning."

CHAPTER FOURTEEN
THE DRESDEN CONNECTION

DeBruycker left Graniteville certain that the Jackal would be pleased. He had played it perfectly with Maddie, gleaned essential information, and had satisfied both his ego and his libido. And yet his mind was in turmoil about what was happening at the Library of Congress that was beyond his control. On the brief train ride back to New Haven, he pondered his options.

New Haven was quickly vetoed as a temporary way station on the off chance that if the Yale library had already discovered that the de Jode map was missing, the police would be looking for someone fitting his general description.

As he awaited Kosinsky's return to Graniteville, Theo decided that the international antiquarian book fair in Boston was the perfect one-day diversion. He was on a winning streak and the fair might provide an opportunity to exploit at least one inattentive dealer.

MADDIE HEARD THE distant rumble of the trains going south and east as she tried to fall off to sleep. How was it that she was in such a melancholy mood when just hours earlier she had been ebullient as they said their goodbyes? It wasn't guilt or self-flagellation but rather a fear that she acted irrationally, giving in too quickly to a latent sexual arousal. It worried her that she may have ruined any chance that d'Arblay saw her as more than the conquest of a pliable American woman who melted before the quintessential European male charms, another notch on the proverbial belt. Time will tell, she said wearily to herself, suddenly philosophical.

She turned on her stomach and buried her head in the sheets, pulling the pillow over her head in an attempt to drown out all distractions. Her muffled voice emphatically saying "No!" startled her and she started to cry softly until her breathing settled into a relaxed rhythm and she fell into an uneasy sleep.

JURGEN EGGEBRECHT MET Woody and Jerry in the lobby of the NCB building. His blonde hair was styled in an immaculate brush cut and his posture was ramrod straight as he approached them. He had a stern look on his face, as if he were a schoolteacher confronting two recalcitrant students. Military training, Woody guessed correctly, as the German crushed his outstretched hand.

Eggebrecht sat stone-faced behind his desk with his hands intertwined in a prayerful position as Jerry recited the story of how he discovered *Little Dorrit* and the murderous event that preceded it. When Jerry finished, Eggebrecht asked to see the novel. While he examined the Hitler bookplate, Jerry recognized the same look he had seen in Fensterwald's office, eyes narrowed and mouth suddenly turned down. "It's always a shock to see a reminder of that dark period," Eggebrecht said softly.

"The curator over at the Library of Congress believes the bookplate is authentic and we've verified that the Kammler family lived in Berchtesgaden," Woody offered.

Eggebrecht nodded and asked, "Exactly where in Connecticut is this town of Graniteville, Mr. Kosinsky?"

"A short drive or train ride from New Haven," Jerry replied. Immediately, Eggebrecht's eyebrows went up and a faint smile creased his mouth. For this stoic German, the facial change was seismic. He started to say something then stopped and looked down at his hands, as if uncertain how to proceed.

When he looked up, he said, "For some weeks now, the police in Dresden have been monitoring the movements of the owner of the Reinhold Auction House. They run a legitimate business for the most part but also trade in stolen antiquities, rare books and maps." Looking at Woody, he continued, "You must know that there is an underground network of buyers and sellers in Europe who traffic in such items on behalf of unscrupulous collectors. During and after World War II, the practice was rampant, a big part of the black market economy in Germany. Back then, people were struggling to survive and such conduct, although criminal, was at least understandable and therefore often overlooked. Not today. Yesterday, Reinhold was being watched as he picked up a shipment at the Dresden airport. It was an aluminum tube containing a rare German map of considerable value."

Eggebrecht paused and looked at the puzzled expressions on the faces of both men. Before he could continue, Woody asked, "And the connection of this Dresden case to the murder of Heinz Kammler? Are we missing something?"

"Perhaps, and perhaps not," Eggebrecht said, his posture stiffening, "but the map in question was stolen a few days ago from a library at Yale University in New Haven. In fact, if you can believe it, the map appears to have been cut out or torn from an atlas. It was shipped the same day from New Haven to Dresden. Now, you might conclude that two antiquity thefts, one successful, taking place ten miles and only days apart is purely coincidental. Others, however, might want to investigate a possible link. As you know, such pursuits are outside our purview here at NCB. However, we did notify our liaison with the FBI late yesterday. They will be coordinating the map investigation with the local police in New Haven as well as our federal police back in Germany and the Interpol office in Berlin."

"Has this Dresden dealer spilled the beans?" Jerry asked excitedly. Eggebrecht looked confused and Woody stepped in. "It's a figure of speech, Jurgen. What my friend wants to know is whether or not Reinhold has given up the name of his accomplice in the hope of receiving lenient treatment."

Eggebrecht smiled and said, "You have been a good, albeit unofficial partner of ours at Interpol, Mr. Meacham, for which we will always be grateful. Reinhold has refused to talk so far but our federal police hope that will change. When confronted with the return address on the package, he laughed. It wasn't long before we understood why. The address used by the library thief was for an individual by the name of Frans van Duyse, who turns out to be an elderly professor at a university in the Belgian town of Leuven. You will not be surprised to learn that Professor van Duyse has never been to the United States and has accounted for his presence on campus for the date in question. One more thing. Your State Department has verified that no one has entered or left the United States in the last month using the van Duyse name. Now, I have shared more than our protocols permit but I feel confident that you will not reveal how you came into possession of this confidential information. I have learned since my assignment to the U.S. that officials here do not like it when someone steps on what they call 'my turf.'"

"This map," Jerry asked, scratching his head and pushing up his glasses, "how the hell did he walk out of the library at Yale University with it and not get stopped?"

Jerry's question caused Eggebrecht to grin broadly and display two rows of glistening teeth. "These thieves are ingenious, Mr. Kosinsky, some of them quite brilliant. I can tell you that the map was somehow extracted from a very large atlas and then taken from the library without anyone noticing. How would you describe such a person who could pull off such a daring heist? In an honest profession, he or she would be highly successful. A frequent mistake is to underestimate them and view them as common crooks. Whomever impersonated Professor van Duyse at Yale University has most likely chosen another identity by now and could prove elusive."

"BOY, I HAD him pegged wrong when he greeted us like a statue. I kept thinking that if you put him in a Prussian military uniform and transport him back to the 19th century, he would hoist his saber and lead a battalion into battle," Jerry exclaimed.

"Yeah, he turned out to be a good friend in a hard shell. He could have made it a perfunctory meeting, stonewalled us, and sent us on our way. Instead, we have an intriguing new lead to pursue with this Yale University heist even if it turns out to be a bizarre coincidence," Woody said, seeking to dampen any premature enthusiasm that Jerry might be feeling.

"Right. Now, I find myself about to repeat something I frequently do when we're together – to wit, what's next?"

THE TWO FRIENDS sat in the airport coffee shop and discussed their plans.

It was agreed that Jerry would stop at Yale University on the way home and try to get a detailed description of the individual who impersonated the Belgian professor. If thwarted by the library, he would turn to Fanny's uncle for help. As the constable of Graniteville several years before the position was made ceremonial, Homer Tulk had cultivated strong relationships with several officers high up in the New Haven Police Department.

"I can't believe it slipped my mind, Jerry. The passenger ships that left Germany before the war were checked by one of my sources and Heinz Kammler's name appeared on the manifest for the *S.S. Bremen* voyage to New York in the Summer of 1939.

"So, I keep asking myself, what possessed him to migrate from New York to Baltimore, Maryland and then move to a small town on the Connecticut coast where he knew no one? Once there, he lived as a recluse while operating a retail establishment. There's no logic to it – unless we assume that his purpose was to hide away in Graniteville.

"Of course," Woody continued, "we need to verify that he emigrated to Baltimore like a good number of other people from Berchtesgaden. If he didn't, then my clan theory is shot to hell and we start over by poring through census and immigration records. We're still in the drudge stage, slogging through mud to get to the facts. Not exactly glamorous but it's the way cases get solved. Trust me.

"I'm going to rent a car and drive over to Baltimore, then head up to Parlor City for a few days. Listen, if it makes you feel better, I have decided not to take on any new cases until the mystery of *Little Dorrit* is solved. If we come up dry in Baltimore, we'll try something else. You can count on me to be at your side to the very end, old man."

"I should have known," Jerry bellowed, unable to resist giving his friend a second bear hug in a matter of days.

CHAPTER FIFTEEN
A DEAD END

◆━━━◆

WHILE WOODY AND Jerry were being briefed by Eggebrecht at Interpol Washington, Theo was on Amtrak's Metroliner train from New Haven to Boston. Deciding that it was important to return to Graniteville that evening to be near his quarry, he had checked his luggage at the New Haven depot.

Before boarding the train, he went into a bathroom stall and put on a jet black wig and a matching mustache, complemented by dark-framed spectacles with clear lenses. Not certain if he might be subject to a spot security checks on the train, he taped his X-Acto knife to his right ankle. Using a hand-held mirror, he carefully applied some burnt umber makeup. When he exited the stall, he checked himself in the mirror over the sink and was confident that he would be unrecognizable to anyone who had seen him in recent days as the old man, d'Arblay or van Duyse.

DeBruycker got off the train at the Boston Back Bay station. Before making the short walk to the convention center, he checked the schedule and purchased a ticket on the 6:00 p.m. train back to New Haven.

The convention center was a massive gray stone structure with a pavilion running the length of the front entrance. It reminded Theo of the dreary train stations that seemed typical in Europe. He walked around the outside of the building and spotted a side exit that led into an adjacent shopping mall. With its heavy foot traffic, it would be an ideal place to disappear into the crowd if he had to make a hasty retreat.

Sitting in the darkened, ornate lobby studying the alphabetical list of exhibitors, he couldn't help smiling when he got to Section C and saw the name of Casaubon. Had they intended to peddle their first edition of *Jane Eyre* at the show? Did he dare to visit their booth and ask if they had any early editions of works by the Bronte sisters? No, while the risk was minimal, it wasn't worth the momentary gratification.

Leafing through the show's catalogue, Theo stopped when he saw a quarter-page advertisement by a book dealer from Ireland. Sheridan & Edgeworth announced that a very scarce 1897 edition of *Dracula* would be on display and available for purchase for $32,000. A thrill raced through Theo's body. Thanks to Renata Peeters, he had for years coveted any early edition of the Bram Stoker novel but today's offering was most unique – a first printing of the first edition in its original cloth binding – and only a short stroll away. He stared at the bright yellow cover with both the title and the author's name in bold red lettering. Theo tore out the ad and stuffed it in his pocket.

Before going into the exhibit hall, Theo retreated to the bathroom and checked his disguise. He pulled off the tape holding the X-Acto knife to his ankle and put the all-purpose tool in his pocket. If asked, who would he be today if he stopped at the Irish booth and engaged with the owners? A glib answer, without hesitation, had to trip effortlessly from his lips to sound authentic. A French-speaking collector from Algiers with an interest in Gothic novels would do. He could speak of his early editions of *Frankenstein* and the *Mysteries of Udolpho* if quizzed about his collection. Certainly, his interest in a priceless edition of *Dracula* would be not just understandable but welcome news to a dealer anxious to make the big sale.

SIMON WEGG STOPPED at a rival dealer's shop on the way to work and saw the "pink sheet" put out by the local rare bookdealers organization, announcing the recent theft at Casaubon's bookstore. Wegg had never been invited to join and liked to quote Groucho Marx' line that he would never want to be in a club that would have him as a member.

Before he went out for lunch, Wegg removed *Jane Eyre* from the locked desk in the back of his shop and placed it in a brown paper bag. He would hide the novel at his apartment until a few more pink sheets came out announcing additional thefts. Attention to *Jane Eyre* would eventually die down, after which he would find an opportunity to unload it on an unprincipled collector.

After interviewing the Casaubon shop manager, the NYPD shared its information with the FBI, along with its composite sketch of Alexandre d'Arblay. If he was indeed a Frenchman, as the manager suggested, the State Department would be able to confirm his date and place of entry into the United States. Border patrol would be notified before the end of the day.

JERRY CALLED THE Thimbletown Inn after he landed at the New Haven airport and told Fanny what they had learned from Interpol Washington about the Yale map theft.

"Do they think there's a connection to the Kammler incident?" she asked.

"Our contact was helpful but equivocal, Hon. Whoever stole the map at the Yale library was impersonating an elderly Belgian professor. Doesn't sound like a vicious killer to me. The good news, if we suppose that the same man committed both crimes, is that every law enforcement agency you can think of is on alert looking for the Yale thief, not just here but in Europe as well. The Yale name has the power and influence that we don't so maybe we just ride along on their tail wind."

Not waiting to hear if this rationalizing had any salutary effect, Jerry asked to speak to Uncle Homer, who provided him with the name of a contact in the New Haven police. The former constable assured him that a Capt. Henry Cleghorn would meet with him when he arrived at police headquarters. Having dealt with the likes of Grantham and Brenner, Jerry concluded that going directly to Yale for information would have proved fruitless and frustrating.

By the end of the 19th century, almost 50,000 Germans from Hesse, Bavaria and the Palatinate had settled in the city of Baltimore, Maryland. By 1930, one-fourth of the city's population spoke fluent German. It was a place like Milwaukee, Hoboken, Minneapolis and Cincinnati where an immigrant from Germany like Heinz Kammler could feel at home as he started a new life.

Before heading to the Vital Records office in downtown Baltimore, Woody placed a call to one of his FBI contacts in Washington, smoothing the way for his visit. When he arrived, a matronly lady introduced herself as Hilda Musgrove and ushered him into a private room off the lobby. She was solicitous from the moment they shook hands, greeting him warmly with "We've been expecting you, Mr. Meacham, and hope we can be of assistance today."

"I'm making a confidential inquiry about an individual by the name of Heinz Kammler. If and when he arrived in Baltimore, where he lived, his occupation. Anything else you can provide would be most welcome, of course," Woody explained.

It was twenty minutes before Musgrove returned carrying several documents. "He arrived in the Port of New York from Bremerhaven, Germany in 1939 and was processed by immigration officials the same day. He came down to Baltimore under the auspices of a sponsor by the name of Oskar Schwammberger. He lived in what was at the time a heavily German neighborhood known as Locust Point, as you can see here," she said, offering the document for inspection.

Woody looked down the page until he came upon the name of Kammler's sponsor and looked up. "This individual, Mrs. Musgrove, can you tell me if he is still alive and, if so, where he is living now?" Musgrove got up and went to a telephone about ten feet away. Woody couldn't pick up the conversation but she would occasionally look over at him and smile.

When she came back, she said, "Schwammberger is in his nineties and now lives at Edenwald, also known among the German population as Greisenheim. It began as a modest old people's home right here in downtown Baltimore but relocated to Towson, a suburb on the north side."

"Kammler's occupation?" Woody asked, pointing to the other papers in her hand. Musgrove shuffled them and her eyes lit up. "Well, I'll be darned. He was a clerk in a bookstore owned by Schwammberger. I was young but I can remember my mother would take me to the shop. They carried foreign language books, periodicals and newspapers, mostly in German. My mother liked to read the news from the old country. She was a Schneider. The place closed its doors years ago, around the time old Schwammberger went to live at Edenwald."

Woody stood up, anxious to see Schwammberger before it got too late in the day. "You've been quite helpful today Mrs. Musgrove. Do you suppose he's –?" Woody stopped short and Musgrove shrugged. "No idea about his mental state but I could make a call out there, if that would help," she offered. Woody preferred the element of surprise and shook his head no.

At the door, she looked at Woody and said, "I was told that the FBI called our Director to make sure we assisted you in any manner possible. I trust that we have done so. It's certainly none of my business and I don't suspect you will feel free to answer me but I am curious, Mr. Meacham. Why all the interest in Heinz Kammler, a man who has been dead for over thirty years?"

CHAPTER SIXTEEN
DEAD OR ALIVE?

◆━━━◆

WOODY WAS SPEECHLESS as he stared at the death certificate for Heinz Kammler. He read the entry of Berchtesgaden, Germany as the place of birth and, under occupation, bookstore clerk. He tried to read the cause of death entered by the medical examiner and handed the certificate back to Musgrove for help.

"Typical doctor scrawl but I've learned to decipher most of them. It says 'unknown.' Pretty typical when there's no evidence of violence or the doctor has no patient history with the deceased. Natural causes was the medical conclusion."

Under the circumstances, Woody was certain that no autopsy had been performed, only adding to the mystery. If Kammler had not moved, or fled, to Graniteville then who would have taken the dead man's identity and why? He thought of Jerry and how he would break the news of this bizarre twist. Would it create a wave of panic in the Kosinsky household when they heard the latest development? Had the impersonator in Graniteville been running from someone in

Baltimore – or even back in Germany? Whomever it was had survived in anonymity on the Connecticut coast for several years before being brutally murdered.

"The parents' names sometimes provide a helpful clue." Woody had been deep in thought when he heard these words and turned to Musgrove with a quizzical look on his face. She was pointing to the death certificate. "Right here, you can see the father's name listed as Siegfried Kammler and the mother's maiden name was Petra Schuster. Looks like they both died when he was just a boy. So, whomever provided this information knew intimate details of the Kammler family. If there isn't another Kammler family member living in the area, my guess is that old Schwammberger was the source."

"I'd like to show the death certificate to Schwammberger and see what he knows. Your supposition could very well be correct. If I come up empty, I might very well impose on you again. You have been quite helpful today, Mrs. Musgrove. Now, if you would be kind enough to write down directions to Edenwald, I will be on my way."

At the door, Musgrove smiled demurely as she pressed Woody's hand. "If you like German food, we still have some excellent restaurants in town, Mr. Meacham. Haussner's was a favorite of my husband's before he passed. Excellent crab imperiale and a famous strawberry pie. Some say the artwork which lines the wall is equal to the cuisine. I'd be willing –."

Before she could continue, Woody smiled benevolently and said, "You've been most helpful today, Mrs. Musgrove, and the suggestion is tempting, but I must be in Upstate New York this evening and will have a long drive in front of me after leaving Edenwald." He had been caught totally off guard by the widow Musgrove and was eager to make his escape.

Jerry's meeting with the jovial Capt. Cleghorn was hardly rewarding. If his view was representative, the New Haven police were highly amused by what the captain called the "hijinks" at the prestigious Beinecke Library. "It's happened to them before, Mr. Kosinsky. The folks at Yale seem to be more embarrassed by the negative publicity than the actual loss of the map. Let's just say that being duped does not reinforce their superiority complex. There's no chance they'll let you speak to the young lady who checked the phony professor into the library. Her vague description of him won't go on a wanted poster, if you catch my drift. All she could tell us was that he was a white man of indeterminate age with grey hair whom she thinks spoke with a French accent. No one else seems to remember the guy. Smart of him not to draw attention to himself. That's it. Now, as a professional courtesy to Homer Tulk, I've told you everything we know at this point. All on the qt, you understand."

Jerry walked to his car, disappointed and discouraged, hoping that Woody was having better success in Baltimore.

At the Edenwald front desk, Woody signed in and asked to see Oskar Schwammberger. The receptionist looked surprised and asked, "He hasn't had a guest in ages. May I tell him who's calling?" Woody had decided what he would say on the ride from Baltimore should there be resistance. He flashed his credentials and said, "I'm here regarding a former employee at his bookstore. Tell him it's a matter of some urgency."

Woody sat in the lobby and wondered if his stratagem had failed, that the old man wanted to keep the past dead and buried, and that he had scared him off. He was about to approach the front desk again when he saw someone in the hallway shuffling toward him while tapping a cane on the floor. He was a lanky man who wore his wrinkled khaki pants hiked up above his navel, the belt a few notches too tight. A grey, unbuttoned cardigan sweater hung awkwardly over a rumbled plaid shirt.

Schwammberger eyed his guest suspiciously and pointed his cane menacingly at Woody's stomach. Unsure of the old man's mental state, Woody stood up and introduced himself as a private investigator looking into the death of Heinz Kammler. Schwammberger scoffed and said, "You're a little late, sonny. He's been dead going on thirty plus years if my memory serves me correctly."

Woody decided to sound perplexed. "That's what they said downtown at Vital Records which puzzled me to no end because I have a Heinz Kammler up in Connecticut who died recently with no next of kin. When I discovered that Kammler came here from Germany via New York, I drove down, hoping to find some relatives, only to learn that another Heinz Kammler died in Baltimore years ago. Look here at the entry on his death certificate. Someone in Baltimore knew him well enough to provide vital family information. Pretty confusing, wouldn't you say?"

While he listened to Woody's fable, Schwammberger's face blanched and his mouth dropped open, revealing sets of oversized, ill-fitted dentures, the uppers slipping down when he hung his head. He looked around and then slowly sat down next to Woody, nervously tapping his cane. "Kammler didn't have family and no one came over with him or I'd have known. Someone back in Germany asked me to sponsor him so I sent a letter or a telegram. Lived with my family for about six months until he found his own place. Worked in my bookstore, steady as can be. I felt sorry for the guy. He limped around with his head down like he was carrying the weight of the world. Every few weeks, he would pick out a book and I would let him have it at cost. Built up a decent collection over the years. This fellow in Connecticut, he's either an impostor or it's the damnedest coincidence I ever heard of." Schwammberger sounded defensive and it gave Woody his opening.

"What do you remember about Kammler's death? The death certificate says 'unknown.' To your knowledge, was he a sick man?" Woody asked in his most sympathetic voice. Schwammberger looked away and Woody noticed that his hands were trembling as he pulled a handkerchief from his front pocket and wiped it across his nose a few times.

"I've no interest in upsetting you, Mr. Schwammberger, but you should know that the Heinz Kammler in Connecticut, impostor or not, didn't just pass away from natural causes. In fact, he was brutally murdered in his bookstore. One theory is that the assailant was looking for something valuable, perhaps a priceless figurine or a rare book, and that Kammler paid the ultimate price by resisting. Now, you have every right to keep certain secrets buried in the past as long as no one is hurt by your silence. However, each day that passes makes it harder to solve this murder case. You will not think me unkind if I say that time is running out for both of us, will you?"

Schwammberger's chest was heaving and Woody could see that both hands were now tightly gripping the cane. He slowly turned his head toward Woody with a look of profound sadness. In a whisper, he said, "A cup of tea would be helpful if I'm going to tell you the whole story."

WOODY SAT IN the tiny living room and watched Schwammberger boil water on a portable burner. Not a word had been spoken since they left the lobby and Woody was determined to let the old man busy himself with the tea-making process as he figured out what to say and how to say it.

"It's my family recipe for Jagertee, passed on from my father and his before him. Black tea with rum and honey. No cinnamon or clove. You sip and I will talk," Schwammberger said, seeming to have calmed himself with his daily ritual. Woody took a taste and smiled, causing Schwammberger to reciprocate.

"When he first arrived in Baltimore, I tried to draw him out, involve him in some of the German clubs in town but he resisted every effort. He was a loner and a recluse. No sense of humor. Life was very serious to him. More than once, he insisted that he was being stalked, that someone had followed him to the bookstore. It made no sense to me since Kammler had no acquaintances in Baltimore, let alone friends.

"One night, Kammler came to my house wild-eyed and frantic, said it was most urgent that I come with him to his apartment. When we walked in, there was a man slouched in a chair who I supposed was either asleep or passed out. It wasn't until I saw the vomit and blood covering his shirt that it occurred to me that he might be dead."

Schwammberger went on to relate what Kammler had told him that fateful evening. The dead man had followed him to the bookstore and subsequently showed up at his apartment a few days later, offering him a substantial sum of money for a book that Kammler had brought with him from Germany. Don't suffer the same fate as your sister back in Berchtesgaden, the stranger warned. To buy time, Kammler said he would comply but that the book had been stashed at another location and it would take him a few days to secure it. On the night in question, Kammler explained that the stranger returned and became violently ill and fell into a stupor.

"It sounds like the man was poisoned, either at Kammler's apartment or prior to arriving there," Woody suggested. "Did Kammler provide any explanation?"

Schwammberger shook his head. "He was highly agitated, in a panic – or so I thought at the time. He said the book was a special gift from his sister and he would die before giving it up. I asked him to tell me the name but he refused. Now, I know the value of books even though I never could afford to collect rare editions. I just couldn't figure out how a pauper like Kammler or his sister came into possession of so valuable a book unless it was stolen. When I pressed him, he told me it was likely that his sister had taken the book from Hitler's library. When he left home for Bremerhaven, she gave him the book to take on his voyage. I got the impression that with the parents dead, she wore the pants in the family, if you know what I mean."

Schwammberger was chewing on his lower lip and seemed ready for the next question when Woody asked, "So, then what happened? There's more to the story, isn't there?"

The old man's lips went back in a tight grimace and he took a deep breath. "I remember everything as if it was yesterday. Maybe I said something sympathetic because Kammler quickly calmed down. He then laid out a plan that later on I realized couldn't have been hatched on the spur of the moment. Why can't this be me, Kammler suggested, pointing to the stranger. You come looking for me when I don't report for work after a few days. Next, you will ask the building manager to check on me. He will discover the body and call the police and you will be notified. By then, I will be gone and, for your protection, to a place you don't know. You will, of course, be asked to confirm that it is me in the chair. Don't worry about the building manager. I haven't seen him since I moved in. You will be saving my life, Oskar." Schwammberger stopped and stared at Woody, the teacup shaking in his gnarled hand.

"And that is what you did, also providing the information for the death certificate?" Woody asked, seeking confirmation. Schwammberger took a large gulp of his tea and nodded yes. "He had the details written down for me, another sign that he had thought everything through. Some of his sister's spunk finally rubbed off on him. Or he was simply taking revenge. I wonder what they'll do with me?" Schwammberger asked rhetorically while staring into his empty teacup.

Woody didn't say that the police, after all these years, were unlikely to investigate and the district attorney would find it difficult to even indict Schwammberger, let alone mount a prosecution. The old man wanted to expiate his sins, to suffer for a while and Woody wasn't about to interfere.

Schwammberger sounded almost chipper when he broke the silence. "I'll call the police after you leave. Accessory after the fact, right? If they put me away, I guess I deserve it but right now I'm feeling a lot better than I did this morning. However, I will miss my Jagertee."

CHAPTER SEVENTEEN
A GOTHIC MOMENT

DRIFTING UP AND down the rows of the exhibit floor, Theo spotted the Sheridan & Edgeworth booth, conveniently located on an aisle where two rows intersected, one of which led to the back of the exhibit hall. Hesitating for a moment, he glanced up at the glass case at the rear of the booth and saw *Dracula*, shining brightly like the North Star.

In the back of the hall, Theo approached the row of concessionaires offering drinks, snacks and sandwiches to accommodate the attendees. The backdrop to these refreshment stalls was a floor to ceiling black curtain which ran the length of the wall. Theo walked to the corner and pulled back the curtain just far enough to reveal dozens of crates with dealers names on the sides. Beyond them, his eyes fell upon the freight elevators and the illuminated red exit signs, one at each corner. "Another escape route," he murmured.

Theo meandered back to the rows of exhibitors and began mimicking the studious collectors who were milling about and continuously consulting their exhibitor guides as they tried to locate a dealer of particular interest. He lingered at one booth to examine a handsomely bound copy of *Dr. Wortle's School* by Anthony Trollope but quickly moved on when the dealer attempted to engage him.

Many dealers teased potential customers with moderately priced books lined up on tables in front, hoping to lure them in to examine the expensive items in the glass cases. If four or five attendees crowded into one of the smaller booths, jostling and maneuvering was inevitable, putting the dealer on alert. Theo was careful to steer clear of any such entanglements and gradually worked his way closer to the corner where *Dracula* beckoned him.

———•———

IT WAS LATE afternoon when Woody stopped on the road to Parlor City and called Jerry. "You might want to grab a beer before I tell you about my roller-coaster day in Baltimore, Jer." Woody heard the phone bang against something hard and a voice in the distance yelling "Be right back." The sound of a pop top being pulled came over the phone line and Woody heard, "Got my refreshments, sir. You may proceed."

Woody related his visit to the Vital Records office and how he had been shocked to initially learn that the real Heinz Kammler had died in Baltimore and that the old man murdered in Graniteville was an impostor. "Who stops to challenge a death certificate? I was convinced that someone had stolen Kammler's identity. That's why I drove to this place outside Baltimore where Kammler's employer, Oskar Schwammberger, lives in a retirement complex. I figured he might be able to tell me about Kammler's friends or acquaintances, anyone who might have a motive to borrow his name and head to Connecticut. That's when I got my second shock."

When Jerry heard about Schwammberger's confession, he yelled "Well, I'll be a monkey's uncle. If you've got more surprises, I might need to grab another beer."

Woody couldn't help laughing. "There's no proof that Kammler killed the stranger that day but it certainly sounds plausible, especially when you consider the revelations about the book he brought with him from Germany to Baltimore. Do you remember that the name of the hotel owner in Berchtesgaden was Karl Schuster? According to Kammler's fake death certificate, Schuster was his mother's maiden name.

"If I had to guess, I'd say Kammler wanted to avenge his sister's murder and poisoned the man's drink while they were negotiating the price to be paid for *Little Dorrit*. Poor Schwammberger carried his guilt for the cover-up around with him for years and wanted to unburden himself. I'm convinced that he never knew it was the Dickens novel. He had no reason to lie to me at this point and Kammler would have been too clever to reveal it. Schwammberger could have just clammed up when I first confronted him. As for Kammler, he was a crafty operator but not clever enough to avoid the same fate as the stranger who hunted him down in Baltimore."

"Goddam amazing, Woody. And to think I felt sorry for Kammler, showed him a little kindness over the years and ended up his heir. That'll teach me to be a hail-fellow-well-met. If it took your digging to uncover the truth, is it feasible that someone else found out that Kammler was still alive and tracked him down here? Or are we back to the theory that his murder was random?"

"Excellent deduction, Watson. Perhaps Kammler's murder was random after all and there is no connection to *Little Dorrit*. It's also conceivable that someone went looking for the stranger killed in Baltimore and figured out that Kammler staged his own death and was on the run. If so, it took him – or her – a few decades to track Kammler down in Connecticut. It's possible that Kammler left Baltimore and hid out elsewhere before coming to Graniteville. Guess we both need to chew on this one. Tell me, what did you learn in New Haven?"

"Fanny's uncle set me up with a Capt. Cleghorn. Seems that the police are as much in the dark as everyone else regarding the library thief. Yale gave a poor description of the perp. It could be any stranger walking around campus. Cleghorn told me Yale would never give me an audience. Pretty frustrating day."

"Where's the novel, Jer?" Woody asked. Jerry chuckled. "You checking up on me, international man of intrigue? Don't worry. It's back in the basement at the Inn, locked in the utility closet. How long will you be in Parlor City?"

"A few days at most then I'll drive down to your place. We both know that she's going to quiz you about what I learned in Baltimore. So, do me a favor and put Fanny's mind at ease at the same time. Stay away from the bookstore and the storage unit until I get back there, okay?"

There was an uncomfortably long silence before Woody asked, "You still there, buddy?"

"I already promised her," Jerry said solemnly, hanging up the phone without saying goodbye.

THEO PAUSED AND looked down the aisle to survey the scene. People were milling in the area where *Dracula* sat perched on a shelf. In the front of their booth, Sheridan & Edgeworth had set up a table with a moderately-priced selection of Irish poetry anthologies by Yeats, Tynan, Kavanagh, Heaney and others. For the first time, Theo caught a glimpse of the other novels on the shelf next to *Dracula*. He read the names *Castle Rackrent*, *Tristram Shandy*, *Rory O'More* and *Gulliver's Travels*, certain they must be early if not first editions. Of course, they could hardly be as valuable as the Bram Stoker novel. On any other occasion, they would all have been of keen interest to Theo but the pocket inside his jacket was only so deep. He remembered and took as a warning the old saying, "for greed, all nature is too little."

On the opposite corner from Sheridan & Edgeworth, the dealer had set up a bookshelf at the front of his booth. Sitting atop it was an easel sign which read, ANY VOLUME – $25. Theo recognized it as another common ploy to engage the undiscerning buyer who might then be enticed into making a more expensive purchase inside the booth. He browsed the bookshelf, randomly pulling out a volume for cursory inspection when, out of the corner of his eye, he saw a middle-aged woman toting a bookbag and coming toward him.

In a flash, the opportunity appeared before him. He stuck out his foot and the lady crumbled to the floor. As people turned to look, he tugged the back of the bookshelf until it swayed back and forth before if came crashing down on the woman's legs. Her screams froze everyone nearby and a crowd quickly encircled her. Someone yelled "doctor" and another "get an ambulance." In the confusion, Theo circumvented the crowd until he was in front of the Irish dealer's booth. It was empty.

Two men were lifting the bookshelf off the woman and bystanders were tripping over the scattered books to get a better view of the unusual mayhem at such a sedate gathering. Much to the chagrin of some antiquarians, it would be the talk of the show for months.

Theo pulled out his X-Acto knife and quickly went to work on the cheap lock holding the glass doors together. It took only a few seconds before he heard the click and *Dracula* was soon in his hands. He kissed the cover and slid it into the oversized, inside pocket of his jacket before his eyes darted to the other novels on the shelf. The binding of *Rory O'More* caught his attention. It was known as an *octodecimo* edition among dealers, small enough to fit into his jacket along with *Dracula*.

The crowd around the woman had grown as Theo exited the booth and moved to the edge, his curiosity aroused. To his amazement, the man who was kneeling beside the woman, the good Samaritan trying to comfort her as she intermittently moaned and cried out in agony, wore a name tag that read Conal Sheridan.

Someone shrieked, "They're here at last. Make room for god's sake." White coats pushed through the throng with a stretcher and medical kits, their arrival bringing together a larger, gawking crowd as Theo slipped away.

CHAPTER EIGHTEEN
THE ESCAPE

THEO WILLED HIMSELF to calmly walk down the aisle that led to the main entrance. No shout rang out from the area of the Irish booth, alerting security that a thief was in the exhibit hall. When he looked back, he was relieved that no one was hurrying toward him.

When he saw the flashing lights of the ambulance on the street, he decided to exit the side door of the exhibit hall. He took the escalator into the elevated shopping area and casually looked back to see if someone was in pursuit. Soon, he gained anonymity amidst the crowd of shoppers and felt the tension in his muscles dissipate.

The restroom symbols on the wall made Theo pause temporarily but he continued walking through the mall. He was now confident that he had not drawn attention to himself and there was no benefit to stopping and altering his appearance. The large clock in the jewelry store window told him that he had thirty minutes before his train departed for New Haven. "I pulled it off! Even the Jackal would be impressed!" he said under his breath, immensely proud of his achievement. If there was no last minute hitch, he would soon be speeding from harm's way.

※

JERRY HAD SHOWN his pique with Woody and immediately regretted abruptly hanging up the telephone. It wasn't that he was jealous of his friend's success in Baltimore but rather that he had failed to make a contribution. Then, Woody's reminder that Fanny deserved to know all the latest developments had set him off. Now, he had to deal with a pending uproar in his own household.

"I want that damn novel sold before the children come home from camp. I swear, Jerry, if you don't do it, I'll give it away. Hell, maybe you should donate it to the Library of Congress even if you can't stand that little twerp who tried to bamboozle it away from you. Let some thief try to break in there and steal it. And if you had any notion that *Little Dorrit* would be on display at your new bookstore, some sort of drawing card, you can forget it."

Jerry put on his hangdog face until his wife finished. "It's going to be *our* bookstore, dear, if it ever gets opened, not a monument to my vanity. I'll sell the novel if you insist but let's wait until Woody gets here from Parlor City. We should get his take on how to proceed. What if one of those antiquarian groups that the FBI notified has a member who steps forward to claim the book? Also, if it's part of a police investigation, are we even allowed to sell it?"

Fanny was cooling down and Jerry could see that she was placated by his reasoning. He had gained a reprieve but it was only temporary so he decided to humble himself a little more. "I'm staying away from the bookstore, day or night, until we figure things out."

She smiled and looked at her husband out of the corner of her eyes. It constituted her "you big galoot" expression and Jerry sighed.

In the next moment, Fanny was frowning and Jerry braced himself for another onslaught. "I'm curious, Jerry. The Yale map thief used the credentials of an old professor from Belgium by the name of Van Duyse to get into the library and the staffer who checked him in said she depicted a French accent."

Jerry nodded in agreement and Fanny continued. "Are you forgetting that we just had a French-speaking professor from Belgium staying at the Inn? Just a coincidence, right? Probably a detail that you two Dick Tracys would surely want to check out even if the Yale thief was grey-haired."

Jerry broke out in raucous laughter and slapped one of his legs. "You are good, Fanny. A regular Jane Tennison, you are. I'm serious. The fact that they were both professors never crossed my mind." Fanny was a big fan, as was he, of the female detective in the tv series *Prime Suspect*. He might have invoked Miss Marple but it would have been a mistake.

"You can humor me all you want but after dinner I'm going over to the Inn to check the guest register. The gentleman who made Maddie all starry-eyed had to show his passport when checking in. If it's not Van Duyse, I'll stop playing detective," she announced.

"That's fine by me but I'm not letting you out of my sight this evening. "We'll go together, buttercup," Jerry said, pulling his wife close.

THEO LOOKED OUT the window of the train as the landscape rushed by, thinking about the Irish book dealer. Here was a benevolent man, this Conal Sheridan, whose instinct was to rush to another human being in distress, a complete stranger no less, and leave his prized possessions in a glass case protected by a flimsy lock. What a contrast to the Jackal. How had Sheridan felt when he turned back to his booth and saw that *Dracula* was missing? Did he notice it right away and cry out? More likely, he sank speechless to the floor, realizing the futility of pursuing a shadow.

All the prejudices Theo had built up over the years seemed to have been justified when he watched the insufferable dealers milling about the exhibit hall, whispering to each other or standing stiffly at the front of their booths like the Praetorian Guard, protecting the treasures of the realm.

Then there was Sheridan, coming to the aid of the woman that Theo had crippled for life, displaying the kind of humanity that challenged his beliefs. But Sheridan was an anomaly and it proved he was correct, didn't it?

He had to admit that in his lust for *Dracula*, he hadn't been affected by the woman's cries of agony. And there was no sense pretending that he felt remorse. The Jackal would have said it was all in a day's work.

Theo thought back to the day some years earlier when Von Paulus had marveled at his boldness, calling him *buchermarder*, explaining that it was a ravenous animal that poaches bird eggs to feed an insatiable appetite. It was a time when two spectacular thefts by Theo had prompted such unaccustomed praise from Otto. Theo had just arrived in Hamburg from the North Sea town of Oldenburg, where he had deployed a miniature knife embedded in the antique silver ring that he was wearing that day. Sometimes referred to as "weapons jewelry," Theo had used it to slice a rare map of Alsace from an atlas in the local library. The week before, there was the escapade at the university library in Darmstadt, a village south of Frankfurt, where Theo had brazenly walked out with rare illustrations of the Rhine River in his oversized coat pocket.

Theo appeared non-plussed by the notion that he had pulled off two daring thefts in a single week when, quoting some writer, Otto had reminded Theo that "Many pause on the brink of a crime who have contemplated it at a distance without scruple."

Theo wondered what Otto would say when he heard about his daring theft of *Dracula*. He patted the books inside his jacket, yearning to pull them out and examine them. But the train was crowded and it was possible that there might even be a book dealer or collector on board who, like him, had left the exhibit hall early. If someone spotted *Dracula* in its distinctive yellow binding, it was not inconceivable that the police would be waiting for him at the New Haven station.

Theo's thoughts turned to the disposal of the two novels. He knew nothing about *Rory O'More* or the novelist Samuel Lover but the edition he seized must have considerable value to collectors, enough so to share a locked shelf with the Stoker novel. He would contact Simon Wegg on his return to New York but would not offer a discount this time.

As for *Dracula*, Theo was ambivalent. It could be the cornerstone of the grand, private library that he had dreamed about as a kid after first visiting the Boekentoren tower at Ghent University. That puerile fervor had abated over the years and Theo had to admit it had been supplanted today by the thrill of the hunt, the dashing and adventurous lifestyle to which he had become accustomed.

Of course, any sale of *Dracula* would have to be handled discreetly through Von Paulus or Reinhold to some "see no evil" collector. Selling it would give him a nice bankroll, a stash for those inevitable slow periods. The theft of *Jane Eyre* hadn't even raised his blood pressure but the excitement of the *Dracula* heist would stay with him. It was a feeling, a high that he never wanted to relinquish.

Theo hadn't given any thought to *Little Dorrit* since he left New Haven that morning and was now feeling emboldened by the success of the *Dracula* caper. Shortly, he would have a decision to make. He liked the freedom of being a solo act, unencumbered by the referrals of auction houses and the demands of clandestine buyers. What if he walked away from the Dickens novel, disappeared for a while into the hinterlands of America? He could change his identity as often as necessary and focus on stealing books of his own choosing, creating his own market. It was an enticing thought.

The instructions in the yellow envelope he picked up in Hamburg came back to him. He was to deliver the novel to von Paulus and, only then, receive his payment of 50,000 euros. With *Dracula* in hand, he could now afford to walk away from the money but that wasn't the problem. He had already used the airline ticket, a portion of the cash and had even made charges on the d'Arblay credit card, all provided by the German client. Plus, there was the issue of Otto, a partner who had vouched for his talent and trustworthiness, put his imprimatur on him. What would happen to him if Theo reneged on his commitment? No, that was a traitorous act, beyond the pale, a mark on his conscience that he could not abide. Even the ruthless Jackal operated with a set of principles – and so must Theo.

When the conductor announced that the train was thirty minutes outside New Haven, Theo knew he had no choice but to complete the assignment that brought him to Connecticut in the first place. He was banking on the likelihood that Kosinsky had returned from Washington, DC and put *Little Dorrit* back in the basement at the Inn. If so, tonight would be quick work, a breeze compared to his risky handiwork in the Boston exhibit hall. By the time he got to Graniteville, Maddie Lever would be on duty. A rendezvous with her would be delightful, a fitting tryst earned after a highly successful and profitable day. But then he would need to retrieve his bag from storage, change his disguise once more, and come up with a plausible explanation as to why he was back in Graniteville. Of course, it was a fanciful idea, one upon which he would not act. Tonight, he would complete his work and avoid any contact with her.

CHAPTER NINETEEN
GOODNIGHT, MY LOVELY

—————

WOODY'S MOTHER NEVER remarried after his stepfather's death and was now retired from her administrator position at the Parlor City Institute, originally an insane asylum for drunkards before the turn of the century but now part of a corporate healthcare behemoth.

Parlor City had changed dramatically since Woody had moved to Spain. He slowed down when he drove past the old familiar haunts that dominated life for Jerry and him as schoolchildren in the fifties. The Pig & Whistle had been leveled, no longer enticing locals with its oversized porcine sign and the smell of sizzling wieners. The aromatic Lattimore's Bakery – the last stop before heading home from his early morning paper route – was now a Quik Pik convenience store offering packaged donuts manufactured in some other city. The park where 10-year-old Woody stumbled upon a gun which he then hid in a horse chestnut tree, and which brought Det. Billy Meacham, Jr. into his life, was still dominating the landscape. Gazing up at that tree gave him a shiver.

The town had struck a deal with a discount furniture outlet to erect a new scoreboard at the Billy Meacham, Jr. little league field. Woody looked away when he caught a glimpse of a bigger-than-life cutout of grinning store owner Milo Shandy perched atop the scoreboard, sitting on one of his cheap sofas, smoking a fat stogie and tossing money into the air. There was no Billy Meacham, Jr. around who cared to look into the relationship between Shandy and a few members of the town council.

The Meacham homestead remained unchanged and it warmed Woody's heart as he pulled into the driveway. Gwen Meacham greeted him at the door, still an attractive woman in her seventies after ten years of widowhood. Her stately carriage and quiet manner rubbed some locals the wrong way, mistaking her quiet, reserved demeanor for arrogance.

Gwen looked at her son and thought he was as movie star handsome as ever, the silver tinges on the sides of his dusky blonde hair adding a touch of elegance. She admired and respected the youthful-looking widow Hannah Cavendish who Woody fell in love with and married. Still, she believed that had he stuck with the pretty young nurse from the Institute, little Meachams would be running around her living room today.

"How's the captain?" Woody inquired, after they were seated at the kitchen table nursing cups of coffee. "Who can tell for sure?" she replied, shrugging her shoulders. "It's his second hip replacement and there were painful complications, not that he would admit it. When I stop by to check on him and bring him food, I catch him grimacing when he doesn't know I'm watching."

"I'll go over in the morning. It will cheer him up," Woody said.

"Just social?" she asked.

Woody smiled. "I came here to see you. The captain will always come second. But yes, mainly social. I do want his advice on a case, though. He's always been a good sounding board."

"He is that, and a lot more, as you know. No one can be the

trusted friend of Billy Meacham, Jr. that many years and not be a stand-up guy in every regard. John appreciates it when you seek his counsel. "You're all mine tonight, son, but you go over there tomorrow morning by yourself. I like to watch CBS with my coffee. That Harry Smith they have on, I like his understated style. Reminds me of the men in my life even though he's bald. But you can deliver some homemade soup for me. Tell John if he doesn't eat it all, he'll not see me for a week."

———

IT TURNED INTO an amorous evening at the Kosinsky household. They had reached an understanding on the disposal of *Little Dorrit* and both parties were purring during dinner.

"Why bother going over to the Inn tonight, babe?" Jerry suggested." I'll walk over with you in the morning and we can check the guest register together to satisfy your curiosity."

Fanny smiled. "Well, it is a slow night with only a few guests and Maddie hasn't called with any problems. C'mon, you big teddy bear," she cooed as she took one of his hands and led him to the stairs.

———

THEO PLACED *DRACULA* and *Rory O'More* in his luggage then rechecked it before catching the next commuter train from New Haven to Graniteville. Determined not to draw attention to himself, even in his latest disguise, he eschewed a taxi and made the short walk to the water as the dusky sky gave way to darkness. Within a few minutes, the Thimbletown Inn came into view.

He entered by the side door and stopped when he recognized the melodious voice of Maddie Lever. How would she react if she suddenly came out from behind the front desk and saw a dark-haired, mustachioed stranger with a swarthy complexion standing in the hallway? A part of Theo craved to see the look on her face.

He walked the few steps to the door leading to the basement and carefully opened it. As he pulled it shut, he heard the hinge creak, causing his pulse to quicken. Flipping on the light switch, he took each step gingerly until he was at the bottom. He looked over to the corner where the utility closet was located and smiled. It had been open on his prior inspection but now it was closed and locked.

It took only a moment for the X-Acto knife to perform its magic for a second time that day. He opened the door and pulled the cord for the overhead light. Looking around, things appeared the same except for one added item – a clamshell storage box, partially hidden by a pile of rags. He was certain that it contained *Little Dorrit* and a peek confirmed it. Theo could hardly believe his good fortune. It was a day, he told himself, that would go down in the annals of book heists as a pinnacle achievement, akin to achieving the treble in football.

Theo turned off the closet light and was about to relock the door when he was distracted by a noise in the hallway above. He crept over to the stairs and slowly ascended each step until he was just below the door. He listened carefully but heard nothing. Confident that the coast was clear, he opened the door and saw Maddie Lever staring down at him.

She stood frozen with her mouth open, looking at those liquid blue eyes that she had lovingly gazed into only a day earlier. It was only a split second, in spite of the disguise, before she knew it was him.

Theo saw the recognition in her face and, in one coordinated motion, dropped the clamshell box, anchored himself by clutching the railing, and grabbed one of her arms with his free hand, violently yanking her forward. Maddie flew past him head-first, bouncing off several steps until she landed with a thud on the cement floor. One of her arms was twisted grotesquely behind her back and her head was wrenched to one side so that she was looking up at him. He must have kicked the clamshell box in the commotion as *Little Dorrit* was laying just beyond her outstretched hand.

Theo started down the stairs, fingering the X-Acto knife in his pocket, praying he would not need to use it. When he got close, he looked into her eyes and knew that she was dead. Back at the top of the stairs, he took one last look at his lover before turning off the light and closing the door.

THERE WAS NO one in the lobby when Theo approached the front desk. Beneath it on a shelf, he saw what he assumed was Maddie's handbag. He rifled through it until he found her keys. Ten minutes later, he was standing in the driveway at her cottage. It wasn't as stylish as the Alfa Romeo two-seater that the Jackal drove from Italy into Paris but Maddie's Fiat sportster would do just fine.

THEO ABANDONED THE Fiat near the train station then retrieved his luggage. Laying the dented clamshell box holding *Little Dorrit* alongside *Dracula* and *Rory O'More*, he couldn't resist taking a prolonged look at his day's handiwork before zipping up the suitcase. He didn't pause to consider the woman he had maimed in Boston or the lover he had just murdered as he boarded the late train to New York City.

CHAPTER TWENTY
SECRET CODES

C APT. JOHN FOGARTY was a retired Parlor City police officer who lived in a cottage he had himself built at a lake on the edge of town. His flinty style and moral rectitude had ensured Fogarty dominance whenever he was among his fellow officers. Some wag in the department who knew him well said that if he had gone west on one of the first wagon trains, wherever he settled would have eventually been named Fogartyville.

It was believed by many, including Woody, that the captain would have courted and possibly won the heart of the former Gwen Pritchard, except that after her marriage to Tommy Braun ended tragically, Billy Meacham, Jr. walked into her life like a conquering hero. John Fogarty had put Woody's mother on a pedestal when she was a young beauty and there she resided to this day.

FOGARTY RUBBED HIS forehead, wincing behind his hand, as he sat and listened patiently to Woody relate the crucial details of the

Kammler case, including the surprising revelations in Baltimore the previous day.

"So, at least two people covet this novel enough to kill for it. Yeah, it could be as simple as an aging Nazi wanting it back because of the Hitler stamp, or whatever you call it, on the inside cover. But I'm not buying it. My guess is that some powerful son of a bitch has sent agents – at least twice that we know of – to secure the book by any means necessary. It tells you how uniquely valuable this particular book is to someone.

"For Kammler to go into hiding for several decades, evading detection before he was finally tracked down a second time, is quite remarkable. I wouldn't be surprised to learn that after leaving Baltimore, he decamped to a number of other cities before ending up in Connecticut. My guess is that he figured out that the comfort of living in a large city with a sizeable German population was outweighed by the danger of being tracked down there. Also, the fact that Kammler held on to the book all these years just shows you what stubborn old men like me will do."

Woody chuckled. The captain, who he would never call by his first name, had a way of distilling cases down to their essence while still keeping an open mind. "Other thoughts?" Woody asked.

"It may not be a productive path to go down but your case got me thinking about how books have been utilized for ages to commit crimes. Old police files are filled with evidence on how the insides have been hollowed out to insert knives, razors, you name it. I recollect a case where a small Derringer pistol was smuggled into a prison in a carved-out bible. But, I'm getting off track, aren't I?" Fogarty said.

Woody didn't mind. He liked to listen to the captain extemporize and it usually generated productive exchanges, even an innovative approach to solving a sticky problem. "Jerry had the novel examined by what they call a Victorian book expert in New Haven and it's a genuine first edition. Except for the Hitler bookplate, the guy didn't notice anything unusual about it – or at least he wasn't saying. In fact, he wanted to buy it on the spot."

"That might have been the brightest move your friend – or Kammler – ever could have made. Pick up some ready cash and unload a hot potato," Fogarty said with a mischievous grin. Woody ignored the dig. There had been bad blood between the ex-Marine and Jerry years earlier when his best friend took off for Canada and then Kathmandu to avoid the Vietnam War draft.

Fogarty regretted his aspersion. "Forget what I just said. Kosinsky's an okay guy. Came home and turned his life around, I gotta give him that. Listen, here's another thought. I'm sure you've already considered the possibility that the Hitler stamp in the front of the book isn't, by itself, enough motivation for the murders. And who hunts down and kills someone to get their hands on a novel by Dickens or anyone else just because it's a first edition? That kind of pursuit costs dough and is fraught with danger, as you've discovered. It'd be a lot simpler to just buy the damn novel from a reputable dealer. No, this particular book holds a secret that only a few people know about – and at least two of them are pushing up daisies.

"Listen, there's an eccentric old chap down at the library by the name of Roscoe Moutard. He runs the local historical society out of space on the top floor. I was checking out some books, stocking up before my surgery, and he buttonholed me in the lobby. Pointed at my stack and started telling me about the secret codes and messages that authors insert into the text. It's like a game, I guess. Moutard's a persistent old codger once he collars you, so don't say you weren't warned.

"Before you leave town, it wouldn't hurt to stop by and talk to him. Do a little unorthodox detective work like an old gumshoe. You know the type, right? What's the popular phrase that drives me up the wall? Oh yeah, think outside the box. One more thing, kid. You've become highly successful of late and I'm damn proud. Billy would be, too. When people were praising him in his heyday, he told me he always had to guard against falling prey to Benjamin's Conceit. I had no idea what he was talking about and he explained that it was an adage by Ben Franklin. Hope I don't butcher it but I'm fairly sure it goes like this: 'The first degree of folly is to conceit oneself wise.'"

Fogarty insisted on hobbling to the door with his arm draped over Woody's shoulder. "I'll call Moutard and let him know you'll be stopping by," he said, grinning broadly. The captain had a way of getting you to take a suggestion as a command order.

"If you don't finish the soup, they'll be hell to pay. You know that, right?" Woody exclaimed with a serious face, before cracking up.

"I'm not so foolish as to dump it, kid. But just between us coppers, your mother puts all kinds of new-fangled vegetables in her soups, so I just eat around the ones I don't recognize. You're not a rat fink, are you?"

―――――•―――――

WOODY FOUND MOUTARD hunched over a book at a long table in the center of a sparsely furnished room. He had a surprised look on his face when Woody said that Capt. Fogarty had called to alert him that he would be stopping by. "I heard the telephone ring but ignore it when I'm busy," he said, pointing to the open book on the table.

"The Captain mentioned the research you do on secret codes and messages inserted into books. It sounds fascinating. A friend of mine just inherited an old edition of a Charles Dickens novel. How does one go about identifying these secrets?" Woody asked.

"It's called steganography," Moutard said, looking annoyed, before adding, "the technique of concealing a message within a non-secret text. We're not talking spy craft here. If you don't have a clue that the writer practiced it, it's easily overlooked – can go undetected for ages, even forever. Lewis Carroll did it for sure with those Alice books and some scholars insist that Shakespeare inserted coded messages in all his plays. Publishers have been known to do it as well without the author's acquiescence. Now, it's interesting that you brought up Dickens. How much do you know about him?"

Woody felt his face redden and wondered if Moutard noticed. He didn't want to mention *Little Dorrit* and tried to recall the name of the Dickens novel he read in high school but it eluded him. Then he remembered the book Jerry had shown him at Trowbridge Cottage. "As I said, it's my friend who has the Dickens novel, *Oliver Twist* if I'm not mistaken. If you can enlighten me, it will assuredly be passed on to him."

Moutard looked disappointed that the man in front of him was a proxy and had no direct interest in the arcane world of literary tricks that dominated his own leisure time. The telephone rang and Moutard ignored it. Here was a didactic moment, not necessarily ideal with an inspired pupil, but he would take advantage of it, nonetheless.

"Most people don't know that Dickens was a court reporter and then a journalist before he began writing novels. His first one, *Pickwick Papers,* made him famous. For his own benefit and amusement, Dickens developed an unusual shorthand using symbols, abbreviations, dots and scribbles, most of which only he could read. He even wrote letters employing his unique steganographic style that scholars are still trying to decipher.

"Dickens enjoyed using the names of his characters to leave a message for the reader. *Great Expectations* is a good example. if you break apart Miss Havisham's name, you get have-is-sham, which describes her empty life, despite accumulated wealth. Get it? Or take *Little Dorrit*, in which Dickens creates a character named Mr. Merdle, a financial fraudster who commits suicide. The French word *merde*, meaning excrement, is the secret. I could go on but you get the idea.

"Now, if the prior owner created some sort of code, your friend could begin by looking for subtle markings on page numbers or letters which are underlined on certain pages in the text in an anomalous manner. Putting them together in a coherent format to decipher the secret message is the tricky part. It's tedious work but can be quite rewarding."

Moutard's soliloquy had been mind-numbing but suddenly fireworks went off in Woody's head and his expression turned animated, causing the old man to think he might actually have recruited a votary. Moutard resumed talking but his words were floating vaguely in the background as Woody brainstormed. What if the individual who removed the novel from Hitler's library knew about – or inserted – a coded message into *Little Dorrit*? Maybe the names of Nazis who had escaped and the countries to which they fled? Or the location of stolen artwork and who possessed it? If he was on the right track, it now made sense why certain people were desperate to get their hands on the novel.

The telephone rang again, bringing Woody back to the moment. "Let's say I wanted to insert a coded message into my friend's Dickens novel. In your opinion, where might I best place it, other than putting a series of markings on selected pages?" Woody asked.

"Oh, one could use various methods, Mr. Meacham. You might insert your message into the frontispiece or the bookplate."

Woody smiled painfully. "Educate me, please do!"

Moutard got up and walked to one of the bookshelves lining the wall. He examined a few volumes before bringing one of them back to the table. "Pull your chair over and see where I've opened up *Masterman Ready* by Captain Marryat. His first name was Frederick but his appeal as a novelist derived in great part from his status as an officer in the Royal Navy. His nautical fiction in the Victorian Era was quite popular at the same time Dickens was gaining fame. Not sure if they were friends but they were acquaintances. Rivals you could say."

Woody was getting anxious as Moutard digressed but he had asked for a tutorial and he was going to get it. Be patient, man, he said to himself. You're way outside the box now.

"So, on the right side, you see the title page, pretty self-explanatory. Note that at the bottom you find the publisher's name and the date the novel was published, often in Latin as you see here. Let's see, hmm. Ah, yes, 1895 for this particular edition. Now, look across at the facing page, That, my good man, is the frontispiece, very often an elaborate and detailed illustration by a noted caricaturist like George Cruikshank or Hablot Browne but not in this case. Hmm, it's not signed. Well, no matter. Notice the intricate detail of the drawing. Some sort of sea nymph hovering above a supine sailor on a boat deck. Marvelous, don't you think?"

Woody forced a smile and the telephone rang again, making Moutard glower. Woody wondered who was so anxious to talk to this guy. Did they know what they were in for?

"Now let's turn to the boards, the cover of the book in layman's language. Here you see the owner of this Marryat novel pasted his personalized bookplate on the inside of the front board. A coat of arms establishing the ownership of someone named Percy Vickers. Long dead, I'd gather. Some people get quite creative. Below his name it looks like a crown with wings and a tree growing out of the top. Very strange. Mr. Vickers was a frustrated artist or had a screw loose.

"So, you see, plenty of places to insert a message or code, in tiny script. Make it part of the design so no one else picks it up except the recipient for whom it was attended. Nothing to see here, is there? My eyes aren't what they used to be. Oh, well."

Woody thanked Moutard profusely and was in a hurry to escape before the telephone rang again. If it did, he would answer it himself.

All he wanted to do now was race over to his mother's house and call Jerry. He would ask him to go over to the Inn, grab the novel and call him back. If there was a coded message in what Moutard called a frontispiece or even in the Hitler emblem, the expert in New Haven and the savant at the Library of Congress had both missed it or were too eager to possess *Little Dorrit* to bother to look.

CHAPTER TWENTY-ONE
A GANG OF ONE

———◆———

When Woody pulled into his mother's driveway, she was standing at the door with a troubled expression. "We've been trying to reach you all morning. John said you left his place and might have gone to the library to meet with someone called Moutard. That guy never answers his phone. Tragedy in Connecticut, son, but Jerry and his wife are okay. There was a horrible incident at the Inn last night. Someone fell down the stairs leading to the basement. Jerry said it was fatal but that's all I know. He said the police are there now."

When Woody was finally able to reach Jerry, there was bustling and loud, indistinct chatter in the background making it difficult to hear.

"How's she doing?" Woody asked, anxious for details.

"She's taking it hard, like it's partly her fault. I called Uncle Homer and he's with her now, sitting across from me in the lobby as we speak. It was her night manager, Maddie Lever. Sweet lady, Woody. Can you believe we were going to walk over here last night after dinner to check on something? If we had, maybe ……..." Jerry's voice trailed off and Woody heard a deep sigh before his friend continued. "I'm just glad it was me who opened the basement door this morning."

"So, an accidental fall down a darkened stairwell. Is that the initial finding? Who's running the show there?" Woody asked.

Jerry didn't hear or was avoiding Woody's questions. He cupped a hand around the receiver and started talking rapidly in a whisper, just loud enough for his friend to hear. "I didn't say anything to Fanny when I first went down to check Maddie's pulse. One look and there was no doubt. Came back up and told Fanny that Maddie had fallen down the stairs and to call 911. She did and then wanted to go down but I stopped her, held her tight. After a few moments, she understood and broke down. When Uncle Homer arrived, I went back down to look around before the cops and medical people started showing up. I know, tampering with a crime scene and all that but I couldn't help myself. That's when I saw that the door to the utility closet was open. I don't have to tell you what was missing."

Woody hesitated for a moment and asked again, "Who's running the show there?"

"Someone from the medical examiner's office is down in the basement plus there are a few Graniteville cops loitering about. What should I do?"

"Well, you've got to tell Fanny about *Little Dorrit* eventually. It's not going to be easy but just try to pick the right time. More immediately, you need to go on the record and inform your local cops about the novel. What they'll do, if they put two and two together, is notify the staties to send in a crime scene unit. You can't appear to be holding back what could be crucial information. Listen, the autopsy report may not show signs of a struggle but I'm guessing that there was some sort of confrontation, not as dramatic as with Kammler, and the woman was either pushed or fell to her death. Can't rule out an accident at this point even though the novel is missing. See if you can get anything out of the ME. Maybe let Homer speak to him. Could be an old relationship that he can work."

"I was a damn fool for keeping it here, Woody. Fanny had better instincts than me about the potential danger and begged me to get rid of the novel – or she would. I had my chance to sell it to Grantham or give it to Brenner but I passed on both opportunities. Last night, we agreed I would either sell it or donate it to a library after we checked with you. Inheriting that damn shop from Kammler has turned into my family's nightmare. I wish I'd never befriended him. She may never forgive me, Woody."

Woody could feel the pain in his friend's voice but didn't have adequate words to assuage it. "We're dealing with a very sophisticated cold-blooded thief, Jerry, who wasn't going to be deterred until he got the novel. Now, it won't make Fanny feel any better right away but with *Little Dorrit* gone, she's going to realize that her family is now out of danger. If it's ever recovered, I'm sure you won't let the novel within one hundred miles of Graniteville."

"How soon will you get here?" Jerry asked, a sense of urgency in his voice.

"I want to check in with my FBI contact before hitting the road. Should be at your place before dark. Stay calm and don't put off telling the police about the break-in, okay? Give some thought about what you want me to do now that *Little Dorrit* is no longer in your possession. If you decide to leave everything in the hands of the police, you'll get no objection from me."

"Looks like we've got an elite ring of book thieves, with foreign connections, working the East Coast, Woody." Without even asking him why he called, FBI agent Aubrey Crockett started updating him on the latest developments, as if he were a member of their team. Woody was too seasoned to inhibit the flow of information from a normally tight-lipped G-man.

"Assuming your friend's novel is a target, and we haven't dismissed that possibility, it's clear that these boys are not intimidated. After the Yale heist, as if that wasn't brazen enough, we believe they hit a book fair in Boston and made off with a few expensive volumes inside an exhibit hall crowded with people. Then, we caught a break on a theft in New York City that occurred before the Yale and Boston incidents. A suspect, as brash as they come, lifted a rare copy of a novel titled *Jane Eyre* from an unlocked glass case at the Casaubon book shop. Instead of fleeing, he hung around while the shop manager stepped away to locate a second novel requested by the thief. Want to guess the name?"

Woody shook his head in disbelief. "Don't tell me it was *Little Dorrit*." Crockett chuckled. "Correctamundo."

When Woody told Crockett about the murder of Maddie Lever and the theft of Little Dorrit, Crockett said, "Damn, there must be a demand for this Dickens novel that we don't yet appreciate. But here's where we caught our lucky break, Woody. The New York thief, not content to walk away with one novel, tells the bookshop manager that he's staying at the Hotel Dorset and to call him there when *Little Dorrit* is available for inspection. The name he gave was Alexandre d'Arblay."

"Couldn't it be one person? Why a ring?" Woody asked, fixated on Crockett's earlier analysis.

"First, the profiles don't match. The New York thief was a well-dressed, very polished French-speaking gentleman with a Van Dyke while at Yale we have an average-looking, clean-shaven, elderly man. Then, you have the daring Boston theft, which points to a two-man job. A bookshelf fell – we think it was deliberately pushed – on top of a woman causing a crowd to gather, thereby prompting a nearby book dealer to exit his booth to provide aid. During the commotion, the accomplice slipped behind the crowd and stole two rare books. Unfortunately, no description so far of either Boston perp. You got any thoughts before I tell you the latest on d'Arblay?"

Woody demurred and Crockett proceeded to brief him on the d'Arblay passport. "It's a valid name all right, except that it belonged to a man who died in a car accident a few years ago. The imposter used it to enter the U.S. by train from Canada several days ago. Our theory is that he either recruited his accomplices when he got to New York or they were lined up in advance. The Casaubon manager didn't recognize the d'Arblay passport photo so at the very least, we are dealing with a two-man team. It appears that they were on a well-planned mission, Woody."

"Any luck tracking d'Arblay's movements?" Woody asked. Crockett laughed. "Yeah, this is what makes his blunder at the New York bookstore inexplicable. We got a court order to monitor his credit card and have receipts for two hotels in the city – neither one was the Dorset – but he was already checked out before we could seize him. We're assuming that the man with the Van Dyke stays at a different hotel from d'Arblay. We'll continue tracking the credit card but it hasn't been used in the last few days. Our assumption is that he's resorted to cash. As for the passport, if he tries to use it to leave the country, we've got him. I think we're definitely tightening the noose. He's bound to slip up," Crockett boasted, sounding confident that d'Arblay would be in custody soon.

"As for Graniteville, it sounds like the other heists, part of a classic 'steal to order' operation, Woody. We see it with artwork, of course, but even with luxury vehicles. I have a buddy in the Newark field office who handled a case a couple of years ago where a thug capped a car thief just because he delivered a vintage Lincoln Town Car without red leather interior. Listen, I'll phone our man in New Haven and he'll contact the state police. If we can establish a connection to the other heists, they'll get our help whether they want it or not."

When Crockett learned that Woody was heading to his friend's house in Connecticut, he said, "Please pass on my condolences. Tell him we'll all be doing our best to help solve the murder and retrieve his copy of *Little Dorrit*."

Woody didn't bother to say that the Dickens novel was the last thing Jerry Kosinsky wanted to see.

———

ON THE RIDE to Jerry's house, Woody mulled everything he had learned in the last 24 hours. He wasn't about to contradict Crockett over the telephone, but the theory of a book theft ring didn't work for him. The only reliable description was this Van Dyke character in New York. The girl at the Yale library had failed to provide anything useful and there were absolutely no descriptions of the Boston thieves, if indeed there was even a pair working in tandem. As for geography, Boston could be reached from New York by train in approximately four hours and New Haven was roughly the midpoint. Woody guessed that the timeline of events would show that a single individual could have easily pulled off all three capers.

That left the enigma of Graniteville. Crockett was right in one respect: the theft of *Little Dorrit* with two murders attached to it simply didn't fit the pattern of the other crimes, all of them committed in public settings. Crockett seemed disinterested in the fact that d'Arblay specifically asked the New York dealer for a first edition of *Little Dorrit* right around the time that Kammler was murdered. Was it supposed to be written off as an extraordinary coincidence?

Woody hadn't shared with Crockett what he had learned in Baltimore and wasn't confident that the FBI team would even consider it germane. Even he was having his doubts. How was it that a single thief or a ring that had pulled off heists in New York, New Haven and

Boston would even know that a Dickens novel was hidden behind a wall at an obscure bookshop in a village on the Connecticut coast?

With so many things churning through his head, Woody had forgotten to ask Jerry why Fanny and he had planned to walk over to the Thimbletown Inn the night before.

CHAPTER TWENTY-TWO
From High to Low

Grand Central Station was practically deserted when Theo got off the train from New Haven. He entered a stall in the lower level bathroom and removed the dark wig and bushy mustache. Standing at one of the sinks, he removed the dark-framed glasses and splashed water on his face, rubbing vigorously to remove the make-up until he was transformed back into Alexandre d'Arblay.

Exiting the terminal onto 42nd Street, he walked the few blocks south to the travel agency where he removed the large suitcase from his locker. Next, he wrapped *Dracula* and *Rory O'More* in clothing and, along with Little Dorrit, put all three novels in his smaller suitcase before placing it in the locker.

Just off 7th Avenue, Theo spotted a small hotel and entered the dimly lit lobby. The front desk clerk was slouched in a chair, sound asleep with his arms across his chest. Theo hit the bell on the counter a few times before the clerk bolted awake. Theo surmised by the scowl on his face that he had interrupted a pleasant dream.

"Credit card and license," he announced in a surly tone without looking up. He examined the d'Arblay passport and then glanced at

Theo suspiciously. Theo was tired and in no mood for a confrontation. "Does this *connard* not realize he is antagonizing a man quite capable of murder?" he said to himself.

"Card rejected, Mr. Dably," the clerk said, smiling as he butchered the name. "It's d'Arblay and I'll pay cash," Theo responded, working hard to contain his growing irritation.

"No can do, Mr. Darbler," the clerk intoned, now feeling triumphant. "We need a card on file for incidentals like long-distance calls and restaurant charges. Surely, you carry a back-up card for emergencies."

A smug, victorious grin was spreading across the clerk's face as he dropped the credit card on the counter. Theo reached forward and grabbed his necktie, yanking the clerk's slender body forward like it was a rag doll. "Give me back my passport before I do something that you will not enjoy."

The clerk was shaking and Theo did not let go until he had the passport in his free hand. By the time Theo was on the street, the clerk was on the telephone with the police. As he described the confrontation, he had pinned down and was throttling his attacker when d'Arblay broke free and ran off.

———◆———

THEO WALKED BRISKLY toward Times Square, now sparsely populated with drunkards, hustlers and street walkers. He realized that his suitcase made him an inviting target so he quickened his pace and had turned onto a side street when he spotted a flickering red neon sign that spelled "OTEL."

He slid a $50 bill across the counter before explaining that his passport and credit cards had been lifted at the train station. He paid in advance for three nights, reasoning that it would give him ample time to sort things out.

It had been a roller coaster day for DeBruycker since he boarded a train that morning in New Haven. He had been euphoric after his Boston and Graniteville successes but now was overwhelmed by exhaustion, as he was beset by a new set of problems.

Ever since his *faux pas* at the Casaubon book shop, he had avoided using the d'Arblay credit card, fearing he was leaving a trail that could be picked up by the police. But with his funds dwindling, after paying cash at the Thimbletown Inn, he had taken a chance at the first hotel and it had backfired.

It seemed inconceivable that the German client had cancelled the card. Was it some sort of machine glitch? He would go out in the morning and try the card again. If it didn't work, he would call Von Paulus. He had not been preserving cash for contingencies because he planned to use the credit card to purchase his plane ticket to Hamburg. To raise additional cash, he could no doubt find another book dealer or library to victimize, plus there was the option to pawn off *Rory O'More* on Simon Wegg. At the same time, with *Dracula* and *Little Dorrit* in hand, Theo understood that it was time to minimize risk.

His thoughts turned back to Otto. The Hamburg dealer would be impressed with Theo's recent successes and would urge him to immediately fly to Hamburg to deliver *Little Dorrit*. But how was he to do so if the d'Arblay credit card had been cancelled? Tired and hungry, Theo fell into bed and was soon fast asleep.

Before Woody's arrival in Graniteville, the medical examiner had identified bruising on one of Maddie's forearms along with finger impressions. While the cause of death was tentatively ruled as blunt force trauma to the cranium caused during the fall, he would not rule out the possibility that she was forcefully yanked by the arm and then pulled or pushed down the stairs. "Okay," said the lead state trooper on the scene, "so we have an accidental death or homicide on our hands. Undetermined cause for now until we see what forensics turns up. Thanks, doc." As they chatted, his team was dusting the entire basement for prints, including the stairwell and railing.

When Woody showed up at the Kosinsky house, he learned that the restaurant at the inn had been closed and its manager was now manning the front desk. Fanny had already retired, eventually falling off to sleep with the aid of a doctor's prescription. It took a while before Woody ventured to ask Jerry why they had intended to walk over to the inn the night before. He wondered if it had struck them yet that had they done so, they might have confronted Maddie's killer.

Jerry explained that Fanny wanted to check the guest register since the library thief and the guest at the Inn who had captivated Maddie were both professors who spoke French and had been at Yale. "She called it the 'French connection,'" Jerry said, smiling wistfully. "You know, the movie," he added unnecessarily.

"Smart thinking. Stay put. I'll walk over and check it out. Never leave a loose end, right?" Woody said, trying to sound positive.

———

Within an hour, Woody had tracked down Crockett and provided him with the inn's guest register entry for Alexandre d'Arblay. Crockett promised to get a copy of the picture in the d'Arblay passport forwarded to the FBI field office in New Haven for Jerry and Fanny to ID.

Before hanging up, Crockett mentioned that after no activity for days, d'Arblay had attempted to use his credit card at a hotel south of Grand Central Station earlier in the evening. "The hotel clerk tried to play the hero and subdued d'Arblay but he broke away and took off. His description matches d'Arblay's passport picture. We've got him cornered now, Woody, and he's getting desperate. It's just a matter of time now until we take him into custody. My guess is that he'll give up his compatriots fairly quickly."

Woody was baffled that Crockett was still fixated on the gang theory but didn't want to say anything that would limit his openness with respect to sharing vital information. Instead, he said, "Send the composite sketch as well as the passport photograph. Who knows what disguise, if any, he was wearing when he checked in to the Thimbletown Inn."

WHEN JERRY HEARD the latest news, he exclaimed, "It's a murderous cabal that desperately wanted to get their hands on the novel, Woody. I'm with the FBI on this one. It's hard for me to believe that this d'Arblay character was operating alone. *Little Dorrit* is a pawn in a larger game, right? Well, good riddance. I've a mind to unload the cursed shop as well. If the novel ever turns up and it's legitimately mine, we'll sell it to the highest bidder and put the proceeds into a college savings account."

Jerry was highly agitated and in no mood to be challenged, so Woody changed the subject. "I've been thinking about what Fanny told you earlier, Jer, recalling her last conversation with Maddie about d'Arblay. He charmed her with talk about Belgium, describing its major cities and attractions in detail. He sounds like quite a lady's man, which is part of his MO, but it also suggests that the path to finding him – and his true identity – could very well lead us through one of those Belgian cities."

"Whoa! Don't tell me you're thinking of flying over there, Woody. If you're doing it for me, don't bother. If his passport was pulled and his credit card blocked, doesn't that mean he's trapped here in the good old US of A? Don't you think the FBI will nab him in New York sooner than later?"

"He's a crafty guy, Jer. Could even have another passport. Because of the other heists, the feds haven't given up on the proposition that there's a team of thieves working with d'Arblay. Even if he's caught, who's to say he'll talk and give up his partners, assuming that they even exist? I'm more interested in who is behind him back in Europe. No, the key to unraveling this case is to find who d'Arblay really is. What's his real name and where's he from? Who are his associates in France, Belgium and elsewhere on the continent besides the auction house owner in Dresden?

"All we know for certain at this point is that someone using the d'Arblay name robbed a bookstore in New York City wearing a disguise and is the likely killer of both Kammler and Maddie which, if true, means that he also stole *Little Dorrit*. It might seem airtight but everything is still circumstantial. We need to wait on the forensic team, to see if they turn up evidence that will prove definitive. Now, let's turn to the Yale theft and hypothesize that d'Arblay pulled it off. Don't forget that, according to Fanny, he told Maddie that he had just been at the university before coming up to Graniteville. Are we really supposed to believe that he wanted to visit the Thimble Islands before returning to Europe? A master thief with a penchant for site-seeing on some obscure islands that most Americans haven't even heard of? Or instead, in criminal parlance, was he casing the joint?"

Jerry shrugged and Woody continued. "You can be sure that the FBI will be showing the passport picture to the lady who checked him in at the Yale library. If I'm right and he resembles d'Arblay, then we potentially have him present at every crime scene except Boston. According to Crockett, not a single attendee or dealer at the exhibit hall could provide a description of the thief or thieves. That would conform with d'Arblay's ability to blend in at such a crowded venue. Are we to believe that it was members of the so-called d'Arblay gang when all the other thefts were apparently handled solo? So, now the question is: How could he manage it?" Woody paused to give Jerry time to absorb what he had just heard.

After a few minutes, Jerry said, "Multiple disguises, of course! You set me up nicely for that one, Woody. Holy smokes, this d'Arblay character, if your theory is correct, is a one-man gang of thieves. A genius with multiple personas. Have you shared this with the FBI yet?"

Woody laughed. "Been chewing on this since speaking with Crockett the first time, before leaving Parlor City. We have a definitive connection between the New York and Graniteville crimes while the Yale link is still tenuous but certainly feasible. Not sure if I'm ready to disabuse the feds of their notion of multiple perps. I am, however, going to suggest that they check with Amtrak for ticket purchases between New Haven and Boston. If the timeline works, then I'll believe I'm not grasping at straws.

"The FBI no doubt thinks he's holed up in some New York dive, laying low while he plots his next move. He doesn't strike me as the kind of operator that will do something rash. Let's see what happens in the next day or so. If there's no sighting of d'Arblay, or his so-called gang, and you're okay with it, I'll fly back to Spain. Maybe I'll take my wife on holiday. I understand Brussels is beautiful this time of year."

CHAPTER TWENTY-THREE
A NEW MISTRESS

WHEN THEO CAME down the elevator the next morning, he was once again disguised as an old man, a reprise from his inaugural visit to Graniteville. In his room, he had practiced slowing down to a halting gait with a slight forward lurch.

Near the hotel, he found a coffee shop with multiple credit card decals on the door. Over breakfast, he debated whether or not it was the right time to try the d'Arblay credit card again. He had spoken halting English to the waitress while examining the menu and she had smiled benevolently. When he finished eating, he presented the card and waited.

The waitress returned to his table shaking her head sympathetically. "So sorry, not good. You have some other way to pay?" Theo acted confused for a moment then reached in his pocket and pulled out a twenty dollar bill. When she returned with his change, she smiled again and walked to another table.

Theo forced himself to sip his coffee, not wanting to leave too hastily and draw attention to himself. He remembered the unusual

American habit of tipping and left a five dollar bill on the table before walking slowly to the door.

ON THE TRAIN to New York the prior evening, Theo DeBruycker had felt invincible, a Medieval French warrior in his *cuirass*. Now, he was exposed and vulnerable, without his breastplate. If the police had the power to block the d'Arblay credit card, wouldn't they do the same with his French passport? If so, both documents were liabilities now and needed to be destroyed. Stay calm and assess the situation, play it cool like the Jackal, he said to himself.

Theo walked a few blocks and spotted a telephone booth. If his calling card had been cancelled as well, he would know for certain that he was a hunted man. He entered his international dialing codes and relaxed when no automated message of declination came on. After dialing Otto Von Paulus' number, he waited nervously.

Otto picked up on the second ring and Theo was relieved to hear his familiar voice. "I've got it, Otto, the prize I was sent here to retrieve. There is much more to tell you but first, I have a problem and need your help."

Theo was talking rapidly when Otto stopped him. "They vill be pleased ven I pass on your message but you must get back here quickly. Augustus Gottfried has inquired about the delay. Also, I fear I'm being followed. I regret bringing you into this scheme, Theo, even though the revords are substantial."

When Otto learned about the credit card and Theo's concern about his other travel documents, he asked, "Are you in a safe place?"

"The best place of all, Otto. I'm in New York City in a neighborhood where anyone can remain anonymous. Certainly, you've heard of Times Square."

"Yes. Yes. Now, stay out of sight. I vill let them know the good news and tell them of your predicament. Surely, they vill find a vay to get you a brand new set of documents right away. It is in everyvone's best interest. Call me back tomorrow at this same time and I vill hopefully have answers for you."

"One more thing, Otto. You know Reinhold in Dresden. I handled a job for him here as well. Please call him and confirm that he received his shipment."

"You vot?" Von Paulus shouted into the telephone. "That vas you that sent him the map? He's been arrested. No doubt the police are pressing him to give up the name of his accomplice. Vot else have you been up to over there? Our client vill not be happy if they learn of these diversions at their expense."

Theo's mind was racing and he grew hot. He was not used to being dressed down. He had been ready to boast about his *Dracula* escapade but couldn't bear to hear Otto explode in anger again. "Listen, Otto, there's no need to panic but you should know that I performed some dastardly deeds to secure the prize. That damn book is worth much more than they're paying us, I tell you, and I intend to find out why."

Otto couldn't believe his ears. "This is crazy talk, Theo. Dismiss it from your mind this instant. Now, take my advice and stay out of sight until ve talk tomorrow. Don't say another vord. Just hang up the phone."

Von Paulus waited until he was certain that Theo had disconnected. When he put down his own handset on the cradle, he didn't hear the second click before the line went dead.

THE BEST THE FBI could get out of the attendant at the Yale library, when shown the d'Arblay passport photo, was "maybe, but he looked much older." Up in Graniteville an hour later, Jerry and Fanny identified him instantly as the guest at the Thimbletown Inn.

Next came the news that Maddie's Fiat sportster had been found in New Haven on a side street near the train station. That discovery sent state troopers to her cottage, scouring it for evidence that might lead them to the killer.

The police and the FBI remained tight-lipped when questioned by the press about the rumored theft of *Little Dorrit* but when word leaked out about the search of Maddie's cottage, speculation quickly spread about a lover's quarrel with a guest from the inn that somehow turned deadly. Seeing Maddie's reputation tarnished in death sent Fanny into a fury before she broke down again, causing Woody to delay his departure for Spain.

WHEN THEO ACCEPTED the fact that he would not be compensated for the theft of the de Jode map, he understood that the consequences were manifold. If Reinhold gave up his name to save his own neck, police would be swarming over his apartment in Bruges. In short order, he would be a man without a country. He forced himself to compartmentalize these troubles and deal with his immediate problem. Until his new travel documents arrived, he was compelled to raise cash by any means possible.

He walked over to the travel agency and retrieved his small suitcase before returning to his hotel. He walked past the library and it beckoned him to come inside but Theo walked on. He had work to do. *Dracula* was sacrosanct but he would scrub *Rory O'More* clean of any identifying ownership markings and take it to the one place where he felt confident he could quickly pawn it with no questions asked.

Simon Wegg was pleasantly surprised that he had not been contacted by the police about the Casaubon robbery. In the past, he felt like he was always the one rousted when a rare book disappeared anywhere in the New York area.

When an old man walked into his shop offering to sell a novel by Samuel Lover, Wegg went to the latest version of *Bookman's Price Index* to ascertain its collectable value. The name Lover was familiar to him as a secondary Irish writer, highly popular in the mid-1800s, particularly for the novel *Handy Andy*.

Wegg looked up from his guide and studied the old man, trying to remember if he's ever dealt with him before. He pegged him as an old immigrant living in a rent-controlled apartment on the Upper East Side or the Bronx, selling off his library a book at a time just to survive.

It was certainly a handsome, first edition of *Rory O'More*, a rarity according to *Bookman*, a near fine copy printed in 1837, with no chipping to the boards and the pages remarkably clean. Wegg wondered if the old man knew its value and decided to offer $100 just to test him. The old man shook his head decisively no and remained mute as Wegg gradually raised the price to $800, at which point he agreed with a subtle nodding of his head. "Cash only," the old man said, his voice trembling.

Wegg retreated to the back and returned a few minutes later with the payment. He watched the old man's hands shake as he counted the bills. "Come back anytime you have books of this quality. I never ask questions unless someone walks in with the Geneva Bible," Wegg said, hoping a little humor would endear him to the old man. Theo glanced at Wegg and left the shop without saying a word.

Theo did not get what he had hoped for from Wegg but he was in no position to bargain strenuously. The fact that he had no idea what

Rory O'More was worth added to his disadvantage and he faulted himself for not looking at the price card sitting next to the novel in the glass case. With anyone but Wegg, he would have wandered through the shop and tried to lift a book, but Wegg was too sly and suspicious to expose his treasures to a stranger walking in off the street.

BACK AT HIS hotel, Theo removed *Little Dorrit* from the clamshell box. He noticed the dent on the side, caused when the box had caromed down the basement stairs at the inn. It made him think of Maddie Lever, not as she lay crumpled at the bottom of the stairs, but as the effervescent woman he made love to at her cottage. If events hadn't gone sideways, he convinced himself that he might even have escorted her around Belgium.

He propped up two pillows against the headboard and opened up the novel, first examining the Hitler bookplate before moving on to the frontispiece drawing and then the title page with its sketch of a waif wearing a bonnet and standing in a doorway. Such an innocent-looking little lady, he mused, to be the protagonist of such a big book for which people had to die.

Without success, Theo skimmed the pages looking for subtle markings in the margins or next to the page numbers which would indicate some sort of pattern that would create a message. Then, he focused on the more than two dozen elaborate caricatures and drawings scattered throughout the novel. The process was tedious and unrewarding and Theo found his eyes closing after a few hours. He laid *Little Dorrit* down next to him on the bed and patted it. "My new mistress," he whispered as he dozed off.

While DeBruycker slept, police were put on alert, with extra patrols in the area between New York City's two train stations. Patrolmen had been provided with the picture of Alexandre' D'Arblay along with the sketch of the suave gentleman with the Van Dyke who robbed the Casaubon shop. Frustration grew when there were no sightings that day or for several days afterwards. No one was on the lookout for the old man who was walking among them.

CHAPTER TWENTY-FOUR
THE LIST

When Theo awoke, he had been dreaming of Maddie Lever and was temporarily disoriented by the early evening shadows enveloping the room. He reached over to touch *Little Dorrit* and it wasn't there. He laid still, looking at the ceiling, moving his hand around the bed.

He sat up and turned on the bedside light before looking back, expecting to see the novel. No *Little Dorrit*. Theo leaped up and stood over the bed, staring in amazement as if waiting for the novel to magically appear. He walked over to the door and saw that the inside lock was still in place. Then, he went to the window and parted the curtain, looking out on the brightly lit spectacle of Times Square. The window was unlocked but he was on the fourth floor in a room with no balcony. "No cat burglar or that spiderman character entered stealthily," he murmured with an uncomfortable laugh.

Theo returned to the door and flipped on the overhead light. When he turned back toward the bed, he saw *Little Dorrit* open on the dark rug, the front and back boards spread eagle, their dark, marbled patterns blending into the carpet. He picked up the novel and sat on the edge of the bed, examining it for damage. A few of the pages in the middle of the book had been folded back during the fall but would smooth out when pressed between the other pages.

When Theo examined the spine, it had pulled apart along the seam where it connected to the rest of the novel. He hadn't noticed it earlier so assumed that it happened when the novel hit the floor. It was a minor defect readily fixed with some acid-free glue.

He grabbed his pocket torch and when he shined it on the top of the spine, he spotted a thin piece of light-colored paper in the crease. Theo went through his bag of book repair supplies, pushing aside jars of shoe polish, Q-tips, solvents and rolls of tape until he found his tweezers.

Returning to the bed, he held the novel upright and gently squeezed the sides of the spine to widen the opening before slowly extracting the paper. It had been folded thrice and was no more than an inch wide and two inches long.

Theo put *Little Dorrit* down and gazed at the folded piece of paper, convinced that it contained a message or information so valuable to Otto's client that he had been sent to America and twice committed murder to secure it. Except, he wasn't supposed to know it was there. He hesitated to unfold it, fearful that it might crumble in his hands. It was only a moment before his curiosity overcame his timidity.

The paper contained a list of first initials and last names, each one followed by a string of numbers. At the very bottom of the page in bold lettering was **Schweizerische Kreditonstalt – Berne.** Theo didn't recognize the name but knew that it stood for Swiss credit institution. In other words, a bank with an office in the Swiss capital. Was it possible that the numbers next to each name represented bank accounts?

He read the list of names: W Rauff; P Schäfer; O Skorzeny; K Becher; and H. Mueller. They meant nothing to him. It wasn't as if he was reading the name of the infamous Heinrich Himmler, in Hitler's inner circle. Somewhere he had read that Himmler was accused of stashing stolen art, jewelry and money in various Swiss banks. Captured by the Russians and turned over to the British right after the war, he committed suicide by swallowing a cyanide capsule.

Was it a leap of logic to assume that, like Himmler, those on the list were Nazi war criminals who had numbered accounts at the Swiss bank? Had all of them been tracked down since the war ended? Were all of them dead? Otto would have some answers. He was a young man during the war and might be able to identify some of the individuals on the list. He would never ask but now wondered for the first time if the Von Paulus family, among many who wanted to bury the past, had been tainted by a connection to the Nazi regime.

Theo applied some acid-free glue to seal up the spine. Next, he copied all the information from the slip of paper and inserted the original in the heel of his shoe.

It was getting dark and Theo was hungry. He donned his old man disguise and headed down the stairs, eschewing the elevator. He walked past the darkened coffee shop until he again found himself in front of the city's imposing main library. Down the street, he saw the lights of a diner. Before leaving the hotel, he had wrapped his French travel documents in newspaper. He saw a trash receptacle on the corner and dropped the bundle in before entering the diner. As of that moment, Alexandre d'Arblay no longer existed.

THE NEXT MORNING, Theo lay in bed staring at the ceiling, contemplating the first day of his new life. When he called Otto, he would hopefully learn that he had a new identity. He had only one more night paid for at the hotel and needed to decide whether to move on or bribe the night manager into extending his stay.

Before he called Otto, he would go the library and research the names on the list found in the spine of *Little Dorrit*. What he learned might influence what he said to his partner in Hamburg. If there was a confirmed Nazi connection to all the names, Theo believed that a much larger payment could be negotiated with the client that would set up Von Paulus and him for life.

THEO WALKED ACROSS the grass of Bryant Park behind the main New York library, unaware that below his feet were millions of books and other documents in underground storage rooms, waiting to be retrieved upon request for the visitors in one of the reading rooms above. With its massive inventory of more than fifty-six million items, it was impossible for even this library that spanned two city blocks to keep its entire collection on display.

He walked around to the main entrance on 5th Avenue and saw the pair of stone lions, carved out of pink Tennessee marble, that guarded each side of the wide staircase. Theo recognized the Beaux-Art style so prominent in Europe in the previous century and it made him nostalgic for home. After admiring the ornate lobby, he headed up the stairs to the Rose Main Reading Room. Seeking out one of the attendants, he filled out a few call slips and waited for his books to arrive. Looking around the room, he was awestruck by its size, the length of a football field. Rows and rows of heavy oak tables already populated with dozens of readers.

Theo learned that the Rare Book Division was housed on the same floor but he had no intention of entering it and yielding to temptation. It was no time to press his luck and endanger his recent string of successes. Besides, the library was now a virtual fortress after an earlier history of spectacular thefts, the most famous being the 1930s purloining of an extremely rare volume of poems by Edgar Alan Poe.

When his reference volumes arrived, Theo learned that many Nazis escaped Germany after the war via the "Kloster line," so named because it was a network of monasteries and convents in Austria and Italy, with apparent Vatican connections, that harbored Nazis until safe passage out of Europe could be arranged.

The genesis of this elaborate escape network was an organization called ODESSA, inspired by a cabal of powerful German industrialists, committed to the survival of Nazism. Aided by *Die Spinne* (The Spider), an underground group that provided false identification papers, ODESSA thrived to the point that only a modest number of high-ranking Nazis ever had to face war crime tribunals.

Many of the escapees ended up in Argentina, where hundreds of thousands of German ex-patriots had been settling for years. Argentine dictator Juan Peron, a great admirer of Hitler and the Third Reich, was instrumental in helping much of the Nazi hierarchy exit Europe via ports in Spain and Italy. Theo discovered that Chile, with its pro-Nazi military, was another favored destination of escapees as well.

The first name on the list he found was a Kurt Becher, an SS Officer who allegedly extorted from concentration camp Jews but was somehow cleared at the Nuremberg Trials. He was now a wealthy grain merchant living in either Bremen or Hamburg. Then, there was Walther Rauff, another SS Officer in the security service who ended up under the protection of the Chilean government until his death in 1984.

Next, he came upon an article describing Paul Schäfer, a colonel living in Chile under the protection of the pro-Nazi military. He was wanted back in Germany on child abuse charges in connection with an orphanage he ran. Otto Skorzeny, Theo learned, was a daring German commando who gained Hitler's favor after rescuing the deposed Italian dictator Benito Mussolini from a mountain retreat. After the war, he spent time in Argentina and Ireland before dying in Madrid in 1975.

Theo read that Credit Suisse Bank was one of the financial institutions that purportedly financed the exodus of numerous Nazis from

Europe. It took time for Theo to locate information on Schweizerische Kreditonstalt. When he did, he learned that the bank dated back to 1856 when it was established to finance railroad expansion and other industrialization projects throughout Switzerland. Even before World War II commenced, it was instrumental in financing the rearmament of Germany in cooperation with the Third Reich. Eager to shed its ignominious past, Schweizerische Kreditonstalt changed its name to Credit Suisse Bank.

Theo looked at his watch and realized that time was running out before his call with Otto. When he came upon an article about the highest-ranking Nazi never found, Theo's mouth went slack jawed. It was titled "Gestapo Mueller."

CHAPTER TWENTY-FIVE
"RUN FOR YOUR LIFE!"

THEO DEVOTED HIS remaining time in the library reading about the elusive and enigmatic Heinrich Mueller. The task of identifying him was complicated by the fact that not only was Mueller the most common surname in Germany but also that numerous Heinrich Muellers served in the German military during the war. As a result, war crimes investigators settled on "Gestapo Mueller," so as to distinguish the high-ranking general from all the others.

It is generally agreed that Mueller was seen at the Berlin Chancellery building, and at Hitler's secret bunker below it, on April 29, 1945, one day before the Fuhrer killed himself and his new bride, Eva Braun.

As Gestapo chief, Mueller ran the much-feared secret police but was also responsible for counterespionage operations and was known in the spy trade as a master of disinformation. Among his lieutenants was the infamous Adolf Eichmann, who he assigned to handle Jewish matters. After being captured by Israel's Mossad agents in Argentina in 1960 and before he died in a Tel Aviv prison two years later, Eichmann insisted that Mueller had survived the war and was in Russian hands.

Evidence surfaced that Eichmann had constructed a series of underground rooms below his office building in Berlin which became known as the "fox lair." This fully stocked, reinforced shelter with heat and lighting was connected to a labyrinth of passages which could be used as an escape route out of Berlin. With Hitler dead and Eichmann in Austria, it was alleged that, before fleeing the city, Mueller and Christian Scholz, one of his top aides, took up residence in the lair as the Russians encircled the city.

However, multiple sources in Germany contradicted this theory, insisting that Mueller was either killed during the Russian's onslaught of the capital city or committed suicide to avoid capture. Some records cited his burial in a cemetery on the outskirts of Berlin in 1945 with identification papers in his pocket. And yet, when the famed Nazi hunter Simon Wiesenthal issued a list twelve years later of the ten most wanted Third Reich villains, Mueller's name was on it.

Police found witnesses who saw Mueller and Scholz in the Chancellery late on the evening of May 1, 1945. Unlike his boss, Scholz disappeared without a trace. It wasn't until 1947, two years after Mueller's alleged burial, that British and American officials ransacked the Berlin apartment of Anna Schmid, his most recent mistress, looking for clues as to his whereabouts. It was Schmid who revealed that Mueller had a prior intimate relationship with his secretary, Barbara Hellmuth, and hinted that he might still be in communication with her.

Then, in 1948, there was the puzzling revelation that an information office staffed by a French contingent in the Allied sector of Berlin set up a regular file on Mueller, suggesting that the search for him continued.

Two years later, in 1950, the Bavarian police issued an arrest warrant for the Gestapo chief that many people had sworn was already dead and buried. German police continued to query western intelligence sources for information on Mueller into the 1960s. When the supposed remains of Mueller were exhumed from the West Berlin cemetery in 1963, a forensic pathologist testified that the bones came from several different bodies and the head was from a man considerably younger than the Gestapo chief.

As late as 1967, the Berlin police conceded that there was no conclusive proof that Mueller was either dead or alive. The police then decided to increase surveillance in the Munich area where many Mueller friends and family members still resided.

Then came the questions raised by a CIA report dated December of 1971, entitled "The Hunt For Gestapo Mueller," portions of which were leaked to a reporter. In it, U.S. intelligence officials speculated on every possible outcome. Was Mueller a double agent, all along, working for the Russians whom he openly despised? Had he escaped to South America, along with Eichmann, assisted by the ratlines in Austria and Italy?

CIA research painted an inconclusive picture while poking holes in all the other theories and investigations concerning Mueller dating back to 1945. The U.S. spy agency mentioned one particular Army investigation where the information collected on all of the other individuals in the German military named Heinrich Mueller was dumped into a single file labeled "Gestapo Mueller," thus making the task of determining the truth that much more difficult.

A witness was found who alleged that the remains in a Berlin morgue identified as Mueller's had been falsified. One defecting Russian agent said Mueller was in Albania doing intelligence work for Stalin's counterintelligence operation, popularly known as "Smersh." After his alleged death, Mueller's son stated that his father told him he had been in touch with the Russians back in 1944. Not one of the witnesses interviewed who saw Mueller and Scholz late on the night on May 1st of 1945 and urged them to flee from the Russian's vice grip on Berlin could swear that they had seen either of their bodies.

The CIA went on to speculate that If Mueller and Scholz had escaped through the passages connected to Eichmann's lair, they would certainly have been wearing disguises and dressed in civilian clothes. As for carrying false papers, that was one of Mueller's specialties.

It had been almost 25 years since the CIA's non-committal report and Theo could not find any later updates. For a brief moment, he entertained the thought that Kammler *was* Mueller until he remembered reading that the Gestapo chief was born in 1900. There was no way that the cantankerous and defiant old man he killed in Graniteville could have been 95-years old. But could Kammler somehow be connected to Mueller through a nephew or even a bastard child by one of his mistresses? All these possibilities for which he had no answers swirled in Theo's head.

Theo left the library baffled and nervous, the moniker "Gestapo Mueller" along with ODESSA and The Spider ringing in his ears. It was one thing to read about dead Nazis in the comfort of the library but quite another to elude them in the real world when your life depended on it. When he called Von Paulus, he would ask him what he knew about this Augustus Gottfried, the emissary of the mysterious German client. Was it possible that Otto knew more than he was telling him?

Theo headed to Grand Central Terminal, only a few blocks from the library, where there were rows of telephones mounted on the walls.

As he entered the train station, Theo recalled Otto's extreme agitation upon learning about the map theft at Yale. Should he even break the startling news about the secret tucked into the spine of *Little Dorrit* or, instead, wait until he was back in Hamburg? Von Paulus was old and cautious, priding himself on his word as his bond. Would Theo's new plan be too audacious for him to accept?

As the connection was made and the phone rang, Theo reminded himself that the purpose of the call was to learn when and how he would receive his new documents. Yes, he promised himself, he would ease into the conversation about *Little Dorrit's* secret and hold back what he had learned about Heinrich Mueller and the others.

Otto sounded somber when he said hello. "Are you still in New York, Theo, at the same hotel near Times Square? A courier vill deliver your new documents and a plane ticket to Hamburg sometime tomorrow. It is time to come home."

"Yes, yes, Otto. I hear you but first you must listen to the most astonishing news. What I have done, such horrible things, to get possession of *Little Dorrit*. Something tells me that the novel holds secrets worth a fortune. We are being paid a pittance and deserve much more, I tell you," Theo declared excitedly, no longer able to remain calm.

"Vere are you now, Theo?" Otto asked, his voice brittle and robotic.

"I'm inside a train station, Otto, but what does that matter? Aren't you listening to me? Does the head of the Gestapo, Heinrich Mueller, mean anything to you? Whomever Augustus Gottfried is representing can afford to pay us much more when they realize that we know their secret," Theo exclaimed, his voice rising.

"I have no interest in secrets, Theo, and neither should you. It's all rubbish. Ve made a bargain and must honor it. Now, vere can the courier meet you tomorrow?" Otto sounded strange. His voice was flat, as if he was a rote actor reading from a script.

"Okay, Otto. We can discuss this matter upon my return. If the courier arrives in time, I will catch the overnight flight to Hamburg tomorrow evening. However, when you see what I have discovered, you will change your mind. I am staying at the Time's Up Hotel, around the corner from Times Square on 41st Street but may -."

Theo was cut short by Otto shouting, "Run, run for your life, Theo!" As Otto's voice grew faint and faded away, Theo heard scuffling noises in the background and then a faint gurgling sound before the telephone line went dead.

CHAPTER TWENTY-SIX
TARGETED FOR EXTINCTION

◆──◆──◆

THEO DROPPED THE receiver and it clanked against the hard wall as it swung back and forth on its armored, jacketed cord. The sound made him look around at the passersby, some of whom were staring at him.

He walked out into the cavernous main concourse of the train station and gazed up at the ceiling with its endless constellation of gold stars. Had he known that the zodiac was painted amidst them, he might have wondered if there was a warning for him, a message presaging his fate. The large brass clock mounted above the information booth in the center of the concourse read almost 11:00 and Theo realized he had but a brief time to act decisively.

It struck him that his current disguise might be his temporary salvation until he remembered the comment by Otto that fateful day in Hamburg. Von Paulus had bragged to Adolphus Gottfried that Theo, "the man with many faces," was the ideal person to send to America. Yesterday, he had told Otto he was staying near Times Square but today he had blurted out the name of his hotel. With Otto most assuredly dead, there would be no courier arriving with new papers. No, they were coming not just for *Little Dorrit* but for him as well. Theo decided that the assassin might already be in New York, awaiting further instructions. It didn't make him feel any better to think they wouldn't kill him right away. Unlike Otto, who was a loose end, he was someone they needed to keep alive until they got possession of the novel.

Theo walked out the side door of the train station onto Vanderbilt Avenue before crossing over to East 43rd Street, forcing himself to walk at a measured pace. He stopped a half block from the Time's Up Hotel and scanned the area but spied no one who looked suspicious lingering near the hotel. What did he expect, a man slinking around in a trench coat, collar up and his head tucked in tight, a cigarette dangling from his mouth? No, Theo realized. More likely, he would be surprised by someone dressed as a deliveryman or a mailman. After taking a deep breath and exhaling, he walked into the lobby and up the stairs to his room.

THEO SAT ON the bed and considered what to do next. Adhering to the instructions of the German client, everything that identified him as Theo DeBruycker, son of Jules, was left behind in his Bruges apartment. It now dawned on Theo that it was a serendipitous demand. If Reinhold broke down and started talking to the Dresden police, the risk of capture using his own passport to cross the border into Canada or Mexico would have been a death warrant – or a sentence of life imprisonment. Theo had learned from the Jackal that one must be prepared and then act decisively when confronted with unforeseen obstacles. Any further delays would be perilous.

Theo took the slip of paper from his heel and folded it inside a piece of hotel stationery then addressed the envelope to himself at his apartment in Bruges.

After quickly packing, Theo slowly opened the door and peered down the hallway in both directions. Knowing that any wrong move might prove fateful, he exited the hotel using a side door and headed south toward the travel agency. Thinking about the clamshell box protecting *Little Dorrit*, he stopped and bought one for *Dracula*.

Convinced that it was now time to travel light, he stored the large suitcase containing both novels along with miscellaneous items of clothing. On the way to the Port Authority Bus Terminal, he spied a post office, bought stamps and dropped the envelope in the outgoing mail slot. When he finally made it back to Bruges, the secret of *Little Dorrit* would be waiting for him.

It was less than an hour after Theo left the Times-Up Hotel that a man posing as a PI approached the front desk, flashed fake credentials and produced the passport picture of Alexandre d'Arblay. It was shown to several of the staff but no one recognized him.

After a few more days in Graniteville and no sightings of either d'Arblay or his alleged accomplices, Woody flew home to Spain. Fanny was back managing the inn and Jerry had resumed renovations at the bookstore. The Kosinsky children were home from camp and every effort would be made to ensure that the remainder of the summer was uneventful. It was understood that there would be no conversation in which *Little Dorrit* was a topic.

CROCKETT HAD CALLED Woody before he left the country and provided him with the FBI's surprisingly upbeat assessment of the case. "We froze the d'Arblay credit card and the passport has been voided, so unless he has unlimited amounts of cash, he'll try to sell one of the novels. Then, we'll nail him. If any of his accomplices are with him, they'll be nabbed at the same time. Every reputable book dealer in the country has been alerted to be on the lookout for anyone selling early editions of *Jane Eyre*, *Little Dorrit* or *Dracula*."

The FBI put up a brave front but were, in truth, baffled and frustrated. d'Arblay had been shut down and ostensibly cornered in Manhattan but no leads were coming in. Interpol had no one in its database with a facial resemblance to the man whose picture was on the fake French passport. It was as if they were chasing a shadow.

The Bureau had taken Woody's advice and directed Amtrak to review its records. It turned out that several tickets had been purchased in d'Arblay's name, the first one being from Montreal to New Haven. Subsequent trips between New Haven and Boston proved that Woody's timeline supporting his single thief theory was certainly feasible. The FBI countered that d'Arblay could have been buying train tickets for his gang to limit their exposure.

When the theft of *Little Dorrit* and the two Graniteville murders were factored in and comported with Woody's timeline as well, the FBI conceded that d'Arblay could have pulled off the quadfecta himself. Still, they clung to their original hypothesis that an elite gang, with d'Arblay as its mastermind, was the most plausible explanation.

The FBI got more bad news when word got back to the Dresden dealer, languishing in prison and starting to wilt under relentless interrogation by the German police, that Otto Von Paulus had been murdered up in Hamburg. Fearful that DeBruycker had somehow orchestrated the hit, any hope that Reinhold would now rat out his accomplice in the de Jode map theft evaporated.

Woody was bewildered by such official FBI optimism but gave

up trying to challenge it. Crockett was young and energetic but not the sharpest tool in the shed which, in Woody's mind, explained his assignment to the Art Theft Team. Stubbornly dull and uninspired, he fit the mold not of an Eliot Ness-style crime fighter but of the cautious, unimaginative bureaucrat.

Surely, Woody reasoned, d'Arblay had changed his appearance since the confrontation with the hotel clerk, so how did the FBI and the police even know who they were looking for? And why were they so confident that he was still in New York City? As for selling one or both prized novels, wasn't d'Arblay too astute to make the mistake of approaching an established bookdealer or reputable collector? If the man needed funds, he was too ingenious not to deploy other methods.

Woody had his own ideas on how the man masquerading as Alexandre d'Arblay might be exposed but he would keep them to himself for now. Before he left Connecticut, Jerry had advised him to give up the hunt, freeing him from further obligation. He loved his childhood friend but it would take more than Jerry's permission to get Woody Meacham, once in, out of the game.

THEO WALKED INTO the bus terminal through the 8th Avenue entrance and stumbled past a body propped up against the wall. Every kind of hustler populated the terminal and the surrounding area, each with their special grift or con. The so-called "gay for pay" boys didn't bother to give the elderly man the once over, nor did the small-time drug dealers and loitering prostitutes as he maneuvered around them. One nervous teen, wide-eyed and sweaty, spotted the suitcase and, for three dollars, offered to guide Theo to one of the dozens of buses queued up outside, quickly lowering his price when he was shooed away.

Theo spotted an Asian man, early to late twenties, lounging against a wall who smiled when their eyes met. He looked out of place with his immaculate and glossy jet black hair, pressed khakis and crisp, patterned shirt.

The Asian approached Theo and whispered "Rolex? Patek Philippe?" Theo shook his head and mumbled "identification papers." The man's eyes lit up, surprised by this unexpected request. He smiled broadly and said, "I am Feng. Can do. You have picture?" Theo shook his head again and Feng smiled. "No problem, see?" he said, pointing to a photo booth across the room from which a young couple was pushing back the curtain and laughing.

They walked over to the booth and Feng motioned for Theo to enter. "How much for a New York driver's license?" Theo asked. "Five hundred dollar, very good quality, no problem," was the response.

"Stand here while I go inside," Theo said, pointing to the spot in front of the curtain.

When the strips of photos came out, it made Theo laugh darkly. An assassin was roaming around Times Square showing strangers a picture of d'Arblay and he was only blocks away creating a new American identity to thwart him as well as the cops.

Theo pushed back the curtain and Feng smiled. When he looked at the two photo strips, he glanced at Theo then back at the photos with a puzzled look on his face. One strip of photographs were of the old man and the second set were of Theo DeBruycker. "That's right, I need two driver's licenses, one for each picture. Now what is the price?" Theo asked.

Feng laughed and said, "You very strange man. I give you best price, a discount, okay? Both licenses for eight hundred dollar. You be very happy. What name?"

"How soon? I need to leave town as quickly as possible," Theo said. Feng frowned. "If we hurry, we do bad job. Need several hours for sure." Theo looked up at the clock. "Okay, I'll meet you back here at 9:00 tomorrow morning."

"No, not here. Bad for business. Meet at top of 7th Avenue escalator at Penn Station. We ride down together and settle our business. You have money ready, yes?"

"Of course," said Theo, feigning indignation.

"You show me now, please? Must be sure," Feng explained, no longer smiling.

Theo turned around and pulled out his money clip, peeling off eight one hundred dollar bills. It was a hefty but necessary expenditure.

The two men huddled so that Feng could examine the bills spread out in Theo's hands. "Two hundred dollar deposit. Shows good faith, right?" said Feng, grinning broadly.

Theo couldn't help but smile, even though he was putting valuable cash at risk by trusting Feng. He pulled out a small spiral notebook and wrote down the name Eduard Vos. "One man is 35 years old, the other is 70," he explained.

The Asian studied the name and said, "Feng means strong in my country." He smiled broadly and held up both arms, flexing his biceps. "What is Vos?" he asked.

"Vos means Fox," Theo explained.

"Ah, you sly and cunning, right? Excellent. I leave first. You wait a few minutes. Don't forget, top of the 7th Avenue escalator tomorrow morning." Feng advised before walking away.

CHAPTER TWENTY-SEVEN
SMALL TOWN THIEF

S EVERAL DAYS WENT by with no sighting of Theo DeBruyker's alter egos – or his alleged compatriots – in and around New York City. The original clue from early Summer when Heinz Kammler had been murdered, describing a white-haired old man washing blood from his shirt at the New Haven train station, had long been forgotten but would have been of vital assistance now.

Feng had come through and Theo now had two versions of Eduard Vos to show on his peregrinations, should identification be required. The police and the FBI continued to pursue the occasional lead based on the photo in the d'Arblay passport and the composite sketch of the man with the van Dyke.

Moving *sub rosa* by bus and posing alternately as a middle-aged man and a septuagenarian, Theo was anything but idle. He limited his ventures to towns within a one hundred mile radius of New York City, returning as necessary to complete transactions with his new *de facto* partner, Simon Wegg. He would sometimes see Feng at the bus terminal and they would smile in acknowledgement.

Theo hit an occasional bookstore but focused his thievery on libraries in small towns along the Hudson River and the northwestern villages of New Jersey where security procedures were minimal or non-existent. He shied away from the rarest collectables that would draw almost immediate attention if they were noticed missing, instead concentrating on later, pristine editions of books bearing the author's signature or some other distinction that collectors found desirable. He was successful in grabbing signed copies of a 1964 first edition hardcover of *Herzog* by Saul Bellow and a 1959 paperback first edition of *Maddie Cassidy* by Jack Kerouac. The name of the Kerouac novel reminded his of his late paramour, giving Theo a momentary pang.

Theo deployed the age-old tricks of book thievery when it was impractical to wear his deep-pocketed blazer in sweltering weather. Techniques as simple as hiding a book in a folded newspaper or covering a rare book with a dust jacket taken off a cheap novel worked like a charm. Before leaving a library, he would go to the card catalog and destroy the record of the book he had just pilfered, eliminating any evidence that it had ever been on the shelf. And, of course, he had his indispensable X-Acto knife to unlock a display case where the risk was minimal.

Theo resigned himself to this new role as Eduard Vos, to the extent possible for a man who was on the run from the police and a hitman. He convinced himself that this interregnum would be of short duration, and he would be able to resume his old life soon.

One day, returning to the bus station from Wegg's shop, Theo walked past a sidewalk bookstall. He spotted a dog-eared, paperback copy of *Little Dorrit* on the $1.00 rack and snapped it up. It was one of the few Dickens novels he had not read. The cover depicted a plain-looking Dorrit of an uncertain age, sitting at a table and sewing a garment. It contrasted with her image on the title page of Kammler's copy, standing at a door, thin and vulnerable in her dark cloak and bonnet, the epitome of selflessness and innocence.

When he started reading the novel, he came to believe that the caricature on the title page was all too real. It depicted her at a prison door, a "child of the Marshalsea" that would define her life. Dorrit would be Theo's companion for frequent bus rides back and forth to the city. Lying in bed at night, the image of the waif was starting to haunt him.

The crafty Wegg, with a keen eye for comrades in crime, was starting to question his original assessment of the enigmatic and pithy old man. Theo's ability to produce a steady stream of books from several genres and periods, some signed by the writer and others which had been out of print for decades, made him question his original theory, namely that he was gradually selling off his personal library out of financial desperation. At the same time, he did not want to say anything to disrupt the flow of merchandise that had proved profitable to him.

One day, Wegg hit on the idea to test the old man by casually remarking that he would pay $5000 for a pristine copy of the first U.S. edition of *Moby Dick* in its original cloth binding. It must include the publisher's advertisements tipped in at the back of the novel, Wegg stressed. Theo quickly saw what Wegg was up to and was non-committal, simply remarking, "I'll check my bookshelves."

Theo understood that if he was fortunate enough to procure the Melville novel for Wegg, he would have ample cash to leave the country and start over as Eduard Vos. He didn't fear that the police were closing in on him but knew that he could also be easily entrapped by his association with Wegg. For Theo, lifting books from small town libraries was no way to live and getting out of the United States was imperative. He would keep his eye out for *Moby Dick* but would not do anything reckless to obtain it.

After returning to his home in the town of Terragona on Spain's Mediterranean Coast, Woody heard little from his contacts at Interpol and the FBI. No one wanted to admit that they were no closer to identifying the individual behind the rare book thefts and murders in the United States. French authorities were equally perplexed. Whoever had used the name of Alexandre d'Arblay on a stolen French passport was a virtual unknown on the continent.

The German federal police, the *Bundeskriminalamt* but better known as the BKA, had no leads in the Otto Von Paulus murder case and were puzzled by the fact that his throat had been cut ear to ear. A professional hit job of this brutal nature in the auction market was not just unusual but unprecedented. Someone was sending a message, but to whom? Von Paulus was suspected of dabbling in stolen books but was known to be discreet.

Woody had not wavered from his conviction that a single master thief had pulled off all of the book heists and committed the murders in Graniteville. It was established fact that the Yale library map thief was working in consort with the Dresden auction house. Learning of the Von Paulus murder, Woody wondered if there was a link to d'Arblay that had yet to be adequately explored. He was no psychologist but speculated about the kind of pathology that could infect a man who treasured rare books, timeless pieces of art, and also possessed a raging, murderous streak.

Strolling hand in hand along the Mediterranean with his wife, Woody announced that he was going to Belgium. The former Hannah Cavendish had inherited a fortune from her late husband upon his tragic death and owned a clothing boutique in the exclusive El Carte Ingles shopping center of Terragona. She knew by the look he gave her that she was invited to accompany him but both understood that it was impractical, it being the busy tourist season for her.

"Something new?" she asked, knowing he wouldn't press her to join him. "No, it's this business with Jerry. I've got to satisfy myself on a few loose ends in the case before giving up on it," Woody explained. Hannah looked away and smiled. She knew what "loose ends" would entail but said nothing as they walked on. When they returned home, she smiled and said, "I command you to find all the delightful places to visit, including the hidden restaurant gems that don't make it into the Michelin guide. Then, we will visit Belgium in the Fall. Without any distractions, my dear."

Woody decided to start in Brussels and then move on to Ghent, Antwerp and Bruges, all the cities that d'Arblay had described to Maddie Lever who had, in turn, recited to Fanny. Had the mystifying man posing as d'Arblay procured a new passport and returned to the continent? It was certainly within his capability. If there was a chance encounter in Belgium, Woody had the advantage. He had a picture of his quarry but D'Arblay didn't have one of the hunter.

CHAPTER TWENTY-EIGHT
WHERE IT ALL BEGAN

WOODY DECIDED THAT the local police didn't need to know that he was snooping around Brussels. Interpol had an office there and he would avoid them as well, at least until he uncovered something worth sharing. He knew that Crockett would salivate if Woody produced a shred of evidence on the true identity of d'Arblay. If Woody was stymied, he would keep his quixotic effort to himself.

He checked into the Marriott Grand Place located in City Centre, convenient to a plethora of bookstores within walking distance. Before leaving Spain, he had prepared a list of shops that specialized in rare books which might have been targets – or even customers – of d'Arblay, on the off chance that he had tried his luck in the Belgian capital. Close by the hotel was the Royal Library of Belgium with its collection of 45,000 rare books, maps and ephemera – another alluring destination for any master thief.

After lunch, Woody made the short walk to the library and noticed that it was adjacent to the central train station, a convenient escape route that would not have gone unnoticed by a person of d'Arblay's experience and talent. In the Rare Book Department, Woody spoke with a reluctant assistant librarian who gave a cursory glance at the d'Arblay photograph and the composite sketch before shaking her head no. He had expected dead-ends and was undeterred. It just felt good to be back in the hunt.

———◆———

THE NEXT MORNING, after sharing his list with the hotel's concierge manager, Woody mapped out visits to several antiquarian bookstores in the downtown area. To his chagrin, many of them were closed, with signs in the window that read "By Appointment Only." Of the two dealers open, he was unsuccessful on both occasions in getting an ID of d'Arblay. The second dealer at least had a sense of humor, telling Woody, "There is an old joke in our industry, sir. 'Every rare book has been stolen at least once.'"

Woody was starting to believe that many dealers were almost fatalistic about the potential theft of a rare book. Even some libraries, if not indifferent, were determined to keep their losses private. In a way, they were all waiting for their number to come up, for that moment when they would be victimized. Witnessing such insouciance, he might have felt justified in giving up on this last ditch effort to find an elusive clue about the identity of d'Arblay, except that he had made a silent vow to Jerry and Fanny to solve the two Graniteville murders.

By mid-afternoon, he was on the train to Antwerp.

———◆———

AUGUSTUS GOTTFRIED WAS in a near panic to find *Little Dorrit*, fearing that if DeBruycker somehow made it back to Europe, he would head to Switzerland and try to get access to the secret, numbered accounts. He didn't believe Theo would be foolish enough to return to

Bruges but did have his apartment surveilled periodically after the Von Paulus murder.

Gottfried sent two more men to New York City to assist in the search for DeBruycker but they were limited by the fact that they had no clue who Theo might now be impersonating. If he was stealing books to raise cash for his escape, it was assumed that he would peddle his wares to one of the corrupt book dealers in the city. It wasn't long before they honed in on a few shops, including the one owned by Simon Wegg.

———

MEANWHILE, AT A bookshop in Cooperstown, New York near the National Baseball Hall of Fame and Museum, Theo lifted a signed copy of Thoreau's *A Yankee In Canada* for which he figured Wegg would pay at least a few hundred dollars. After the euphoria of *Little Dorrit* and *Dracula*, his recent successes felt trivial, even belittling. At his current pace, he would be stuck in the United States for weeks. Theo also had to acknowledge the fact that even though he could not return to Belgium for a considerable time, if ever, he yearned to be back in Europe.

The routine of hustling small town libraries and holing up in squalid motels was also taking its toll on Theo. His evenings consisted of removing library card pockets from the books he had stolen and then scraping off telltale signs of their existence with a chemical mix. Looking at the title of the Thoreau book, he decided that until he could afford a plane ticket to Europe, the French-speaking province of Quebec was his best option.

Theo returned to New York City to finalize plans for his departure from the U.S. He found a rundown hotel near the Hudson River that rented rooms by the hour or the day. When he saw that the chain lock had been ripped from the door frame, he wedged the straight back chair under the doorknob and pushed his suitcase up against it.

Over the clanking of the air conditioner, the roar of trucks and buses could be heard through the ill-framed window. Theo pushed aside the shade to get a view of the river named after the famous English explorer but it was growing dark and all he could see was streams of light racing by in both directions on the road below.

He sat on the bed and propped up two thin pillows against the wobbly headboard. After examining the sheets, he decided to remain fully clothed and sleep on top of the bedspread. He opened his tattered copy of *Little Dorrit* and started to read. When he got to the section in the novel where the villainous Frenchman Blandois committed a murder in London and then disappeared, Theo dropped the book into his lap and looked at his surroundings. It took a fictional character to remind him that the Jackal would take bold action to extricate himself from danger. Hiding out in Canada was only a temporary solution, a last, desperate option. He needed to get back to Europe.

The next morning, he would go to the travel agency and check the price of flights to Paris and ask the agent to hold a seat for him. He would sell *Dracula* to Wegg but wouldn't make foolish demands.

It was painful to relinquish one of his treasures but *Little Dorrit* was infinitely more valuable to him than the Bram Stoker novel, as rare as it might be. Harsh reality had taken hold of Theo DeBruycker.

CHAPTER TWENTY-NINE
A Momentous Discovery

❖

I N DOWNTOWN ANTWERP, close by the River Scheldt that flows through France and Belgian and then passes through Holland before emptying into the North Sea, Woody visited several bookstores. In an attempt to gain sympathy and cooperation, he described d'Arblay as a rare book collector who had gone missing, raising concern in his family. No one recognized the man in the photograph but one shop owner suggested that he pay a visit to the Hendrik Conscience Heritage Library. It was a long shot, but someone in the library's rare book department may have had dealings with him.

❖

RENATA PEETERS HAD been dead for several years but was still revered at the Hendrik. In fact, one of the tables in the rare book reading room bore a nameplate in her honor.

Renata's niece had been a library intern at the Henrik during the period when Theo DeBruycker was being tutored by her aunt. Nathalie was a plain-looking, gangly teenage girl back then. She had a hidden crush on the handsome young stranger who frequented the library but her extreme diffidence made her unnoticeable. Now approaching forty, and following in her aunt's footsteps, she was working in the rare book department when Woody Meacham walked in. Her face turned crimson when he produced the d'Arblay photograph and Woody knew instantly that he had caught the break he needed.

Nathalie recalled how her aunt mentored the teenager who had shown an unusually keen interest in and knowledge of rare books for someone so young. She remembered how disappointed Renata was when, after intervening to secure him a position at a nearby university, he abruptly disappeared, never to be seen by them again. Struggling to remember the young man's name, Woody urged her to keep talking until she blurted out, "Theo DeBruycker!"

CONTINUING TO STUDY the d'Arblay photograph, Nathalie recalled her aunt telling her that Theo had come to Antwerp as a teenager from his hometown of Ghent to live with his uncle after his father's death. Around the time Theo vanished, stories appeared in the Antwerp papers about the uncle's criminal activity and his disappearance.

When Woody pressed for details, Nathalie took him to the library section where old newspapers were archived. Pulling up copies of the *Het Laatste Nieuws* from the period in question, Nathalie found articles on the disappearance of Luc DeBruycker, patiently translating them from Dutch into English as Woody took notes. A few sidebar stories confirmed that the nephew of Luc was exonerated from any involvement in his uncle's criminal enterprise. A tidbit in one of them caught Woody's attention when it described Theo's father as a bookstore owner in Ghent.

When he left Nathalie, Woody had an incomplete but useful picture of Theo DeBruycker's tragic early life and how it might have influenced his development into the man masquerading as Alexandre d'Arblay. To fill in the blanks, he would need to go to Theo's hometown.

———◆———

On the train to Ghent, Woody mulled over what to do with his momentous discovery. Should he immediately provide the name to the FBI as definitive proof that Theo DeBruycker was the man behind the d'Arblay façade? What he had so far were some newspaper articles about the uncle and the years-old remembrances of a woman who had, through her aunt, only an indirect connection to DeBruycker. If she was mistaken, he would be sending Crockett and every other law enforcement agency on two continents on a wild goose chase. Alternately, if DeBruycker and d'Arblay were the same man, he needed to be nabbed as quickly as possible.

There was no guarantee that a Belgian passport had been issued to a Theo DeBruycker but if one had, Woody knew that if its photograph matched d'Arblay's, it would clinch the deal. Woody had established a good relationship with a senior official at Interpol headquarters in Lyon, France. This person would, if it existed, secure the picture on the DeBruycker passport from Belgian authorities. If Woody got this vital confirmation, he would then notify Crockett and Interpol so that the manhunt for Theo DeBruycker could commence on both sides of the Atlantic.

———◆———

Theo was at the travel agency when it opened. He learned that there was a late flight to Paris the next evening and he convinced the agent to hold a seat for him, promising to return in the afternoon with payment. After retrieving his large suitcase, he headed back to his hotel to prepare for his meeting with Simon Wegg.

Back in his room, Theo removed the white wig and peeled off the grey eyebrows and mustache. From the large suitcase, he unstitched part of the false bottom and took out the black priest robe and laid it out across the bed, smoothing out wrinkles with the palm of his hand. Next to it, he placed the cross belt, the capelet and the white collar he had purchased at the theatrical costume shop weeks earlier.

Before he got dressed, Theo removed the ageing cream and dark lines under his eyes and applied the umber shade make-up that had served him well in Boston. Fully outfitted, he surveyed himself in the mirror as he positioned the wide, circular brim hat on his head. "Yes," he mouthed softly, remembering how the disguise had worked perfectly in the past. Theo knew enough Spanish to intersperse with broken English to pass himself off as a padre from a village outside of Madrid.

Wegg would certainly be aware of the recent theft at the Boston book event and might wonder how a "man of the cloth" from Spain came into possession of a most rare copy of *Dracula*. Theo was banking on Wegg's avarice quickly overcoming any ownership qualms. Short of murder, Theo was sure that Wegg would do anything to gain possession of the Stoker novel.

THEO FELT THE sun burn through his heavy, dark clothing as he walked the several blocks from the hotel to Wegg's shop. He worried that the perspiration he felt under his broad brim hat might impair his make-up. Pre-occupied with how he would initiate negotiations with Wegg, Theo didn't immediately notice the two men who were stationed near the shop, one diagonally across the street and the other a few doors down from the entrance.

Whatever it was that caught his eye and caused him to look around, Theo could not recall as he relived the events of the next few minutes over and over in his mind later that day. Of one thing he was certain. Had he entered Wegg's shop and was followed in by the two men, he would not have come out alive.

But Theo did glance across the street as he approached Wegg's shop and noticed a man smoking a cigarette and staring not at him but at the clamshell box under his arm. Theo watched him crush the cigarette under his foot and hurriedly cross the street toward him. It was then that Theo saw the other man less than 50 yards away on his side of the street, watching him intently.

Theo panicked and started running down Broadway. He looked back and saw the two men, now side by side, gaining on him. Picking up his pace, Theo felt the bottom of the cassock brush against his shoes and then catch on the toe, causing him to trip, the clamshell box tumbling to the ground a few feet away.

He crawled over to it just as the two men came up and hovered over him. One of them stepped on Theo's outstretched arm then bent down to pick up the clamshell box. When Theo tried to get up, he was pushed back down to the ground by the other man who flicked open a switchblade and held it next to his leg for Theo to see. A few people slowed down to survey the scene and gawk at the priest sprawled on the ground. Theo was helpless and alone as the two men disappeared up the street.

THEO HOBBLED BACK to his hotel, his knees aching and his mind racing. His first depressing realization was that he would not be flying to Paris the next evening unless a priestly miracle occurred. He thought through all the details of his close encounter. The men reminded him of the thugs that surrounded his Uncle Luc, the kind of gangsters that the

German client would employ, automatons who would follow orders and ask no questions. Had it been a side street, not a busy New York thoroughfare, Theo had no doubt that he would have bled out on the sidewalk, the gleaming knife thrust deep into his ribcage. And yes, the same fate would have befallen him had he been cornered in Wegg's shop.

He thought back to that fateful meeting in Otto's office. Had his partner bragged about Theo's talent for transforming himself into an old man, a distinguished professor with a Van Dyke, a beggar, a policeman – even a priest?

It all made sense now. The German client was clever and determined. His thugs must have been watching certain bookstores for any sign of DeBruycker, hoping he would eventually show up. With his reputation, Wegg's shop would be near the top of their surveillance list.

Luckily, they had made a colossal blunder, running off with the clamshell box without first looking inside. It seemed likely that the thugs had immediately called Germany and had been directed to open the box and confirm the contents. Any feeling of elation would have been short-lived when it was learned that *Dracula*, not *Little Dorrit*, was inside. The client might think that Theo had pulled off a clever ruse and deserved their begrudging respect by switching books. In fact, luck had been on his side, as it had been for the Jackal, in so many close encounters.

One thing was certain. The client had gambled that he was still in New York and had patiently waited for the opportunity to corner him. When Theo realized that the hunt for him would be renewed with increased fervor, he knew that he had no choice but to get out of New York City as quickly as possible and never return.

AFTER STRIPPING OFF his clerical garb and removing his make-up, Theo changed back into his old man disguise, figuring that it was his least risky option for getting out of the city undetected by either the police or the thugs. Of one thing he was sure: time was now his enemy.

He was down to less than four hundred dollars, enough to get him a one-way airline ticket to Montreal or some distant American city. But then he would be left with nothing to live on. He concluded that hiding out in Quebec, until he could raise money for a flight to Europe, was once again his best option.

Theo placed *Little Dorrit* in the small suitcase along with his traveling essentials and the blue blazer with the "Pichler pocket." Everything else went into the large suitcase, including the expensive grey charcoal suit he had worn for the Casaubon caper. On the way to the bus terminal, he saw a Salvation Army thrift store and tried to sell the large suitcase and its contents. When he learned that he could only receive a tax deduction in lieu of cash, Theo smiled forlornly, handed the luggage key to the attendant and left.

CHAPTER THIRTY
THE ACTOR

———◆———

IN THE GHENT neighborhood where the DeBruycker family had resided, Woody found someone who remembered Theo's father as a simpleton who was rumored to have dabbled in the stolen book trade. As for the boy, he was described as a bright but dour young man and a loner before he went to live with his uncle in Antwerp.

In the shadows of the Boekentoren, the owner of a bookstore recognized the d'Arblay photo and remembered the adult Theo as a tall, well-dressed man who carried himself in a very dignified manner, affecting an upper class pose, even wearing an ascot on occasion. The dealer conceded that he might even have purchased a few rare books from DeBruycker but was certain that he had first quizzed him on their provenance. Any early editions with library or private collector markings would have raised suspicion and been rejected, he assured Woody.

It was very odd, the book dealer commented, in thinking back on a particular conversation he had with DeBruycker. "I told him he looked very prosperous but much different than I remembered him when he first returned to Ghent. He smiled very strangely and said

– and this I never forgot – 'just call me the Jackal.' I said zot under my breath and asked no more questions."

Woody didn't pick up on the allusion and asked the owner to repeat the word. He laughed and pointed to his head as he ran a circle in the air above it. "Zot. It is a Flemish word. You know, crazy in the head." It was Woody's turn to laugh. "Zot is a great word. We have nothing like it in the English language but the Jackal, what did he mean?"

"I assumed it was a reference to the movie about the man who tried to kill De Gaulle. The assassin was known as the Jackal in English. In French, it was Chacal. Very popular movie here in Belgium, maybe because the Jackal commissioned his rifle in Brussels and then went to the Ardennes for target practice. DeBruycker must have developed a fondness for him. As I said, zot." At the door, the owner told Woody that he never saw DeBruycker after that meeting and heard later that he had moved to Bruges.

Woody puzzled over this latest revelation. He had seen the movie *The Day of the Jackal* after reading the Forsyth novel when it appeared in 1971. He was at Thorndyke College then and remembered that everyone was obsessed with the political thriller. As he recalled, the main character in the novel and the movie was an English assassin, a master of disguise, who had been hired by a disgruntled military clique to kill Charles De Gaulle. Was it possible that the Jackal had been, and still might be, the inspiration for Theo DeBruycker? It would help explain not just the penchant for disguises but also the two Graniteville murders.

He tried to conjure up an image of the actor who played the part of the Jackal. What the hell was his name? As for DeBruycker, if he was "zot," as the shop owner suggested, wasn't he liable to do something crazy again, sooner rather than later?

WHEN WOODY CHECKED in with his Interpol contact, he learned that a Belgian passport had been issued to DeBruycker with an address in Bruges. So, the shop owner was right about him moving there. The passport photograph and address were being sent to the Interpol office in Brussels where Woody could pick them up.

The train from Ghent to Brussels took a little more than thirty minutes. If the photographs in the two passports were a match, Woody was certain he had his man. If DeBruycker had somehow made it out of the United States and back to Europe, would he be bold enough to return to his apartment in Bruges?

AS THE GREYHOUND bus passed through the town of Coxsackie in route to Albany, it came to Theo that, with *Dracula* lost, he was left with no safe way to raise immediate cash except by selling *Little Dorrit*. He had come to cherish the Dickens novel and its rich characterizations, despite the chaotic plot. He would have loved to place Kammler's first edition on his bookshelf in Bruges if and when it was safe to return there. Then, he was buoyed by the thought that if he did sell it, he would make it his mission when he was back on friendly soil to purloin another first edition – this time without the odious Hitler bookplate adornment. Besides, what was important about Kammler's copy had already been extracted.

Before leaving New York City, Theo had studied the bus schedule going north to Montreal and saw that Albany was the only major city before crossing the border. When he learned that it was the state capitol and also the home to several universities, he assumed that there would be an abundance of bookstores as well. It seemed like a good place to stop before entering Canada. All he needed to do was to find another Simon Wegg, some scoundrel venal enough to purchase *Little Dorrit* without asking questions.

※

THE GREYHOUND BUS brought Theo to a desolate stretch in downtown Albany, just west of the Hudson River. After checking into a rundown hotel a few blocks from the bus depot, he was out the door to catch a local bus for the short ride to the campus of the University at Albany.

At the English Department reception desk, Theo repeated the story he had concocted on the bus about inheriting an old copy of a Dickens novel which he was desirous of authenticating. After a few whispered calls, a pale-looking, desultory PhD candidate with an unruly beard, emerged from a warren of cubicles. He was behind in his thesis research and annoyed that he had been delegated to meet with this stranger. It was just another example, he grumbled, of how graduate teaching assistants were treated like indentured servants or chattels, serving at the whim of tenured professors.

He picked at his beard as he examined the boards and spine of *Little Dorrit*, his eyes darkening when he glanced at the Hitler bookplate. He went to the title page to confirm the publishing date, then leafed ahead to page 371. There, he saw the telltale "B2" at the bottom of the page, confirming the printer's signature mark which only appeared in the novel's first edition. Color now suffusing his cheeks, he flipped ahead until he saw the note inserted by the publisher, explaining that Dickens had mistakenly used the wrong name for a character for the next several pages, an error that was corrected in later editions of the novel.

The graduate assistant hadn't looked up as he examined the book until he heard, "Is it worth anything?" Theo's voice was soft and plaintive. His false humility had the desired effect and caused the interlocutor to smile benevolently.

"My thesis is on certain prolific Victorian novelists, like Dickens and Thackeray, and how they were motivated by and felt the pressure to write faster as lesser novelists were gaining in popularity. Charles Reade and even Dickens' best friend, Wilkie Collins, come to mind. Hope to finish it this year," he concluded, suddenly turning sullen when he thought about the committee of professors who would rake him over the coals during his oral presentation.

Theo was getting impatient. His question had been ignored by the self-absorbed assistant but he was determined not to show his pique before getting the information he came for. "Very impressive and way beyond me, I'm certain. Must confess, I'm not much of a reader but a friend said I should get the opinion of an expert like you about the value of the novel. Can you think of anyone in the area who might be interested in buying it?" Theo asked, hoping that flattering would do the trick.

The assistant pulled on his beard for a moment and said, "Unfortunately, I am not aware of any antiquarian book dealers in town but if you don't mind chaos, you might try Sam Winkle's Books Galore. It's located downtown. They have a large used book section and I've heard that some of their stock is early editions. Not sure if this will be an obstacle but Winkle's is certainly worth a visit," he said, opening the cover and pointing to the Hitler bookplate.

After perfunctory goodbyes were exchanged, Theo put *Little Dorrit* back in its clamshell box and took the next bus heading into the city.

EVEN BEFORE WOODY picked up the DeBruycker passport photo at the Interpol office, he was convinced that it would match d'Arblay's. He was right.

The FBI liaison office was located in the American Embassy

and Woody headed there next. He had heard the chatter about Gyles Oliphant, the resident agent, but had never worked with him. Oliphant was known as a stiff, a tool that no one had any use for – unless you needed a cover your ass report packed with every bureaucratic cliché ever conjured up. It was common knowledge that Oliphant had connections high up in the hierarchy and few people were willing to jeopardize their careers by calling him a jackass to his face.

Woody preferred to work alone but his professional career would be hampered if he did not notify Crockett and Oliphant, then follow the necessary international protocols. No one else was yet aware that in the last forty-eight hours, he had uncovered the true identity of the individual responsible for at least two murders and several thefts. Woody Meacham would not let overweening pride interfere with his duty. He shrugged and told himself to accept the fact that for all intents and purposes, his independent investigation was at an end and the suits would take over.

―――◆―――

IN NEW YORK City, a newly badged Port Authority cop, just coming on for his afternoon shift, was shown the d'Arblay photograph and was almost certain that he had seen the man, or someone who looked like him, in the station the previous day. It took almost 24 hours before the possible sighting of Theo DeBruycker reached Crockett at the FBI.

CHAPTER THIRTY-ONE
Buried In Books

———◆———

When Crockett heard Woody's news of the discovery of the DeBruycker passport, coupled with his sighting at the New York City bus terminal, he leapt into action, immediately notifying all FBI field offices and police departments east of Ohio. U.S. Customs Enforcement and the U.S. Marshall's office were also put on alert, along with the feds regional fugitive task force. With particular attention placed on bus traffic into Canada along the New York and New England borders, Crockett was starting to feel confident, assuring Woody that if DeBruycker tried to fly, drive, walk, swim or levitate across the border, he would be apprehended.

In Europe, Interpol put out a Red Notice to every police department on the continent, providing a photograph and detailed description of the Belgian national as a fugitive wanted for murder, assault and grand theft in the United States.

Oliphant dutifully contacted Capitaine Roland Escrinier of the Belgian Federal Police, or Gendarmerie as they were known. Escrinier pressured a judge to quickly issue a search warrant for DeBruycker's apartment. The local police in the district where DeBruycker resided were also brought into the loop so they could share in the glory of solving, if only tangentially, a double homicide in the U.S. that might have been committed by a resident of Bruges.

At the insistence of Crockett and Escrinier, despite grumbling by Oliphant, Woody Meacham was allowed to accompany the contingent that would descend on apartment 6 at 41 Jagersstraat in the city of Bruges.

Sam Winkle's Books Galore was located in an abandoned bank building several blocks from the bus depot. Theo was not thrilled about his prospects as he looked up at the faded sign which hung precariously over the front door and seemed to sway with each gentle breeze.

A girl with stringy, dark air in pigtails and wearing a sleeveless peasant dress, sat on a high stool at the door. Next to her was a table with a receipt pad and a cash box. She was working a wad of gum while reading Michael Crichton's *The Lost World* and didn't bother to look up when Theo walked in.

Theo stopped and looked around but couldn't believe his eyes. Books were jammed haphazardly into every corner, in some places piled high toward the vaulted ceiling. Separated by narrow aisles, there were long rows of shelving the length of the floor but whatever they housed was obscured by the clutter and disarray in front of them. Theo turned back to the girl and asked, "Is Mr. Winkle in?" Her arm went up and she made a jabbing motion toward the back of the shop.

Theo found an aisle where no one was browsing and started to slowly navigate his way through a sea of books, careful not to bump against any of the protruding piles and set off an avalanche. Looking ahead, he saw a middle-aged man sitting at a desk with a metallic sign bolted to the front that read, "Samuel Winkle, Proprietor." He was enjoying himself as he barked mockingly at an elderly woman, as if he were dealing with a recalcitrant child. "That's all you get, Mrs. Rudge. You know how it works. We sift, we weigh and then we pay. Run along now." The woman stuffed some bills in her purse and shook her head dejectedly while she waddled toward the exit door a few feet behind Winkle's desk.

Winkle was patting and smoothing a slick gray comb over which started close to his left ear and traversed his head before culminating just above the right ear. When he glanced up and noticed Theo, he assumed he had overheard the prior conversation and decided to explain his business model. "A typical supplier," he explained, shaking his head in dismay.

"All of them out there, digging and scrounging, looking for the Holy Grail that will earn them big bucks so they don't have to come back here. Me, I buy 'em by the pound. People pull up back here and unload their trunks every day. They rummage through garage and yard sales, grandparents' attics, dead relatives' basements, you name it. Mostly paperbacks. Of course, we toss out anything that's ripped, frayed or damaged in any way before they go on the scale. It can cause a little hard feeling, like with the old lady that just left, but I've got an image to protect, you understand."

When he saw the clamshell box under Theo's arm, he abruptly stood up and stuck out his hand. "Well, what do we have here, my good man? Something unique, the chalice that dreams are made of? Let's have a look, shall we?"

Theo removed *Little Dorrit* from the clamshell box and handed it to Winkle. He wasn't going to make up some story about how he came to possess the novel and he was sure that Winkle wouldn't care. So, he kept quiet and waited for the shop owner to react. It was no surprise that Winkle's bushy eyebrows shot up when he saw the Hitler bookplate. He gazed suspiciously back and forth from Theo to the bookplate a few times before saying, "Okay, what's your game? You add this to the inside cover to squeeze a few extra dollars out of me?"

Winkle intimated, poking his finger at the bookplate accusatorily. His nature was to be suspicious of everyone and the thought that the tables might be turned, with himself the victim of a scam, terrified him.

"Look closely, Mr. Winkle. You are holding a very unusual first edition of a Dickens novel. Who but the German leader would place such a bookplate on the inside cover of such a valuable item? You are an astute buyer, no doubt, so I will show you further evidence that the novel is genuine." Theo reached over and turned to the title page with the 1857 publication date. Winkle still looked wary so Theo continued.

"Students of history know that Hitler maintained several libraries which contained literature from many countries. All of his books bore the bookplate you see here. After the war, thousands of his books disappeared, many of them brought home by American soldiers. With this knowledge, I will let you draw your own conclusions. If you are still not interested, I am confident that there is a discerning buyer who would jump at the opportunity to possess the book you are holding in your hands right now."

A smile started to spread across Winkle's face. He wasn't sure that he was buying everything this stranger was saying but it didn't matter now. A grand promotional idea was taking shape in his head.

"I'm quite a showman, sir. Some people refer to me as the P.T. Barnum of used books. Look around you. The anarchy you see is by design. I have no signs or rows dedicated to history, biography, literature or any of the sections you find in a typical bookstore. For my customers, it is a treasure hunt the moment they walk in the door. I've had college students on a dare dive into a pile of books headfirst and buy whatever books they grabbed before surfacing. Yes, this book just might be the ticket for a big splash. I can see it now."

Winkle was waving his arms in grandiose motions, imagining hordes of shoppers searching for a book from Hitler's library among the clutter. The publicity would be priceless. He had almost forgotten that Theo was sitting across from him until he heard his guest clear his throat.

Winkle realized he had talked too much and quickly manufactured a stern look. "Of course, there are risks associated with promoting any book connected with Hitler and I do have a reputation to protect. What are you asking? Don't try to highball me now, you hear?"

"One thousand in cash and it's yours," Theo said without blinking. Winkle stood up and tried to look offended before turning gregarious. "C'mon now, be reasonable. That Hitler stamp could make the thing damn near worthless. Gives me the heebie-jeebies just to look at it. Now that I think about it, a lot of people in this town might be offended when they learn I own a book once in the library of the most reviled man in the world. I'm taking a big gamble. Take $200 and be happy you got that much."

It was Theo's turn to take umbrage. He reached over for *Little Dorrit* and put the novel back in the clamshell box. As he turned to leave, Winkle said, "hold on" and unlocked the top drawer of his desk. "One, two, three, four and five. I'll meet you halfway. It's my final offer, take it or leave it," he demanded, waving the bills in front of Theo's face.

Theo doubted he would find another buyer in Albany. Time was running out and all other options had dried up. Still, he resented being played for a sucker by a two-bit huckster. "Half-way, as you say, would mean six hundred dollars. Add one more of those and we have our deal," he said, staring intently at Winkle.

Winkle broke out into a laugh to complement his phony contrition. "Sorry about that. Hey, you might want to exit using the door behind me," Winkle said, smiling unctuously as he pulled another Benjamin from the top drawer. "I would hate to see you trip and fall trying to make it safely to the front door."

Theo walked to the Greyhound Station wondering who Barnum was. If he was a cheap conman like Winkle, the bookstore owner would be in good company. Checking the timetables, he saw that there was a bus to Montreal leaving the next day at noon. To avoid suspicion, he bought a round-trip ticket so he could demonstrate that he was on holiday. The ticket agent had been to Montreal and recommended the Bon Marche Parc Hotel on the Rue St-Hubert, close by the train station. Theo thanked him for the telephone number and would make a reservation that evening to further solidify his story.

He learned that the border crossing where passports and other identification papers would be checked was just beyond the town of Champlain, NY when the bus entered Canada at St. Bernard de Lacolle, Quebec. From there, it was forty miles to the safety of Montreal. He had been dispirited by the recent loss of *Dracula* and now the forced sale of *Little Dorrit* to a wormy little man who cared no more about great books than a trash hauler. He found solace in the fact he would soon be in a French-speaking province where he felt he could operate with impunity and gradually restore his fortunes. It might take more time than he hoped but he would eventually make it back home and begin anew For all practical purposes, Theo DeBruycker was now dead.

CHAPTER THIRTY-TWO
NO WAY OUT

WHILE THEO WAS negotiating with Sam Winkle, it was near midnight under a dark, moonless sky as storm clouds rolled into Bruges off the North Sea. With Woody and Oliphant following, Capitaine Escrinier and a member of his team, joined by a few officers from the local Belgian police zone, cautiously approached the apartment building on Jagersstraat. All were on guard, wondering if they might confront a ruthless killer who had somehow snuck back into the country – all except Woody, who felt certain that the wily DeBruycker was somewhere else, most likely still in America.

Oliphant couldn't hide his annoyance at being required to leave the comfort of his own apartment back in Brussels and join the search. It was because he viewed himself as more a part of the embassy staff than a law enforcement official. His job description required close coordination with the State Department and he relished the mantle of diplomat more than crime fighter. If Woody had learned that Oliphant was nettled because he had to get up early the next morning to catch the express train to Luxembourg-City, where he was leading a seminar on inter-governmental cooperation, he might have mocked him to his face.

After there was no response to repeated knocks, a forced entry was made into Theo's apartment. It was quickly evident that the place was empty and tensions eased. Woody followed deferentially behind the Belgians as they moved from room to room. In the bedroom, the wall opposite the bed was dominated by a large movie poster in bright yellow. It showed a blond-haired man staring intensely down the scope of an unusual looking sniper rifle which was pointed at a circle in the top corner of the poster. Inside the circle, depicting what the shooter would see in his rifle sight, was a red silhouette of French President Charles De Gaulle. Looking closely, one could see that the shooter had zeroed in for a head shot.

Along the bottom of the poster was a black strip with *The Day of the Jackal* in bold red letters. Smaller print below the title of the movie read: "Edward Fox is the Jackal." Woody walked over to the side of the bed and gazed back at the poster. He imagined DeBruycker lying in bed, absorbing the image of the assassin before drifting off to sleep.

In a dresser drawer, one of the local police found several promotional photographs from the movie, showing Edward Fox in various scenes as he meticulously planned the assassination. Buried below rolled-up socks was Theo DeBruycker's passport along with his Belgian driver's license. Smiling triumphantly, the officer held up the passport and the license for all to see, as if his discovery signified that the case was somehow solved. If this was how success was measured, Woody wanted no part of it.

Woody pulled Oliphant aside and urged him to contact Crockett asap. "Tell him resources are being wasted looking for someone presenting DeBruycker's passport. He'll want to notify Customs Enforcement and everyone else who has been put on alert. Of course, DeBruycker was too smart to bring his own documents with him and d'Arblay can't be his only false identity. He is sure to have a back-up." Oliphant didn't like taking orders from a PI and sauntered out of the room to place the call in private. Woody was certain he would make some disparaging remarks to Crockett but he was beyond caring at his age.

Woody paced the bedroom, racking his brain for ideas. When he walked back to the door, he saw Oliphant still talking on his phone in the next room. When Woody turned back, the gendarme who came with Escrinier had spread the contents of the drawer onto DeBruycker's bed and was photographing them. There were two rows of movie studio pictures showing Edward Fox in action. Looking at them brought certain scenes from the movie back to Woody. He looked over at the movie poster on the wall and remembered the comment that DeBruycker made to the bookdealer in Ghent. "I am the Jackal," he had boasted. Of course, DeBruycker had taken the phrase almost verbatim from the movie poster.

So, there it was, staring him in the face. Was it possible that DeBruycker wasn't so much obsessed with the Jackal as he was with his portrayal by the English actor? Looking at the poster and the photos, he had to admit that there was a certain resemblance which could be enhanced by make-up and hairstyle, certainly modifications to his appearance that DeBruycker had proven he was talented enough to make.

Escrinier walked into the bedroom and Woody motioned him over. Pointing to the wall poster, he asked, "How do you say Edward Fox in Dutch?" The Capitaine smiled and pronounced the name in a clipped, nasal accent. Woody pulled out a pen and notebook from his breast pocket and handed it to Escrinier, who commenced to write in clear block letters the name EDUARD VOS.

———※———

WHILE HIS APARTMENT in Bruges was being turned upside down, Theo was waking up from a nightmarish dream of Maddie Lever pleading for her life as she tumbled down the stairs at the Thimbletown Inn. He struggled to shake off this eerie sense of foreboding and focus on the final details of his imminent departure from the United States.

THEO FOUND A diner close to the hotel and sipped black coffee at the counter, hoping it would help shake off the lingering images of his troubled sleep. He was glad he had made the decision to travel light. If he got into a precarious situation, he needed to be nimble.

Back in his room, he unstitched the lining of the suitcase and removed the Belgian passport and driver's license which identified him as Eduard Vos. After putting the blue blazer into the opening, he restitched the lining. If there was a spot search of his luggage at the border, nothing would be found that would identify him as other than a Belgian tourist on holiday in North America.

WOODY RUSHED FROM the bedroom and found Oliphant still on the telephone. "I need to speak with Crockett," he said, reaching for the phone. The agent had a bemused look on his face and turned away. Woody grabbed the phone from behind with a menacing look and put out his free arm to discourage Oliphant from reacting. "Crockett, it's Meacham. Not sure how much you've been told so far but will assume you know that DeBruycker will not be using his own travel documents. My instinct tells me he has at least one more identity to use. I can explain it all later but my hunch is that he may be traveling under the name of Eduard Vos. That's Edward but with a u instead of a w. No, not B. It's V as in victory then os. Just one s, got it? What, you're breaking up? Yes, Belgian passport and other supporting documents.

All forgeries, and likely damn good ones. I'm going to stay in Bruges tonight and will call you when I get back to my hotel."

Oliphant hadn't moved since Woody commandeered his phone but had been contorting his face to express his skepticism over what he was hearing. Woody smiled and tossed the phone to him. "Crockett hung up. Guess he was done with you."

———◆———

It was noon when Theo left the hotel and started walking to the bus station. He was wearing tan leather boat shoes, drawstring khaki pants and a grey t-shirt with "I Love New York" printed in red across the front. On his head was a well-worn navy blue baseball cap bearing the bright yellow and red flag of Belgium. On the way, he stopped at a trash can and tossed in the two Eduard Vos drivers licenses produced for him by Feng.

The Greyhound was only a few minutes late when it pulled into Albany. There were a handful of other passengers standing with DeBruycker, waiting on the platform to board. Theo was pleased when he saw an empty row in the back of the bus from which he could observe everything in front of him. He didn't foresee any difficulties getting safely across the border but the narrow escape outside Wegg's shop had shaken him enough to exercise caution.

———◆———

It was almost 2:00 a.m. in Bruges when Woody was able to reach Crockett. The FBI agent had been on the phone with multiple officials, spreading the word to be on the lookout for anyone who looked like Theo DeBruycker but traveling as Eduard Vos on a fake Belgian passport. "I've stuck my neck out for you on this one, Meacham. If he's not traveling as Vos, all we have is the photographs from the d'Arblay and DeBruycker passports to ID him. Busy agents are trained to scrutinize the details of the passport but rarely study the face. If he slips over the border, there will be a great deal of finger pointing and my next assignment will be in Wyoming."

Crockett had surprised Woody so he wasn't going to observe that cautious people didn't catch bad guys. It made him think of his stepfather, Billy Meacham, Jr., who wasn't nicknamed the "boy wonder" detective for playing it safe. At times like this, Woody liked to think that some of that risk-taking derring-do had rubbed off on him.

"I guess you've heard from Oliphant by now," Woody said. Crockett laughed. "That prick went over my head to file a complaint. Not surprised, really. It's out there that he's angling for a job in the State Department. A real stiff with Ivy League connections all the way to the top floor of the Hoover building. I'm sure you won't lose any sleep over it."

Woody was starting to like the guy. Maybe he had pegged Crockett wrong. Well, there wasn't anything more to do except wait and see what happened next. If DeBruycker was on the move or still hiding out in New York City, even if he wasn't traveling as Eduard Vos, his picture was everywhere and he was bound to make a mistake sooner or later. With this final thought, Woody stripped off his clothes and fell into bed.

———◆———

THEO STARED OUT the window as the Greyhound passed Saratoga Springs, Glens Falls, Lake George and a town called Peru. After a stop in Plattsburgh at the edge of the northern Adirondack Mountains, the terrain turned sparse and the towns were few and far between. He saw a sign for Point Au Roche and for a moment thought he had dozed off and magically passed into Canada. But the bus hummed along past

West Chazy and Chazy until it reached the New York border town of Champlain which connects with St. Bernard de Lacolle just ahead on the Canadian side.

Over the intercom, the drive reminded the passengers that the bus would be stopping shortly at Canadian border patrol. Theo pulled down his suitcase from the overhead rack and held it close to his seat. In a few minutes, it would all be over and he could think more clearly about how he would proceed once in Montreal.

At St. Bernard de Lacolle, the bus emptied and everyone dutifully marched inside the customs office with their luggage. Theo tried on a friendly smile for the border agent who examined his passport and his declaration form with a passive expression. The man was tired of looking at strangers faces and wasn't going to pretend that he was happy to see another foreigner entering his country. After checking Theo's return trip bus ticket and asking where he was staying in Montreal, the passport was stamped and a perfunctory examination of Theo's suitcase ensued.

Theo let out a sigh as we walked back to the bus and returned to his seat. It was a short ride to Montreal and he would soon be having dinner among French-speaking people. After surviving on American cuisine for days, he anticipated a more appetizing repast.

When he looked out the window, he saw that the Canadian agent who had examined his passport had come outside and was standing near the bus, talking to a plainclothes man in a dark suit who was holding something in his hand. They both looked up at the same time and the Canadian agent pointed into the bus where Theo was sitting.

The other passengers reboarding the bus were pulled back and Theo watched with alarm as they were hurriedly escorted into the border patrol facility. A few people were standing in the aisle, putting away their luggage, when two men climbed the stairs and shepherded them off the bus. Outside, Theo saw a vehicle pull up with the U.S. Customs insignia on the door panel. Then, he saw the flashing lights of more vehicles with uniformed officers leaping out and flanking the bus.

Theo DeBruycker knew in that instant it was all over for him. He envisioned rotting away in a U.S. prison for the remainder of his life. Heinz Kammler and Maddie Lever flashed before his eyes, then Otto Von Paulus, all in rapid succession. He thought of the Jackal and how his life had ended in what Theo once thought was a blaze of glory. But Theo had only one dramatic option left to him. He reached down and pulled back his sock, ripping away the X-Acto knife taped to his ankle. When he looked up, the two men had reboarded the bus, this time with their guns drawn. They were starting to make their way down the narrow aisle, one after the other, when Theo flipped open the X-Acto knife and ran it savagely across his neck.

Epilogue

―――――

Back in 1938, it was "Gestapo Mueller" who Gerda Kammler had seen in Hitler's library that fateful day. The general rarely paid visits to the Berghof but had his operatives and spies among the troops guarding the mountain retreat who knew how to circumvent the increasingly powerful and ubiquitous Martin Bormann.

Despite the failed assassination plot in July of 1944 when Hitler miraculously escaped death after a bomb was planted near him at the Wolf's Lair field headquarters in East Prussia, Mueller sensed that the end was near. It prompted him to send a trusted aide to Berchtesgaden the next month on a special mission: to retrieve a book from Hitler's library.

Mueller's aide was escorted to the library by the same valet who had seen Gerda with *Little Dorrit* in her hands on the day of General Mueller's visit five years earlier. Now the novel couldn't be found.

A few days later, Gestapo interrogators took Gerda and Anton Albrecht to a remote guard house in the Obersalzberg. It was Anton who quickly succumbed to the torture and told the story of how Gerda had taken *Little Dorrit* from the library in 1939 and given it to her brother. Within a few days, it was confirmed that Heinz Kammler had been a passenger on the *S.S. Bremen* bound for New York in August of 1939. For the time being, Kammler was beyond Mueller's reach.

After Hitler entered the Führerbunker below the Berlin Reich Chancellery in January of 1945, Mueller started destroying several secret files and formulating his own end game. The file on Heinz Kammler was sent to his long-time secretary, Barbara Hellmuth, then living in Munich. Mueller added a personal note advising Hellmuth about an important detail omitted from the official file – the secret hidden within *Little Dorrit* and where the novel could be found. From that day forward, Heinz Kammler had a target on his back.

When Germany surrendered and the Gestapo general disappeared, Hellmuth was concerned that she would be interrogated and even put on trial once the Allies learned of her close association with Heinrich Mueller. There were rumors but no proof that Hellmuth had been not only the secretary but also the secret lover of the Gestapo chief, resulting in the birth of a boy in 1942. Amidst mounting fears, she decided to give the file to her friend and confidante, Augustus Gottfried, for safekeeping.

Simon Wegg's shop did not escape the wrath of the men who accosted Theo on a New York City street and then rushed off with the wrong novel. Apprised of their error by an apoplectic Gottfried, they visited the Wegg shop that same evening and, venting their pent up rage toward Theo DeBruycker, rampaged through it in their frantic search for *Little Dorrit*. When they got to the locked desk in back, they pried open the drawers and, not finding the prize, mutilated several rare books, including a first printing of *The Red Badge Of Courage* and a signed first edition of *The Rise Of Silas Lapham*, both destined for private collectors. In the end, all Wegg was left with of any significant value was the copy of *Jane Eyre* that he had purchased from Theo.

Before disappearing into the bowels of the subway at 14th Street, the thugs left the clamshell box containing *Dracula* on a bench in Union Square Park.

———◆———

THE DAY OF DeBruycker's suicide, Sam Winkle was putting the finishing touches on his grand promotion. Unlike P.T. Barnum, he did not have the benefit of a General Tom Thumb, the dwarf that the famous impresario began featuring in his shows back in 1842 when he was just a five-year-old boy and not yet two feet tall. But Winkle did find a blurry picture of Hitler as a schoolboy which he proceeded to blow up and put on a large poster in the shop's front window with the following caption across the top in bold red lettering: WHO IS THIS INFAMOUS HISTORICAL FIGURE? RARE AND PRICELESS BOOK FROM HIS PRIVATE LIBRARY HIDDEN INSIDE THE SHOP. WHO WILL BE THE ONE TO FIND IT?

Along the bottom of the poster, the public was advised that the shop would be closed for this private affair the coming weekend, at which time one could gain admission by paying a $5.00 entry fee. Once the poster went up, Winkle contacted all the media outlets within a one hundred mile radius of Albany to announce his promotion. Flyers were stapled and taped to telephone poles, streetlamps and vacant buildings throughout the city.

On the weekend of the promotion, one local tv station did send a crew when it learned that a large, raucous crowd had formed outside Winkle's shop, where the owner could be seen dressed as P.T. Barnum. Winkle sported a black top hat, a red velvet jacket and silk ascot, all the while waving a cane at the giant poster in the window. On the front door, he had placed an outline of a book wrapped in black paper with the words TREASURE HUNT in bold red lettering across the middle.

The first day brought in several thousand dollars. Inveterate suppliers of Winkle's inventory enjoyed the festivities, some searching diligently for several hours, hoping to find that one rare book that eluded them in their regular hunts. Most newcomers, unconditioned to the topsy-turvy scene inside, spent a few minutes wandering around before leaving.

After a humorous bit on the evening broadcast, the crowd at Winkle's shop was even bigger for the last day of the treasure hunt. For Winkle, it was another big pay day. No one found *Little Dorrit* because it was never even hidden in one of the massive, impenetrable piles that proved daunting to even the most aggressive scavengers. And how was one to know? Winkle never told a soul the name of the novel or its connection to Hitler. Nonetheless, he was pleased with his subterfuge, believing that a showman had an innate license to go beyond hyperbole. Winkle would wait a few months and rerun the event to see if it had any staying power. If the reprise bombed, he would look for a collector of Hitler memorabilia to buy the Dickens novel.

It was not long before the press got tipped off about a confrontation at the border that involved both U.S. and Canadian authorities. First reports speculated that a crazed man had been shot on a Greyhound bus after a struggle with police.

Someone had gotten close enough to the bus to take a photograph of DeBruycker with a gaping neck wound and a blood-saturated shirt. At the bottom of the photograph, one could see a blood-spattered paperback book on his lap. When this gruesome picture made it into the newspapers, a Canadian government official confirmed that the individual had committed suicide by cutting his own throat.

Questions immediately arose as to why U.S. officials were swarming an area under the jurisdiction of the Province of Quebec, prompting speculation that, in cooperation with the Royal Canadian Mounted Police, they had been in pursuit of a jihadist on America's terrorist watch list.

It wouldn't be long before the terrorist rumor was debunked and the press reported, relying on anonymous sources, that an astute FBI agent based in Brussels had discovered that a Belgian citizen by the name of Theo DeBruycker, wanted for at least two murders in the U.S., was using a fake passport in the name of Eduard Vos in an attempt to escape the country.

Once the coroner completed his examination, there was the issue of what to do with the *corpus delicti*. The Belgian Embassy in Ottawa directed investigators to the Belgian Consulate General offices in Montreal, where it was confirmed that Theo DeBruycker was a Belgian citizen with no known relatives. With no one to claim the body, it was taken to a nearby hospital morgue for "official processing." Eventually, he would be buried in an unmarked grave at a municipal cemetery. The Canadians would milk their limited role in the saga until DeBruycker's body was finally in the ground.

When Theo's suitcase was searched, there was little to see. Investigators spreading open the blue blazer that Theo had deployed so ably during his New Haven and Boston crimes were puzzled by the wide pocket that encompassed its entire right side from the armpit down to the bottom hem.

CROCKETT WAS DISPATCHED to St. Bernard de Lacolle to coordinate with Canadian police and was directed to share just enough background on their DeBruycker investigation to secure their cooperation. The FBI was eager to get the fingerprints that they hoped would connect Theo to the two Graniteville murders. Crockett spoke to Woody before heading to Canada and apologized for the bogus press reports on the prowess of Gyles Oliphant. Woody just laughed. "I don't want or need any publicity. In fact, I am more effective if I work in the shadows." Woody was thinking of Capt. Fogarty's warning about Benjamin's Conceit. He was disappointed to learn that *Little Dorrit* wasn't found in the suitcase, which convinced him that the Theo DeBruycker saga was far from complete.

———

WOODY HAD NOT spoken to Jerry since leaving Connecticut. He wanted the Kosinsky household to enjoy its well-deserved tranquility until he could report DeBruycker's capture. Now, he called his friend with the news of d'Arblay's true identity and his suicide on a bus at the Canadian border. He was not surprised that Jerry didn't ask about *Little Dorrit* and, instead, quickly changed the subject.

Jerry was excited to announce a planned opening of the bookstore on Labor Day. Fanny and he had settled on Trowbridge Books as the name for the shop. As you walked in, there would be a narrow glass case which would hold *Oliver Twist*. Since Cyrus had gifted his cherished first edition of the Dickens novel, Jerry was determined to honor his mentor and felt that he was purging the history of *Little Dorrit* at the same time.

"I've been expecting your call. It's no surprise to me that you didn't return home and sit on the couch. What else can you tell me, my friend?" Jerry asked, after hearing that Woody was in Bruges when Theo DeBruycker's identity was confirmed.

"You'll learn all the sordid details, if you care to, when you bring the family over here for vacation. Hannah told me she would be calling Fanny to work out arrangements. In the meantime, take with a grain of salt whatever you read in the papers or see on television."

❖

Prof. Fensterwald was prompted by Jerry's visit to undertake a new book project which, with the encouragement of Thorndyke College, would require him to take a one-year sabbatical. He would visit Germany for the first time since his family fled the country before the war and then proceed to Austria, where he would conduct extensive research into all the Hitler family branches. Fensterwald's goal was to produce a detailed expose on the Fuhrer's life *before* society labelled him the most diabolical man in modern history.

❖

In their efforts to burnish their reputation in Europe, the effete Gyles Oliphant was puffed up and lauded by the FBI suits in DC as "the epitome of the agent who displayed excellent inter-governmental talent in working with America's allies to solve a complex case of international import." The higher-ups in the agency, in talking to Oliphant's superiors, admitted it was all bunk but one thing they had learned from Hoover was that nurturing the agency's public image was sacrosanct. When the coveted FBI liaison post in Berlin opened up and was dangled in front of Oliphant as a way to generate more favorable news coverage, his colleagues were thankful that he turned it down. A few days later, it was announced that the State Department, acting on the strong recommendation of the U.S. ambassador to Belgium, had offered Oliphant a diplomatic assignment in France, relieving a thankful FBI of his rhetorical skills.

❖

Once the Belgian press learned the identity of Theo DeBruycker, they fed off articles in the American media describing his exploits in the U.S. The bookstore owner in Ghent, who described Theo to Woody as a self-styled Jackal, was a sought after source of information. Pictures of the actor Edward Fox in his movie role appeared alongside the DeBruycker and d'Arblay passport photographs. As a result, the two horrific murders in Connecticut were overshadowed by this image of a dashing man of mystery who purloined rare books with ease on both sides of the Atlantic. The false identities of Alexandre d'Arblay and Eduard Vos only added to the intrigue. He was no ordinary glib talking grifter, people said, but a charming professional in the tradition of Victor Lustig, who once sold the Eiffel Tower to a gullible investor and even had the nerve to con Al Capone.

———◆———

The endless newspaper articles and television segments on DeBruycker's exploits, including his connection to the auction houses in Dresden and Hamburg, sent bookdealers and libraries throughout Belgium and Germany on a fervent hunt through their collections. Any volume that was missing was conveniently assigned to the handiwork of this world-famous thief. How could they be expected to guard themselves, they explained, against such a masterful charlatan who had recently outwitted such a prestigious institution as Yale University?

With DeBruycker dead, German police pressed Reinhold for the names of the customers for whom he procured rare collectables. On this line of questioning, the Dresden auction house owner remained tight-lipped. Many of these private collectors were successful businessmen and highly placed government officials who would go to any lengths, if necessary, to silence Herr Reinhold.

One Germany tabloid, *Bild*, covered the story extensively, even dispatching an eager young reporter to New York to dig up as much detail as possible on DeBruycker's movements on the days leading up to his suicide. With DeBruycker's picture appearing daily in the local Albany newspaper, the PhD student at the university, emerging from his cubicle, saw it and contacted the police. This latest development made headlines and thousands of people in the area who knew the name of Charles Dickens but had never read a Victorian novel would be talking about *Little Dorrit*. Sam Winkle didn't want to talk to anyone. He closed up the shop and left town before the inevitable visit by the police.

Augustus Gottfried and the mysterious client closely followed the extensive news coverage, in Europe as well as the U.S., as the movements of Theo DeBruycker in the days leading up to his suicide were chronicled. When it finally came out that he had visited Albany University and shown *Little Dorrit* to a graduate teaching assistant, it caught their attention. The assistant told police he was convinced that the novel was a genuine copy from the first printing. When he revealed that Hitler's bookplate graced the inside cover, it made front page news.

Temporarily out from under the shadows of his professors, the assistant went on to say that he recommended DeBruycker visit Winkle's bookstore in downtown Albany as he seemed eager to sell the novel.

This latest development gave Gottfried hope that *Little Dorrit* might still be secured. If DeBruycker had sold the novel to Winkle, the bookstore owner could certainly be persuaded to give it up. When two men showed up to chat with him, the shop was dark and Winkle was nowhere to be found.

When Winkle returned to Albany after a one week absence, he had his story ready for the police. Yes, DeBruycker came by and tried to peddle what he insisted was a Charles Dickens novel from Hitler's library. He laughed him out of the store when he demanded an outrageous price. Winkle, unable to control his overweening pride, couldn't resist boasting that the incident gave him the idea for his bogus promotional extravaganza. The police weren't buying Winkle's fable but when they looked around the shop, they concluded that even if the novel was buried somewhere within, it would take hundreds of man-hours to find it.

Crockett made a visit to the bookstore and, agreeing with the police, was skeptical of Winkle's specious tale about *Little Dorrit*. He tried and also failed to get his boss to approve the cost of sending a team to tear apart Winkle's shop. The FBI bigs were satisfied. Their murder suspect had been cornered at the border, the agency had been praised for its vital role and DeBruycker had committed suicide. It wasn't as if the Belgian had stolen the Mona Lisa and the world was clamoring for its return, Crockett was advised. Play nice with the Canadians, tie down any loose ends and come home.

The title of the Dickens novel had never been mentioned in Winkle's promotion and now the book was tucked away at his mountain cabin in the Adirondack Mountains. Store traffic was up and the name of Winkle was now well known as a successful impresario beyond the confines of the state capital.

The hubbub surrounding Theo DeBruycker had died down and Winkle relaxed. When two strangers walked into Winkle's Books Galore one evening right before closing, they found the owner smoking a cigar while tallying up the day's receipts.

It was after dark when a shaking Sam Winkle was hustled out the back door for a ride into the mountains. His remains were found by some hikers several weeks later.

―――◆―――

IN MUNICH, THE overnight Lufthansa flight from New York landed on time at Franz Josef Strauss Airport. The man in Row 16 had not checked any luggage and breezed through customs without incident. His carry-on bag holding *Little Dorrit* receiving only a cursory glance.

He boarded the next train to city centre and went directly to the Platzl Hotel where Augustus Gottfried had finished his breakfast and was sipping his Dallmayr coffee. Gottfried did not look up when the man placed a package on the table and kept walking.

An hour later, the binding of Little Dorrit was carefully pulled apart with no success. Then, amidst loud curses castigating Theo DeBruycker, the spine was ripped open in an increasingly frantic search for the slip of paper that would make Gottfried and Dolph Hellmuth, the alleged bastard child of Heinrich Mueller and his secretary, two of the richest men in all of Europe.

―――◆―――

IN PARLOR CITY, Woody's mother and Capt. Fogarty raised celebratory glasses of bubbly in salute to the man who once again proved his mettle while receiving none of the laurels. If Billy Meacham, Jr. was still alive, they both knew he would be beaming for the new "boy wonder."

―――◆―――

IT WAS EARLY September when Woody and Hannah flew to Brussels to begin their long-delayed vacation. Their itinerary mirrored the one that Theo had outlined for Maddie back in Graniteville, when he was softening her up. Woody could talk freely now and Hannah always looked forward to a "post facto" recap of how the hunt for *Little Dorrit* unfolded.

They visited the Henrik library in Antwerp so Hannah could see the place where young Theo had been tutored by, and had taken advantage of, the kindly Renata Peeters.

In Ghent, they visited the Boekentoren, a short walk from where Theo grew up and where his father ran his bookstore. Neither of them could know about Theo's visit to the book tower as a boy and its profound influence on his life.

After touring the Rubens House museum in Bruges, the Meachams were cruising the canals of the city, when something made Woody think back to the police raid on DeBruycker's apartment. It had struck him at the time that there was no mail in the lobby box and none on the floor when they entered the apartment. Was it possible that DeBruycker had stopped delivery when he left for the U.S. and his mail sat unclaimed in the local post office? Woody contacted Capitaine Escrinier in Brussels and he agreed to meet Woody the next day.

Bills and advertisements dominated the bundle of mail that had accumulated for DeBruycker over the last several weeks. As the two men sorted through it, Woody saw the letter-sized envelope with the name of the Times Up Hotel in the top left corner. Looking closely, he could see the faded circular postmark of New York, New York.

Escrinier opened the envelope and the two men read the names and sets of numbers on the slip of paper in silence. "So," Woody said to himself, "DeBruycker found the secret hidden somewhere inside the Dickens novel and before leaving New York City mailed it home, thinking at the time he would make it back to Bruges one day and cash in. Roscoe Moutard in Parlor City would be duly impressed."

Finally, the Capitaine looked at Woody and they both smiled. Later forensic ink and paper analyses would confirm that the slip of paper came from the 1940s but both men, standing there in the Bruges post office, knew it was merely a formality. They understood that Theo DeBruycker had uncovered a secret of shocking magnitude and that the mystery that began fifty years earlier with the disappearance of Hitler's copy of *Little Dorrit* from his mountain retreat in the Bavarian Alps was far from over.

Finis

Made in the USA
Middletown, DE
16 July 2023